TIME TO KILL

'The way things are going, Pippa,' said Ralph Allen, 'it's quite possible you'll get a visit from Detective Chief Inspector Anderson soon and if you don't know some things then so much the better.'

'There are things which wouldn't look good if they came out,' his secretary replied. 'What do I do if he starts questioning me about the financial state the company's in, or was in before your wife's death?'

Ralph's face went scarlet. 'The last thing I want is for Anderson to know I needed the money I'll inherit now Lisa's dead. You'll have to lie. And lie convincingly. Anderson dislikes me and if he can pin anything on me over Lisa's death he will.'

CRIME & PASSION

A MOMENT OF MADNESS
A TANGLED WEB
Fairfax and Vallance mysteries

DEADLY AFFAIRS
INTIMATE ENEMIES
A WAITING GAME
TO DIE FOR
TIME TO KILL
John Anderson mysteries

TIME TO KILL

by
Margaret Bingley
A John Anderson mystery

CRIME & PASSION

First published in Great Britain in 1997 by
Crime & Passion
an imprint of Virgin Publishing Ltd
332 Ladbroke Grove
London W10 5AH

Crime & Passion series editor: Pan Pantziarka

Copyright © Margaret Bingley 1997

The right of Margaret Bingley to be identified as the
Author of this Work has been asserted by her in accordance
with the Copyright, Designs and Patents Act 1988.

ISBN 0 7535 0164 3

Typeset by Avon Dataset Ltd, Bidford on Avon, B50 4JH
Printed and bound in Great Britain by
Mackays of Chatham PLC, Chatham, Kent

*All characters in this publication are fictitious and any resemblance
to real persons, living or dead, is purely coincidental.*

This book is sold subject to the condition that it shall
not, by way of trade or otherwise, be lent, resold, hired
out or otherwise circulated without the publisher's prior
written consent in any form of binding or cover other
than that in which it is published and without a similar
condition, including this condition, being imposed on
the subsequent purchaser.

For Alan and Alex,
who helped more than they'll ever know.

ACKNOWLEDGEMENTS

I am extremely grateful to a number of people who have helped me with this book. My thanks go to my brother-in-law, Derek, for all the information on heart rhythm problems, to John Bratt for a great evening during which I learnt, among other things, about ladder making, to Roger Latter of H. H. Cox for his sartorial advice, to Phil and Stan of The Music Box, to Tony Scrimshaw who gave me advice despite being in the middle of lambing, to Pan and Pete F. who were always on the other end of the phone and finally to Jo who, as usual, managed to make sense of the original manuscript, scribbles, arrows and all!

ONE

Detective Chief Inspector John Anderson surveyed himself in the full-length mirror on the wall at the foot of his bed and nodded in approval. He was one of those men who are born to wear dinner suits and he knew it, but he was particularly pleased with his new waistcoat that had slim crimson stripes running through it, and the low-cut front was the latest thing in design. He rather doubted if anyone else would be wearing a waistcoat like it tonight, and that thought too gave him pleasure.

A dinner dance at the new squash club in Dorking, where he had recently become a member, was not his idea of a good night out, but Karen was very keen to go and as he was keen on Karen it was a sacrifice he was prepared to make. He knew when a compromise was worthwhile.

Karen and he had met by chance, drawn as mixed doubles partners in one of the competitions the club ran to help new members get to know each other. In truth Anderson had no desire to get to know anyone there particularly well. Joining had been part of his new regime, designed to eliminate what he thought might possibly be the beginnings of very slight middle-aged spread. It had a much higher standard than his previous club, and good competition made the journey worthwhile. The energetic sport combined with extra running had certainly seen an end to any excess weight, and with the arrival of Karen on the scene things were looking up on the sexual side as well.

A thirty-five-year-old divorcee, tall and rangy with excellent bone structure and almost perfect legs, she was also classy, intelligent and wealthy in her own right. She was no clinging vine, but on the other hand she seemed to like to look up to the man in her life, and that suited Anderson perfectly. So far they'd been out about half-a-dozen times but without sleeping together. However, he had the feeling that tonight was meant to be the night and he was looking forward to it with keen anticipation.

He checked himself in the mirror one more time, noticing that the silver in his hair was increasing, and then glanced with satisfaction at two Chinese paintings on glass that he'd acquired the previous week and were now hanging above his bed. Their subdued colours and subtle tones were restful on the eye and the artwork exquisite. He'd had to wait a long time before he could afford them but that only made the final possession all the sweeter. He supposed it was no different from pursuing a special woman or a clever criminal: the waiting and planning were an intrinsic part of the final pleasure.

He walked briskly down the four flights of stairs from his top-floor apartment in the Mill, climbed into his silver BMW and drove off to collect Karen Raybould. She lived a fifteen-minute drive away in a modern Georgian house set back off the main road and well protected by burglar alarms and security lights. He approved of that. These days it was only common sense to protect yourself as much as you could. Robberies were rarely solved. The burglars might be caught but real valuables usually remained missing. The loss was what owners tried to avoid, unless they were into an insurance swindle, but that was an altogether different story and not something that he imagined had ever crossed Karen's mind. She enjoyed her money and her possessions, and although her taste was more ostentatious than Anderson's, he accepted that his preferences were far more minimalist than most people's. At least Karen had good taste, and that was something that no amount of money from an ex-husband who'd run off with a younger replacement could supply.

Hearing Anderson's car coming up the long gravel drive, Karen felt a flutter of excitement in her stomach. It had been over a year since she'd felt like this about a man, but at last she was physically alive again and she hoped that tonight she'd find out if he was as good a lover as she'd imagined. She didn't think he'd disappoint her; he wasn't the kind of man who ever disappointed. If he said he'd telephone, then he did; if he said he'd pick her up at a certain time he was always there on the dot, and she was certain he'd be just as skilled at sex as he was at driving his BMW. In her experience you could tell a lot about a man from the way he drove. Her husband had driven like an overexcited teenager not quite in control of a powerful car. He'd also been like an overexcited teenager when he ran off with a nineteen-year-old girl, raving about her youth and freshness as though they were unique to her rather than a gift nature bestowed on most girls that age.

She sighed. Despite it all she'd loved him and it hadn't been easy going back out into the world as a single woman, although the generous divorce settlement had helped and she had no children to cramp her style. John Anderson for one wasn't the kind of man who would have been interested in a divorced mother-of-two. He hadn't ever said anything about children, but anyone with such a passion for neatness and order in his world would have found life with children unbearable.

Just as Anderson had earlier, Karen gave her reflection in

the hall mirror a quick glance. She was wearing a full-length navy halter-neck dress by Nicole Farhi, and where the slim collar straps joined the top of the bodice the jersey and the straps were threaded through a large silver ring. Quite apart from creating an excitingly erotic image of collars and subservience, something she again sensed would appeal to Anderson, this meant that the sides of the top of the dress dropped sharply away revealing just a tasteful hint of the sides of her breasts, if you were standing to one side of her. From the front it was perfectly decorous and unlikely to raise any eyebrows at the squash club. Silver hooped earrings and a narrow silver bangle on her left wrist were her only jewellery.

Draping a cream mohair wrap over her arm she let herself out through the front door and stood in the porch watching Anderson get out of his car. His dark blue, frequently unfathomable, eyes lit up at the sight of her and he smiled.

'You look stunning,' he said admiringly, and at the sound of his dark, perfectly modulated voice her stomach did another flip.

'Thank you,' she said softly, going round to the far side of the BMW as Anderson opened the passenger door for her. 'I like your waistcoat,' she added.

Anderson was pleased she'd noticed. 'Do you know many other members?' he asked as he drove swiftly but carefully out on to the main road.

'Not many,' she confessed. 'That's partly why I thought it would be a good idea if we came tonight. It will give us a chance to meet more people and widen our social circle.'

Anderson didn't answer. He had no intention of widening his social circle to include the members of the squash club. He was a man who when not working enjoyed his own company. Neither did he like the way Karen was using the word 'we' as though they were already a couple rather than two adults just reaching an exciting moment in the early stages of what was unlikely to be anything more than a short-term relationship. She was far too wealthy to ever become a permanent part of his life. He wouldn't like the financial balance to be tilted in that direction if he ever chose to form a steady relationship again.

As he'd guessed it would, his silence led Karen to chatter more. It was a useful tactic when interviewing suspects, and sometimes he felt a twinge of conscience when he did the same thing socially, but it was a deeply ingrained habit now.

'Of course, you might already have masses of friends,' she said quickly. 'I don't though, it's quite difficult for single women, and this way I hoped . . . Well, I just thought it would be nice.'

'Quite,' Anderson said, taking pity on her and not wanting to spoil the evening before it had begun. In any case, she looked extremely sexy in her halter-neck dress and her perfume — Coco by Chanel he thought — was sensual and arousing.

The main function room at the squash club was large and, Anderson had to admit, unusually well decorated. The decor was light and the framed pictures, curtains and furnishings discreet but tasteful. The bar itself was thick with cigarette smoke and as he ordered drinks for himself and Karen he wondered why it was that despite the government's best efforts people still chose to pollute the air for themselves and others. Sheer bloody-mindedness he suspected. It was like telling children not to do something: you immediately made it even more attractive. He wouldn't have minded if they hadn't been polluting his lungs and making his clothes reek of tobacco smoke as well. The man next to him at the bar failed to notice that his cigarette ash was about to fall and Anderson moved his arm only just in time to prevent the ash from falling on the sleeve of his dinner jacket. The man glanced at him as though he'd been insulted.

'I was avoiding your ash,' Anderson said with a polite smile, his eyes flicking down to the bar counter where the offending ash now lay.

'Really? Don't I know you?' asked the man.

Anderson's heart sank. It was possible they'd met during some investigation or other but the last thing he wanted tonight was a discussion about the total inability of the police to solve any crime. 'I doubt it,' he said. 'I'm a new member.'

'Not here, somewhere else,' pressed the man. 'My name's Ian Forster, I'm in insurance.'

'Sorry, it doesn't ring any bells with me.' Anderson grabbed his drinks and moved as swiftly as possible through the crush of people.

'Someone you know?' Karen asked as he handed her a schooner of dry sherry.

'Someone I've probably met,' Anderson said, smiling down at her. 'That's one of the hazards in my line of work. He wasn't happy, but the chances are he'd have been even less happy if he'd remembered where we'd met. Very few people have happy memories of their encounters with the police, even when they're the victims of a crime. Or possibly especially when they're the victims,' he added.

'Never mind,' Karen said consolingly. 'Be thankful you're not a dentist. A friend of mine's married to a dentist and she loathes meeting new people because of the way they react when they hear what Mike does. She says it's like being married to a criminal. Everyone says: "How can you bear being a dentist? Don't you mind being hated by everyone?" ' She laughed, showing her very white, even teeth and Anderson put an arm round her bare shoulders, leading her over to a less crowded part of the room.

'Done anything exciting since we last met?' Karen asked him.

Anderson shook his head. 'It isn't like people think, you know. An awful lot of my time is spent filling in forms, working out statistics and going to meetings.'

'That's not what I've heard,' Karen retorted. 'Someone told me that you're a real action man, always where it's at, as they say in America.'

Anderson felt considerably flattered by this description; it was how he liked to think of himself. 'Who said that?' he asked with interest.

'I'm not telling,' Karen said. 'I value my secret source. Oh good, it looks as though it's time to go through. I'm starving. I haven't eaten a thing since breakfast.'

Anderson had already glanced at the seating plan, but none of the names at their table meant anything to him, and when they sat down no one looked in the least familiar. Two of the couples clearly knew each other well. They were both young, in their early twenties, and made no attempt to introduce themselves when Anderson sat down with Karen.

Seated on his right was an immaculately made-up blonde young woman, whose extremely attractive curves were emphasised by the pale-pink strapless dress she was wearing. It clung to her like a second skin, and a thin strip of semi-transparent material ran down the middle of the top half of the dress like an imitation zip, hinting at the creamy skin beneath.

She smiled warmly at Anderson. 'Hello, I'm Lisa Allan,' she said in a slightly breathy voice that reminded him of Marilyn Monroe, although it wasn't as irritatingly girlish. 'This is my husband, Ralph,' she added, turning her head in the direction of the man on her right.

'I'm John Anderson and this is Karen Raybould,' Anderson replied. 'We're both new members so we don't know anyone else here.'

'Neither do I,' Lisa said. 'I'm not a member at all. Unfortunately I'm not allowed to play squash, and Ralph's only just joined. He's fighting the flab,' she added with a gurgle of laughter.

Her husband, who looked a lot older than his wife, didn't laugh. A big, heavily built man, he was handsome in a flashy way but Anderson noticed that his waistcoat was covered in an over-gaudy floral pattern and his expensive suit was too tight. It was clear to Anderson that the man had more money than taste.

'What line of business are you in?' Ralph Allan asked Anderson, his voice as loud as his waistcoat. Next to him, Lisa seemed to draw in on herself physically, as though the sound grated on her.

'I'm in the police force,' he replied quietly. 'How about you?'

'The police force!' bellowed Ralph, who had clearly already drunk a great deal. 'Good job I'm not driving home then or you'd probably be rushing out with a breathalyser. What are you, a sergeant? Or something impossibly important, like an inspector?' He seemed to find this highly amusing.

'I'm a Detective Chief Inspector,' Anderson murmured. Ralph's heavy-lidded dark eyes sharpened, and Anderson wondered if he was quite as drunk as he'd thought at first.

'One of the brainy lads? That's what I like about this place, you only meet the best sort of person, even when it comes to the police. If there is such a thing as a "best sort" of policeman, that is.'

'What do you do, Ralph?' Karen asked, tactfully. Anderson was grateful; he hated talking about his work when out socially.

'Me? Oh, I'm a self-made man,' Ralph replied, his eyes skimming over Karen with obvious appreciation. 'I inherited a small ladder-making business from my father and I've built it up into something quite impressive, even if I do say it myself.'

'Which he does, frequently,' Lisa said with another little gurgle of laughter.

'At least I don't bore everyone senseless with details of

my health,' said her husband, shooting a look of annoyance at her.

Anderson was relieved when the food arrived, and although the meal was of the poor standard that he expected from mass catering it at least kept Ralph, whom he instinctively disliked, quiet. The man attacked his food as he probably attacked everything in life, with concentration and gusto, which meant that Anderson was free to chat to both Karen and Lisa without too many interruptions.

By the time they were down to the coffee and mints, Anderson was feeling as close to relaxed as it was possible for him to get. He was enjoying having an attractive woman on each side of him, and Karen's shoulder-length brunette hair and slender body were an intriguing contrast to Lisa's short blonde crop and opulent curves. He thought that Lisa was somewhere in her mid-thirties, while Ralph looked to be in his mid-fifties, and he wondered if she was a second and 'trophy' wife, although her husband's behaviour towards her was hardly that of a doting older man bewitched by her relatively youthful charms. Human relationships fascinated Anderson, and he wondered what it was that had brought the pair of them together.

'About time,' Ralph commented as the band began assembling. 'Now it should liven up a bit. Do policemen dance?' he asked Anderson with a look of amusement.

'Not on duty,' Anderson said, keeping a perfectly straight face. Karen laughed but Ralph didn't, and next to him Lisa quickly stifled her giggle.

'How long have you two been an item?' Ralph continued, looking at Karen.

Even Anderson was surprised by the crass question, but Karen was quite up to coping with Ralph. 'We're not an item,' she said with a polite social smile. 'Items are things I put on my shopping list.'

'Right, but you're not just good friends are you? That would be a wicked waste of such a gorgeous young lady.'

'We're very good friends,' said Karen. 'Now, perhaps you'd like to tell me about you and your wife? Are you just good friends?'

Anderson smiled to himself. Ralph however was completely unfazed. 'No, in fact I'd say that right now we're not feeling at all friendly. That's the way it is with married couples. There are more bad days than good, isn't that right, Lisa?'

Lisa, who appeared to Anderson to have gone rather pale, seemed startled by the question. 'I'm sorry, what was that? I was miles away,' she murmured.

'Having one of her turns, I expect,' Ralph sneered. 'She's got some strange illness that stops her doing anything she doesn't want to do but allows her to have fun when she feels like it. Oh yes, and stress makes it worse, so no one must upset Lisa. An interesting illness, don't you think, John?'

'I'm afraid I don't know anything about medical matters,' Anderson said, completely shocked by the man's attitude and feeling a surge of protection for Lisa, who was plainly not well at that moment.

'Only dead bodies, I suppose,' Ralph concluded, suddenly getting to his feet and pulling his wife on to the dance floor despite her protests.

'What a pig,' said Karen the moment they were out of earshot. 'What on earth does she see in him?'

'I've long since ceased to be surprised by the kind of men women are drawn to,' Anderson murmured, as he led Karen out to dance. 'In any case, I'm more interested in us than in Ralph and Lisa tonight.' Karen moved closer to him and tucked her chin into his shoulder. They moved well together and Anderson felt himself stir at her closeness. He couldn't wait for the dinner dance to end.

Before it did he had a dance with Lisa Allan. She was much smaller than Karen and her head fitted beneath his chin. It made him feel even more protective than he had earlier, and when their bodies touched there was a sudden surge of sexual energy between them that took him completely by surprise. Lisa drew back and looked up at him, her eyes wide with shock. Her face turned pink and her breathing became shallow and rapid. Anderson allowed her to keep the extra space between them for the rest of the dance, but they both knew what had happened and they were both equally startled.

'There, that's brought the colour back to your cheeks,' Ralph remarked as she sat down at the table again. 'I keep telling you that you should take more exercise rather than wrapping yourself in cotton wool.'

'I know you do,' Lisa murmured, glancing briefly at Anderson from beneath lowered lashes.

Anderson and Karen were among the first to leave and during the drive back to her house Karen said very little. Anderson didn't know if she was nervous or if she'd picked up on something between himself and Lisa. He hoped not. That had been an aberration, one of those things that happen perhaps once or twice in a lifetime and are best forgotten. His relationship with Karen was something quite different and with growing excitement during the entire evening he had been anticipating making love to her.

He stopped the car outside her front door, and to his surprise she reached for his left arm and looked at his wristwatch. 'I hadn't realised it was so late,' she said quietly.

Anderson said nothing. If she was having a sudden attack of nerves then it was better that he didn't put any pressure on her. If she wanted him to be the one to make the first move, she'd be disappointed. He'd sent out all the right signals, now it was up to her to pick them up. He'd never yet had to push himself on a woman and didn't intend to start now.

'Are you on duty tomorrow?' she asked. Anderson shook his head. 'Then perhaps you'd like to come in for a nightcap,' she suggested.

'That sounds like a very good idea,' he said warmly, and

as Karen unlocked her front door he immobilised his steering wheel and then locked his BMW.

Karen led him straight through to her drawing room. It was bright without being garish; the damask-rose-coloured walls were adorned with prints by Modigliani, while above the vast multi-coloured sofa covered in Le Rocher by Braquenite there was a huge print of Raoul Dufy's painting of the Bastille Day celebrations, its blues and splashes of dark pink perfectly complementing the rest of the room. With a sigh of contentment Anderson lowered himself on to the sofa.

Karen flicked through some CDs and settled on Rimsky-Korsakov's *Sheherazade* and *Le coq d'or*. Anderson nodded his approval and then took the brandy glass from her outstretched hand. 'I love this room,' he told her with a smile. 'There's something about it that relaxes me.'

Karen settled down next to him, but her body was tight with sexual tension and Anderson put an arm round her narrow shoulders, letting his slim fingers gently caress the fine bones of her shoulders and the nape of her neck.

Karen's eyes slowly closed as she let herself drift into a pleasant haze of sensuality. She felt his lips brush the end of her shoulder and then his hands were lifting her hair up and away from her body so that he could plant tiny kisses on the skin beneath. When he deftly unfastened the halter top of her dress she could have cried with relief that at last she was going to find out what he was like as a lover and her body, starved for so long of true sensual contact, began to awaken at his clever touch.

Anderson looked down at Karen, at her closed eyes and half-parted lips and felt his own arousal grow. Slowly he bent his head and lightly kissed each of her nipples in turn before letting his tongue run lazily over the undersides of the breasts themselves.

Karen made a tiny noise of pleasure low in her throat

and then her eyes flew open as she felt Anderson move away from her.

'Just wait a moment,' he said reassuringly and she watched as he removed his own clothes, folding them carefully and placing them on the nearest chair. She'd imagined them going upstairs to make love, but now she was as anxious as him that the spell shouldn't be broken.

When he was naked he returned to the sofa and settled himself with his back against one end of it before drawing Karen on to his lap where he proceeded to ease her dress over her head before carefully draping it over the back of the sofa.

Feeling suddenly shy she bent her head but Anderson put a finger beneath her chin and forced her head upward. 'Look at me, Karen,' he said firmly, his deep voice husky. 'I want to see the expression in your eyes when I'm making love to you.'

Looking into his deep blue eyes, Karen shivered with excitement. Her husband had never behaved like this, not even in their early days together, and when Anderson drew her on to his lap and she felt the lean hardness of his thighs beneath her buttocks she gave herself over to him with total trust.

He caressed her entire body for a long time, taking special care when teasing her nipples, a part of her that he quickly realised was highly sensitive, and then he slowly entered her. It was sooner than she'd expected, but she was more than ready for him. However, once inside her he lowered her back along the length of his outstretched legs until her head was resting on a cushion at the opposite end of the sofa. Then his hands were free to continue their delicious exploration of her body while she lay quivering with mounting excitement as hundreds of tiny electric shocks coursed through her.

For Anderson the position meant that he was able to watch Karen's face the whole time; more than half of

Anderson's pleasure in sex came from pleasing women, so that watching them in their moments of ecstasy was as exciting as the time leading up to that moment.

When Karen, after a series of small orgasms, finally exploded into total release he watched the pink flush of arousal suffuse her breasts, neck and throat, saw the pupils of her eyes dilate as though in incredulous shock and felt her body twisting and arching, while his own moment of release drew nearer and nearer. Then, when she was suddenly still he allowed his hands to move her unresisting body back and forth along his thighs as he drove towards his climax, but only the smallest of sounds marked the moment he felt his orgasm rush through him.

When it was over, Anderson gathered Karen up and held her close, well aware of the importance of ensuring she still felt wanted and needed. He knew that after her disastrous divorce her self-confidence, however much she managed to conceal this in daily life, must be low and it was vital she didn't feel she was discarded the moment the sex ended.

Resting his mouth on the top of her head he blew softly into her hair. 'Wonderful,' he breathed, his right hand cradling her left breast.

Karen sighed with pleasure. 'It was even better than I'd . . .' Her voice trailed off.

'Than you'd what?' Anderson asked with interest.

'Imagined,' she admitted.

Anderson smiled to himself. It was flattering to think that she'd been imagining the pair of them together in such detail, and even more flattering to know that he'd exceeded her expectations. He'd enjoyed it too, especially the way in which she'd been almost shy about taking her pleasure. There was something in his make-up that Anderson only half-understood, but it meant that whenever a woman was reticent or even semi-reluctant about sex he became far more excited than if she was as relaxed and upfront about it as most women were meant to be these days.

'Can you stay the night?' asked Karen anxiously. 'Only to sleep,' she added quickly. 'It's just that it would be nice, after this, if we could spend the night together.'

Anderson's mind flicked through his Sunday agenda. The morning run, breakfast on the balcony, some papers to be read; in other words nothing urgent, but just the same he didn't want to give up too much of one of his precious days of solitude.

'I'm afraid I'll have to leave by ten,' he apologised.

Karen's face lit up. 'That's fine. It will be lovely to have someone sharing my bed again. I miss that physical closeness. Would you like another brandy before we go up?'

'Coffee will be fine,' said Anderson, wondering why it was that many people craved constant companionship whereas he found it stifling and uncomfortable. The thought that this might be a weakness on his part and not on theirs never occurred to him.

As they climbed the stairs some fifteen minutes later he was working out whether or not it would be a good idea to make love to Karen again in the morning before he left. Probably not, he thought. It would be better to leave her wanting more, and if they became too well acquainted with each other too soon she might either start to lose some of the sexual docility that appealed to him or fight against it. That had happened to him before and he was now more wary of the dangers of letting women realise quite how much he liked to be in control where sex was concerned. Just the same, he was very pleased with the way the evening had gone and was feeling generally at peace with the world.

There was no such peace inside the luxurious house where Ralph and Lisa Allan lived. They had stayed on at the squash club for half an hour after Anderson and Karen had left, but then Lisa had complained of feeling tired and a reluctant

Ralph had been forced to call them a taxi.

As soon as they were inside the front door he turned on his wife. 'Why is it that whenever I'm enjoying myself you feel ill?' he demanded. 'Just because your admiring policeman had left, did we have to go? Couldn't you have found someone else to massage your ego for a while?'

Lisa, whose face was still pale, sighed and ran her fingers through her short blonde hair. 'I'm sorry, Ralph, but I really don't feel well. I should have rested this afternoon, but somehow the time went by and I never got round to it. You know what the doctor says –'

'I know what you tell me he says,' Ralph snapped. 'On the few times I manage to get a word with him he always says that you're doing well.'

'Yes, doing well in view of my condition!' Lisa shouted, walking through into the front room. She sat in an armchair. 'Ralph, I'm exhausted, let's not have an argument now.'

'I'd like to know why you couldn't rest this afternoon,' Ralph persisted, standing a few feet away from her and looking down with an expression of mingled annoyance and bewilderment. 'You weren't at the health club by any chance, were you?'

Lisa flushed. 'Of course not. You really are dense sometimes, Ralph. As though I'd go to the gym when I knew I was going to be at a dinner dance in the evening.'

'So what stopped you from resting? I was out playing squash, both the kids were out and doing domestic chores has never exactly been your forte even before your "delicate condition" was diagnosed.'

'I had things to do,' Lisa snapped. 'The washing doesn't do itself you know. Clean shirts don't just appear by magic in your wardrobe.'

'The machine washes them and Tracy irons them,' Ralph said acidly. 'You make it sound as though you have to go down to the river and pound everything against rocks by hand. You don't have to do anything, Lisa. You have a lifestyle most women would die for, so why couldn't you take time out to rest before tonight?'

'You never understand how busy I am,' complained Lisa. 'We do all eat meals, and I prepare those.'

'Marks and Spencer prepare them,' retorted Ralph.

'Look, if you're trying to say something specific come out and say it,' Lisa shouted. 'I didn't video myself this afternoon. I can't show you what I was doing, but you sound as though you think you know, so please tell me.'

'I think you were seeing that blue-eyed, over-muscled health freak,' Ralph yelled. 'You seem to spend most of your life searching for male admiration. How many men do you need to captivate before you're happy?'

'You're talking bloody rubbish,' Lisa said. 'I mean, why would any woman married to a superstud like you need to look elsewhere for anything? You're so charming, so protective, caring and understanding that I'd have to be insane to need any kind of sympathy from anyone else, wouldn't I?'

'Sympathy? I've given you sympathy by the bucket-load. I've given you sympathy until I've none left, and for what? You're not even a proper wife to me any more.'

'I'm ill!' Lisa reminded him in an exhausted voice.

'And don't we all just have to remember it.' Ralph's voice was getting louder and louder and Lisa got up to leave the room, but then saw Deborah standing in the doorway. She attempted a smile. 'Hello darling; I didn't hear you come in.'

Deborah stared at her mother and stepfather. At eighteen she was almost an exact replica of her mother at the same age and she stared at Lisa with her blue eyes carefully blank. 'I'm not surprised,' she said quietly. 'You were both making such a noise I doubt if you'd have heard a team of burglars breaking down the door.'

'We were just talking about the dinner dance,' Ralph said, his voice bluff and hearty. 'How was your evening?'

Clearly embarrassed by what was going on, Deborah began to edge backwards into the hall. 'Fine, great. I'll be off to bed now. 'Night.'

'Goodnight, sweetie,' Ralph said affectionately.

The moment her daughter was out of sight Lisa turned on him. 'Why is it that you're always so nice to her, and never to me?' she demanded. 'No, don't bother to answer, I know the reason.'

'Do tell,' Ralph said sarcastically.

'It's because you want her to like you. Everyone has to like you, don't they? That's why you always buy more rounds than anyone else in the pub, and take your staff out to ridiculously expensive meals at Christmas, because you want them all to think you're a "jolly good bloke". It's pathetic.'

'At least I'm not mean with my money,' Ralph said accusingly.

'Here it comes,' Lisa said, pacing round the room but keeping a good distance between herself and her furious, slightly drunk husband. 'I knew it wouldn't be long before we got on to the question of my money. God, you really hate me for not giving you it, don't you. My mother's right, that's the only reason you ever married me, and now you're stuck with me because you like everyone to think you're a superstud who keeps a young wife happy, and heaven knows how many other stupid women as well, so a divorce would be out of the question. Unless I divorced you, of course. Now there's an interesting idea. That would get you out of a marriage you no longer want without any blame being attached to you. Actually I'd like to divorce you, but I'd never give you that satisfaction,' she ended viciously.

Ralph took a step towards her. 'You enjoy making me miserable, don't you? Well, you should be careful. You might get a nasty surprise one of these days.'

'Like what? I'd have thought I'd had most of those already.

You ignore my health, chase other women and are nothing better than a bully.'

'And you're nothing but a tart,' Ralph shouted. 'I saw you on the dance floor tonight, pressing yourself up against that stuffed shirt of a policeman. I suppose he's more your type is he? Looked like a queer to me.'

'You always say that about any man who possesses a modicum of sensitivity,' Lisa replied. 'Now get out of my way, I want to make some coffee.'

'It's bad for your condition,' Ralph sneered.

'I do have decaffeinated,' Lisa retorted. 'That's another of those things I do that you seem to think just happen. I shop for us all, and let's face it, your son takes more feeding than a normal family of five on his own.'

'I'm still growing,' said a voice from the hall and Lisa, who hadn't seen her stepson in the shadow, gave a sudden start.

'God, Tom, you frightened me. Do you have to creep around like that?'

'I wasn't creeping,' he said awkwardly. 'You and Dad were talking loudly, that's why you didn't hear me.'

'Talking loudly? What a lovely euphemism,' Lisa said, laughing for the first time since she'd left the squash club. 'What a tactful boy you are, Tom. I can't imagine where you get it from; it certainly isn't your father.'

'Perhaps it comes from mother,' Tom muttered.

'Perhaps it does,' Lisa agreed. 'I've really no idea.'

'No one has any idea,' he said as he turned away to go up to his room. 'It sometimes seems to me that she never really existed.'

'Well she did, because I certainly never gave birth to you,' Lisa said sharply. 'It's a pity she didn't leave you a note or something before she killed herself, but perhaps she felt too guilty. I can't imagine why; I can quite see that death would be a welcome release from your father, providing you were the one to choose that particular line of escape that is,' she added as Ralph loomed up behind her.

'Nice time, son?' Ralph enquired. 'Where were you tonight?'

'Out with the crowd,' Tom muttered, as anxious as his stepsister to get away from Ralph and Lisa.

'That's right, don't get tied down to one woman too soon,' Ralph shouted as Tom climbed the stairs. 'They all change once you marry them.'

Once Tom was out of sight he followed Lisa into the kitchen. 'Don't you bloody well dare talk about Eve like that to Tom. You never even met her. I treat Deborah as though she's my own daughter; why can't you treat Tom like your own son?'

'Because my feelings for Tom are quite different from yours for Deborah,' Lisa said coldly. 'Far healthier, but different.'

'What the hell are you on about now?' Ralph asked. 'Sometimes I think this illness has affected your brain.'

'Oh, you do accept I've got an illness then?' Lisa remarked, plugging in the kettle. 'What a relief; then perhaps you wouldn't mind bringing my drink up to me once I'm in bed. I'm completely shattered and ought to be resting.'

'Just sod off!' Ralph snarled. 'I ought to let your blond boyfriend live with you for a week or two, he'd soon change his mind about you.'

'Drop dead,' Lisa said wearily.

With that they ceased talking and within an hour were both fast asleep, each isolated in their own private misery.

TWO

Anderson arrived at the station on Monday morning in a good mood. His relationship with Karen was progressing exactly as he'd hoped and it was a warm early June day without any hint of humidity. Perfect weather in fact; excess humidity played havoc with his linen suits. He tapped perfunctorily on Detective Superintendent Parrish's door and out of the corner of his eye noticed a slim young woman with tousled chestnut curls sitting on a chair in the corridor. She smiled at Anderson but he looked away. There was no telling who she was, besides which she wasn't his type and her clothes looked as though they'd come from a charity shop.

At the sound of his superior's voice he walked into the room and found Parrish looking out of his window, his bulky shoulders blocking out most of the light. The seams of his jacket were straining across the armholes and Anderson wondered if Parrish would make it to his retirement date or if his ulcer would force him to go early. It didn't bother him either way; he loathed the man and knew the feeling was mutual.

Slowly Parrish turned and looked at Anderson. He was

smiling, and this was the first indication Anderson had of the bombshell that was about to be dropped. Parrish never usually smiled at him.

'Nice morning,' Parrish said cheerfully.

Anderson kept his face carefully blank. He couldn't remember the last time the pair of them had exchanged platitudes about anything. 'Is it?' he asked.

Parrish shook his head. 'There you go again; even a polite remark calls forth a question from you. No wonder you've succeeded in annoying almost everyone who matters in the course of your career. You're impossible to talk to, a social disaster. When was the last time you went out for a drink with your team?'

'I really can't remember,' said Anderson, well aware that his attitude towards socialising with other members of his force went down badly, but totally unable to explain to this moron that he hadn't joined the police to become some kind of highly ranked lager lout. He'd joined it because he had ideals, beliefs, and a strong sense of justice. It offended him that the rule of law, so necessary in a civilised society, could be broken with apparent impunity and he wanted to make a difference, to contribute towards making life more orderly, and safer for the average law-abiding citizen. None of this showed on his face, he simply looked bored.

'Exactly!' Parrish said triumphantly. 'You can't remember, and nor can any of your team, I imagine. What's the matter with you, Anderson? Don't you ever learn? No, don't bother to answer that. It doesn't matter anyway. I've come up with the perfect solution, something that will force you to make a bit more of an effort for a few weeks. It will do you good, stop all that solitary introspection you're so keen on.'

'You mean I've got a new sergeant?' Anderson asked. He'd heard that Detective Sergeant Pat Fielding was at last nearly well enough to start a desk job but still missed her far more than he'd ever anticipated. She'd been the perfect partner for him, and he wasn't looking forward to learning to work alongside someone new.

'No, something far more exciting than that,' Parrish said.

Anderson wished the man would stop smiling, an expression that didn't suit him at all, making him look rather like the Cheshire Cat in *Alice*. 'Did you see a young woman waiting outside, pretty little thing with curly hair?'

'I saw a young woman with curly hair,' Anderson said smoothly.

'Well, she's a postgrad student working on a thesis about the role of our police in modern society compared with fifty years ago. As part of her thesis it's been agreed that she can spend some time with a police officer, following his progress on cases, that kind of thing. I can see you get the general idea. The thing is, in the end I decided you were the best man for the job. She'll be working alongside you for the next six weeks or so.'

For a moment Anderson quite literally couldn't breathe and stared at Parrish with undisguised hatred, but he lowered his eyes as a flash of satisfaction crossed the other man's face. He knew this was a carefully calculated insult. He was a man who prided himself on efficiency and order. The prospect of having some stupid young woman trailing him in order to finish a thesis that would have no relevance whatsoever to the real world was more than he could stand.

'I'm afraid I think that's a very bad idea, sir,' he said at last.

'Really? Why's that?' Parrish enquired with mock surprise.

'She'll only get in the way, quite apart from being a possible danger to herself and other people.'

'Not expecting an American-style shoot-out in the streets are you?' Parrish queried, his pleasure obviously mounting with every second that passed. 'If you are, I'd better warn the chief constable.'

Anderson bit on his bottom lip. He was well aware that all his colleagues would see this as a form of humiliation, designed to teach him a lesson for keeping aloof from the normal camaraderie of the station. For a moment he thought of refusing point blank, but then he remembered that Parrish would soon be gone, and that Chief Superintendent Eyer wanted Anderson to take his place, despite opposition from other officers.

It crossed his mind that Parrish might also be fearful this could happen and was trying to force him into making another mistake which would totally ruin his chances. Breathing slowly and steadily, Anderson finally managed to regain his composure. 'It doesn't sound as though I've got much choice,' he said flatly.

'None at all. Cheer up, Anderson; you might even like her. She's a cheerful sort of girl, good fun and certainly not the kind to turn faint at the sight of blood or anything like that. I wouldn't mind having her by my side, I can tell you.'

'Not much point in that, sir, is there?' remarked Anderson. 'After all, you don't do anything.'

Parrish's face turned scarlet. 'What do you mean by that?' he snapped.

'Only that you're rather tied to your desk by all the paperwork required of your rank,' Anderson said calmly, mentally notching up a point for the first time since he'd come into Parrish's office.

'Quite. And if you understood what your job was meant to be about, you wouldn't spend so much time dashing off to crimes. You'd learn to delegate more and concentrate on the paperwork too.'

'Then I'd have missed this opportunity to work with an over-age student, wouldn't I?' Anderson said smoothly.

Parrish gave up. 'Her name's Chloe Wells, she's twenty-seven, single – which might or might not be of interest to you – and highly intelligent. You might get some good conversation out of her, if you remember to speak to her that is.'

'Perhaps we'd better be introduced,' Anderson said, wondering why on earth he'd ever thought this was a good day.

Parrish went across to his door, opened it and called in the waiting young woman. She had a slightly bouncy, athletic walk and despite her business-like skirt and blouse it was plain she had a good figure. It was also plain that the skirt was a little too large and the blouse a little too small, which was why Anderson suspected they were bargains picked up at one of the numerous charity shops that sprang up almost overnight in the town.

'Chloe Wells, I'd like you to meet Detective Chief Inspector John Anderson, one of our most experienced officers,' Parrish said. Experienced was clearly the most flattering adjective he could bring himself to utter, thought Anderson. He certainly wasn't going to say successful, and after recent events that was hardly surprising. If he was going to get Parrish's job then he had a lot of ground to make up. 'John, this is Chloe, a shining example of what's best about our young people today.'

Even Chloe looked as though she felt Parrish was going a bit far, but she smiled brightly at Anderson and held out her hand. 'Hi, I'm really excited about this I can tell you. I hardly slept last night.'

'I'm afraid you'll find most police work is pretty boring,' Anderson replied as they shook hands. 'I hope you're not a devotee of some of the TV programmes. We don't work like that here, as I'm always trying to tell people.'

'You certainly don't dress like Columbo!' laughed Chloe, and Parrish snorted with amusement.

Anderson, who'd taken particular delight that morning in choosing his pale aubergine-coloured linen suit with its two-buttoned, double-vented jacket and then teaming it with one of his new poplin shirts with double cuffs, in this case a pale green one with a cut-away collar plus a green and mauve Liberty print tie, wasn't amused. He thought that if this was her idea of humour she'd be better off working on a thesis about TV game shows, and if it was an example of the fact that she was a plain speaker then he considered it extremely rude given that they'd only just met.

'I'll show you where you can get some coffee,' Anderson said.

Chloe's mouth turned down at the corners in mock dismay. 'It was a joke,' she said brightly.

'I never laugh on Monday mornings, I'm afraid, not even if a joke's really funny,' Anderson replied, smiling thinly in order to cover up his irritation.

His remark didn't appear to have affected her. 'I suppose this is quite unusual for you,' she said chattily as Anderson showed her the canteen.

'What?' Anderson asked.

'Having a member of the general public around while you work.'

'It's certainly never happened to me before, but I can't speak for other officers in other forces.'

'You don't sound as though you're looking forward to it much. I won't be a nuisance, honestly. It's just that the thesis needed something to make it a bit different, some extra authenticity, and when your chief was so helpful and said he had an officer who'd be delighted to help I assumed he meant it.'

'He must have had someone else in mind,' Anderson said shortly. His head was beginning to ache and all he wanted now was the peace of his office and a chance to finish his notes on a case due in court at the end of the week.

Leaving Chloe to her coffee he made his way to his room, and saw Detective Sergeant Philip Walker coming towards him. Walker had only recently joined them, having just been promoted to the rank of sergeant. With his fair hair and light blue, guileless eyes he looked too young to have joined the force, although Anderson had no idea what he was like at his job and hoped he wouldn't have to find out. Once again he longed for the familiar presence of Pat Fielding. He must visit her, he thought to himself. For some reason he kept putting it off. Her forthcoming wedding to Daniel had something to do with that; he knew this was ridiculous but it had made him aware that perhaps his feelings towards her had been deeper than he'd imagined.

At five to one, with most of the paperwork satisfactorily completed, he was about to go for lunch when DS Walker put his head round the door.

'The Super wants a word with you straight away, sir,' he said breathlessly. 'I think there's a bit of an emergency come up.'

Anderson's pulse quickened. It would be nice to have some action for a few hours, although emergency was bound to be an exaggeration. Walker looked like the type of policeman who made a drama out of a crisis.

Superintendent Parrish seemed relieved to see Anderson. 'I thought you might already have gone to lunch,' he said. 'Something's come up out at Kingswood. It might be something or nothing, hard to tell at the moment, but you'd better get over there right away.'

'Kingswood?' Anderson queried. 'That's a bit out of our usual area isn't it?'

'They're short-handed due to this bloody flu and your opposite number's tied up on a complicated fraud thing. They've asked for our help. What's the matter? Does the idea of a twenty-minute car drive worry you? Frightened your suit will crease?'

'It's only that I don't know the people there,' Anderson pointed out.

'Well, you'll have to get to know them, won't you? Besides, you can use our men as long as you liaise with the local lot. For God's sake, Anderson, get moving. Walker's got the details, you can take him with you. And don't forget Chloe Wells.'

Anderson couldn't think of anything he'd ever done to make him deserve his designated companion. He only hoped that DS Walker was more intelligent than he looked.

Outside the station, Walker was waiting for Anderson by the BMW.

'Where's that mature student woman?' Anderson snapped, his eyes running over the information sheet he'd been handed by Superintendent Parrish.

'She's on her way, sir,' replied Walker nervously. He'd heard exactly what kind of a bollocking to expect if he ever kept Anderson waiting and suspected that if Chloe Wells was late he'd be the one to take the blame. A civilian could hardly be torn off a strip in the same way as a junior officer.

'Get in,' Anderson said shortly. 'I'm not hanging around waiting for her. The longer the delay between the crime being reported and us getting there, the greater the chances that someone will ruin a vital piece of evidence. I'm afraid a thesis doesn't come high on my list of priorities right now.'

'Here she is, sir,' Walker said with relief. He knew that Chloe Wells was meant to trail Anderson everywhere, it was the talk of the station, and he didn't want the responsibility of being driven off by Anderson without her. All in all he was feeling very nervous about the entire situation. He just hoped that he'd pick up some good tips from Anderson. The general opinion at the station seemed to be that he was good at his job, but was a less than popular officer.

'Sorry!' Chloe said cheerfully, climbing into the back of the car and hastily pulling her door shut as Anderson drove off. 'I couldn't find my voice-activated tape recorder.'

'Corpses don't say much,' Anderson said dryly.

'Is it a murder?' Chloe asked excitedly.

'It's a dead body. We'll have to wait and see if it's murder or not once we get there.'

'Well, they wouldn't send for you if someone dropped dead of old age would they?' asked Chloe, quite reasonably Walker thought, but Anderson sighed impatiently.

'They might, if the old person wasn't expected to die. It all depends on the circumstances. You don't need to be found dead in a river with your hands tied behind your back and concrete boots on before they call in a detective inspector.' Walker smiled to himself and Chloe's bubbly enthusiasm was sufficiently dampened to silence her for the next five minutes.

'Got the address?' Anderson asked, weaving swiftly and skilfully in and out of the traffic on his way to the M25.

'Yes, sir. The house is called The Chilterns and it's in Mile Road at Kingswood. Apparently that's a very select area, all large houses with plenty of ground, a swimming pool, that kind of thing.'

'Not much good to you once you're dead,' Anderson commented.

'No, sir,' Walker agreed. 'I just thought you'd like to know a bit about it, as it's not our usual patch that is.'

'You were quite right,' Anderson conceded. 'It was a joke. I appreciate your enthusiasm; without it a policeman will never get anywhere.'

Anderson left the M25 at Junction 8 and travelled north on the A217.

'Turn right here, sir,' Walker said after about three minutes, and Anderson swung off the main road and into a tree-lined road that had been hidden from the main road by scrubland. Large houses were set well back from the road itself and about thirty metres along there was a Panda car and a Ford Fiesta outside a pair of wrought-iron gates. 'Looks like we've found The Chilterns,' remarked Anderson, easing his foot off the accelerator and slowing the car. They drew up behind the Panda car and waited as a uniformed constable came towards him.

Anderson wound down his window and showed his

identification. 'DCI Anderson,' he said shortly.

'We were told to expect you, sir,' the constable said. 'The entrance to the drive's been sealed off. Would you mind following me and I'll show you the line of approach.'

Walker could see a look of relief on Anderson's force and knew it was because things had already been done to keep the scene of crime as near its original state as possible.

They walked over the front grass and then across a marked strip of the drive past a Rover. 'Whose car's that?' Anderson asked.

'It belongs to the house owner, the husband of the dead woman, sir,' the constable said.

'Fine. Well, we'll go through and you'd better get back to gate duty,' Anderson said.

'Super house,' Chloe said, following the two men into a vast entrance hall.

'Super,' Anderson repeated ironically, and despite his nerves Walker couldn't help smiling again. He just hoped the dead woman didn't look too much of a mess. He'd seen only two badly mutilated bodies in his whole career and both times he'd disgraced himself by throwing up. He didn't want that to happen in front of Anderson. The man seemed to have ice rather than blood in his veins.

As they stepped into the parquet-floored hallway a slim young woman with short, straight black hair and almond-shaped brown eyes came towards them. 'DC Lin Ford, sir,' she said. She'd clearly been told of their arrival by the constable on the gate, but Anderson still showed her his ID before putting on a pair of disposable gloves from his jacket pocket.

'I doubt if there's any need for that, sir,' she said briskly. 'It doesn't look like foul play after all. I think the husband panicked when he called the police; he should have called a doctor or an ambulance.'

'You mean no one's dead?' asked Anderson, managing

to keep the astonishment out of his voice but privately working out exactly whose head would roll for sending him to Kingswood on a wild goose chase with Chloe Wells there to witness it.

'No, we've got a body,' she replied. 'The police surgeon's looking at it now, but it seems it's probably natural causes.'

'I think I'd better take a look,' said Anderson, wondering if things could possibly get any worse as he remembered Chloe's joke about him not being called out when old people died of natural causes.

'Of course, sir,' she said calmly. Anderson approved of her tidy appearance and composed manner. It reminded him a little of Pat Fielding, but these days a lot of women reminded him of her.

Despite what DC Lin Ford had said he felt the familiar stirring of excited anticipation as he walked into an immaculate pine kitchen with a double oven, hob, vast areas of worktops and polished wooden racks that held yellow plates and mugs that were probably never used. In fact, the entire kitchen looked unused, like a show kitchen with its bowl of exotic fruits, vases of red flowers and large-headed imitation sunflowers in various jugs.

'Very nice,' Chloe breathed. '*Ash Provence* by Mark Wilkinson. Someone's got good taste.'

Anderson glanced briefly at her. 'Don't touch a thing,' he warned. 'Not a light switch, a door knob or a surface. Keep your arms by your side and stay out of everyone's way, otherwise you'll have to wait in the car, understood?'

Chloe nodded. Anderson suspected that his warning was unnecessary. She looked pale and he guessed that her first sight of a scene of sudden death was affecting her more than she'd expected. Touching anything in the room was probably the last thing on her mind.

'Chief Inspector Anderson, Surrey Police,' said Anderson, approaching the police surgeon, who looked up at him with a brief smile.

'John Stevens, family GP and occasional police surgeon. I won't be long and then your boys can take their photos and the scene of crime officers can get cracking. I doubt there's any real need but . . .' His voice trailed off.

Realising the man was busy Anderson stepped round him to take a better look at the body. Nothing could have prepared him for the shock of seeing Lisa Allan's lifeless body lying in a crumpled heap in the corner, the back of her head resting against the wall with her legs stretched out in front of her as though she'd slid down it before finally collapsing on the tiled flooring.

She was wearing a pale blue cropped halter-top and white jeans. Her exposed midriff was lightly tanned, as though she'd recently been on a sunbed, and her blue eyes were still wide open, staring ahead of her with an expression of apparent horror.

Anderson swallowed hard and struggled to keep his voice under control. 'How long's she been dead?' he enquired.

'Not long,' Stevens said casually. 'She was still warm when her husband found her, and he rang through about half-twelve I think. You'll have to check that with Detective Sergeant Kirby. He's in the front room with the husband at the moment.'

Anderson's eyes were scanning the kitchen. 'Has anything been moved?' he asked sharply, trying to disassociate the body on the floor from the woman he'd danced with two days earlier.

'Not as far as I know. Kirby's good, and he was the first man here.'

There wasn't much that could have been moved. Anderson couldn't see a single item out of place, with the possible exception of a mobile phone on the worktop nearest to Lisa's body.

'Any idea about cause of death?' he asked, having seen no marks of violence on Lisa's body.

'I've got an idea, but that's because I'm her GP so I've

got a bit of an advantage,' Stevens admitted. 'Mrs Allan has – or I should say had – suffered for some time now from cardiac arrhythmia, a problem related to the mechanisms of the heart. Sometimes the missed heartbeats caused loss of consciousness and even, once or twice, convulsions.'

'You mean she was expected to die?' Anderson asked in astonishment, remembering Ralph's cavalier attitude to his wife's ill health.

'Certainly not. In fact, I'm astonished. She'd already had a pacemaker fitted you see, and she was on beta-blockers, which helped to iron out the irregularities. There were still problems, which was why she was going to have a defibrillator fitted. That kick-starts the heart with an electric shock if it stops, but she wasn't high on the waiting list because her condition seemed to be under control as long as she followed medical advice and kept taking her drugs.'

Anderson forced himself to study Lisa's body again. Her right arm was twisted upwards as though fending off someone or something and his eyes narrowed as he saw a small bruise on the inside of her wrist. Bending down closer he noticed a bruise on the left hand side of her neck. It looked more recent than the one on her wrist.

'What about the bruises?' he said to Stevens.

The police surgeon glanced up at him. 'I think we'd better wait for the full autopsy report before we get too worked up about small bruises. Look, I'll be finished in a couple of minutes, then she can be photographed and taken away. Do you want to stay here, or would you rather have a word with the husband while you wait?'

Anderson realised that the doctor was surprised by his interest in the body and knew that if he hadn't previously met Lisa and been attracted to her he wouldn't be hanging around getting in the man's way. 'I'll see the husband,' he said briskly. 'It seems he believes the death to be unnatural. Perhaps I'd better find out why.'

'Human nature,' Stevens murmured, suddenly bending

closer to the dead woman's body. 'He was always in a state of denial about her condition. You'll want forensic to go over her clothes I imagine?'

'Given her condition, yes I will,' Anderson said. 'She'd have been easier to kill than your average woman, I take it?'

'Physically not necessarily, but emotionally yes. Stress was very bad for her. Mind you, beta-blockers help cope with that.'

As Anderson walked out of the kitchen, closely followed by Detective Sergeant Walker, DC Ford stepped towards him. 'I'll show you where the husband is. Sergeant Kirby's been talking to him in the front room.' She looked at Chloe. 'Are you . . .'

'She's on secondment to me,' Anderson said, unable to utter the words 'postgrad student' at a moment like this. Chloe didn't protest. She didn't look as though she wanted to speak at all. At least something could shut her up, thought Anderson with satisfaction.

DS Luke Kirby was in his mid-fifties with the unflappable look of the old-school detective. He wore an ill-fitting suit, a thin, badly knotted tie and a shirt with frayed collar and cuffs. Just the same, he looked reliable.

'The husband's in a bit of a state,' he told Anderson after introducing himself. 'It seems he came home unexpectedly to collect some papers for work and found his wife dead on the floor. He called us straight away.'

'I'd better speak to him,' Anderson said.

The front room of the house was overcrowded. There were too many chairs, too many ornaments and too much material at the windows, but the thing that struck Anderson was the change in Ralph Allan from the night of the dinner dance.

The overwhelming impression then had been one of a larger-than-life personality, both in build and manner. At this moment Ralph, sitting hunched on the end of the sofa, seemed to have shrunk in on himself and his naturally high colour had vanished, leaving him looking pale and drawn. He lifted his head as DS Kirby and Anderson entered, but the look of weary numbness that was on his face vanished the moment he set eyes on Anderson.

'What the hell are you doing here?' he demanded, his voice raw with pain.

'I'm here in my official capacity,' Anderson explained, holding his ID in front of Ralph Allan's sunken eyes.

'Of course, you're a policeman, I forgot,' Ralph muttered.

'If you feel well enough, perhaps you wouldn't mind going over a few points with me, sir,' Anderson continued smoothly, sitting on a chair opposite Ralph. The man certainly seemed to be in shock, but shock could be caused by many things, and if Ralph was in any way involved in his wife's death then now was the moment when he was most likely to make a mistake.

'I've been telling the sergeant all about it,' Ralph protested.

'I know that, but there are one or two things that need clarifying,' Anderson persisted. 'Of course, if you don't feel up to it we can get the doctor to look at you once he's free, and I can come back and talk to you tomorrow. Would you prefer that?' He held his breath, hoping the man wouldn't say yes.

After a brief pause Ralph Allan shook his head. 'No, I'd rather get it all over with in one go. What do you want to know?'

'Exactly what happened, sir. Perhaps you'd like to start at the beginning. Was it usual for you to come home in the middle of the day?'

'No,' Ralph said. 'Sometimes I did, but not that often. And most times when I was coming home I'd have told Lisa in advance. This time I needed to pick up some papers that I'd left behind. They're needed, were needed I should say, for a meeting at three o'clock. I rang home a couple of times from work to ask Lisa to get them out for me but there was no answer. When I got here I shouted her name as I came in, but she didn't answer so I went straight through into the kitchen.'

'Is that where your papers were?' asked Anderson.

Ralph looked bewildered. 'Of course not, but it's where I expected to find Lisa. She loved to sit there drinking her decaffeinated coffee and looking out on to the garden.' His voice cracked.

'What happened next?' Anderson pressed, his voice gentle but authoritative. Now was not the moment to let the apparently grieving husband off the hook.

'Well, I went in and at first I couldn't see her, but then I did. I thought she'd just passed out – she did that, you see, it was something to do with her heart condition – and I put my hands on her shoulders and tried to lift her into a more upright position but when her head fell back against the wall I realised . . . It was then that I . . .' He stopped and dropped his head into his hands, making a kind of choking noise as though fighting back tears.

Anderson paused for a moment. 'I know this must be very painful for you, Mr Allan, but there's something I really do need to know. Why did you call the police?'

Ralph Allan lifted his head and stared at Anderson in astonishment. 'That's what you're bloody well there for, isn't it? My wife was dead, for God's sake. I had her body lying there in front of me and no idea what had happened to her. I did what every normal person would do in the circumstances and rang for help. I used the mobile because it didn't matter, I mean Lisa was already dead, but it wasn't mine. I never bring mine into the house; it's dangerous, you see, for her condition. We're all very careful about our mobiles because Lisa gets . . . got in a terrible state if there was one near her. She took the booklet from the hospital very seriously. We all did.'

'So you were surprised to see a mobile phone in the kitchen?' asked Anderson.

'Not at first, all I could think about was that Lisa was dead; later, after I'd rung the police, yes I was surprised. I can't think who it belongs to, but mine's in my car. It's been a house rule here ever since Lisa was first in intensive care. We leave our phones in the car and take off our shoes when we come into the house.'

'And did you?' Anderson asked, wishing that Chloe would stop fidgeting in his line of vision.

'Did I what?'

'Take off your shoes?'

'No, no I didn't. That's in the evenings, when we're coming home to eat. It was a figure of speech, for God's sake, not a literal statement'

There was a tap on the door and DC Lin Ford put her head into the room. 'Dr Stevens would like a word with you before he leaves, sir,' she said softly.

Anderson got to his feet and straightened his jacket. 'That's all for now, Mr Allan. Are there any other members of the family here at the moment?'

'Tom, my son. I heard him arrive a few minutes ago. I don't think Debs is here. She's probably not back from horseriding. She's got a horse of her own which I bought for her and spends most of her free time exercising it.'

'How old is your daughter?' Anderson asked.

'She's my stepdaughter and she's eighteen, why?'

'I always thought it was younger girls who were horse mad, but never having had children of my own I wouldn't really know. We'll talk to them later, after they've had a chance to take in what's happened. How old's your son?'

'Twenty-two,' Ralph said. 'Not that you'd know it. Debs seems older than him.'

Sensing the usual story of father and son locked in the age-old battle for supremacy, Anderson refrained from comment. Leaving DS Kirby with Ralph Allan he went out into the hall, where John Stevens was waiting for him.

'I've finished and your scene-of-crime lads are busy now.

I'm afraid I can't give you a definite answer until there's been a full postmortem. I've got a feeling it's going to turn out to be natural causes but I can't possibly write out a certificate at this stage. She certainly wasn't expected to drop dead, not by me or her specialist, but we're not infallible as you and I both know only too well.'

'How long before you can let me know?' Anderson asked.

'Forty-eight hours, give or take the odd hour.'

'I'll tell the husband,' Anderson said.

The doctor nodded. 'Fine. How's he coping?'

'He seems shocked but he's bearing up. Are you his GP too?'

Stevens shook his head. 'This isn't the most united family you'll find, Anderson. If Lisa Allan used me as her GP then her husband probably went elsewhere to show he thought she'd made the wrong choice. He certainly never liked what I told him about her condition, but then men don't like having wives who are ill, especially when they're second wives and meant to be young and active.'

'Really,' Anderson said. He had already worked that out for himself but liked having his opinion backed up by another professional.

'I'll get in touch as soon as the results are through,' Stevens promised as he left.

Anderson glanced into the kitchen and saw that the officers were all busy with their individual tasks. Some were dusting for fingerprints, or photographing the body and objects in the room while others were checking for any kind of forensic evidence they could find.

'A lot of work for a natural causes,' DS Walker said.

'Natural causes?' Anderson asked.

Phil Walker was flustered. 'Yes, sir. I mean, the doctor said it's almost certainly natural causes didn't he? And she had this heart condition so I thought –'

'It's best to go on the facts, and wait and see how they

come out, Walker. Unless you can think clearly and logically perhaps it's a good idea not to try. Preconceived ideas can be very dangerous and lead to mistakes,' said Anderson. Walker blushed

'The poor husband,' Chloe said suddenly.

Anderson turned his penetrating blue eyes on her. 'Why do you say that?'

'It's bad enough finding your wife dead, but then to be told there's going to be an autopsy, that she's going to be cut up . . . ugh.' Chloe shuddered.

'If he's got nothing to worry about then he should be pleased we're taking such care over the case. After all, he was the one who called the police in. We have to assume he wanted to be sure it was natural causes too.'

'He said it was an instinctive reaction,' Chloe protested. 'You make it sound suspicious.'

'Do I?' Anderson asked.

Now it was Chloe's turn to be thrown by a question. 'Yes, you do,' she said firmly.

'Perhaps I think it is then. Or perhaps I'm just doing my job and being thorough. You'll have to work out which it is for your thesis, won't you.'

Chloe bit on her bottom lip and then followed Anderson back into the front room where Ralph was now standing by the drinks cabinet and drinking a large brandy.

'The police surgeon's gone now but there's still quite a lot going on in the kitchen,' Anderson explained. 'I'm afraid I'll have to ask you all to stay out of there until we've finished. It shouldn't take too long.'

Ralph looked blankly at him, as though he had no idea what Anderson was talking about.

'Dr Stevens says he'll have to have a postmortem before he can give the cause of death,' Anderson continued, watching Ralph Allan closely. 'We should know the result within forty-eight hours.' Rather to Anderson's disappointment there was still no reaction. As Anderson left he heard

Ralph asking DS Kirby what he should do about the funeral arrangements.

Before leaving the house he went into the kitchen again. The body had been removed but the outline was clearly marked and Anderson remembered with hideous clarity the moment of almost electric sexual magnetism that had flashed between him and the dead woman less than forty-eight hours earlier.

'I want that mobile phone bagged and taken to forensics,' he said sharply. 'If there are any clues in this room then they're probably on that. The husband's already admitted touching the body and trying to move it, which makes life a damned sight harder for us.'

'If the doctor thinks it was natural causes you won't need the evidence, will you?' Chloe asked as she, Anderson and DS Walker got into Anderson's car.

'No, but if it isn't the evidence isn't going to wait around until I come back another day,' replied Anderson.

'I wonder why they sent for you?' Chloe mused. 'It doesn't look at all suspicious.'

Anderson, who had a pretty shrewd suspicion that Parrish had sent him for precisely that reason, swung the car back on to the A217 before replying. 'I think there's more to it than meets the eye,' he said slowly. 'No one expected Lisa Allan to die, least of all her doctor. And no one, according to her husband, ever took a mobile phone into the house. In my opinion that combination makes it look decidedly odd.'

'The autopsy will show whether you're right or not,' Chloe said, 'but personally I'd have said it was just one of those terrible things that happen.'

'Put it in your thesis,' said Anderson. 'Write it tonight, then you can crow if you're right.'

'Or look a fool if you're wrong,' Phil Walker muttered.

Anderson smiled to himself.

★

Later that day, when all the police had gone, leaving the kitchen still sealed and out of bounds, Ralph, Tom and Deborah were gathered in the drawing room.

Deborah's eyes were red-rimmed from crying, but Tom's face was blank and pale with shock. Ralph had regained some of his normal colour, and his voice was stronger again, although the hand holding his brandy glass trembled when he lifted it to his lips.

'Who the hell left their phone in the kitchen?' he demanded, glaring at both Tom and Deborah.

'Not me,' Tom said. 'When I got back I left mine in my car, the same as I always do. You can come and see it if you like.'

'What about you, Deborah?' Ralph asked.

Deborah's lips trembled. 'Why would I have left my mobile there? I loved Mummy. I'd never have done anything to hurt her.'

'No one's saying you would,' Ralph said. 'The phone didn't kill her, Debs. I just want to know what it was doing there, and the police will want to know as well.'

'It isn't my phone!' Deborah shouted. 'Mine's in the bedroom. I left it there last night. It must be yours or Tom's.'

'We'll soon settle that,' Ralph said. 'Come on, we'll go and look in the cars.'

With tears welling in her eyes Deborah followed her stepfather and stepbrother out to the front of the house and watched as first Ralph and then Tom produced their phones. They both looked at her, waiting for her reaction.

'So what?' she sobbed. 'That doesn't mean it was mine. I'm not the one who was arguing with Mummy last night, you are, Ralph. Who's to say you didn't go out and buy another phone?'

'Why the hell should I?' Ralph demanded.

'Are you sure yours is in your room?' Tom asked his stepsister.

Without another word Deborah ran back into the house

and up to her room, while the two men followed slowly behind her. After a long time she came back into the lounge and now she was crying and shaking uncontrollably. 'It isn't there!' she wailed. 'My phone's gone, but I know it was there last night. It isn't fair. I'm the only one in this house who really loved Mummy. I'd never have done anything to hurt her.'

Ralph went across to his stepdaughter and put an arm round her shoulders. 'No one's saying you did hurt her, Debs. You must have brought it down with you this morning and left it in the kitchen by mistake. It doesn't matter. Your mother almost certainly had a fatal convulsion while she was alone in the kitchen. It was just a dreadful accident and now we've all got to try and be brave and carry on the way she'd have wanted us to. We've got to show that we can still be a happy family.'

Tom stared at his father in disbelief. 'I've never heard such total crap,' he said at last. 'We weren't exactly the Waltons when Lisa was alive, you know. Christ, the way you and Lisa were going for each other last night no one would have thought you'd ever been in love. Why the hell should her death improve things? Don't be such a fucking hypocrite.'

As he pushed past his father and out of the front room there was a long silence and then Deborah fled to her room in tears, leaving Ralph alone, his expression thoughtful.

That evening Anderson sat in the peaceful solitude of his fourth-floor penthouse flat with Couperin's *Concerts Royaux* playing quietly in the background as he mentally went over the events of the day.

When Karen had rung just after he'd arrived home he'd postponed their scheduled meeting that night pleading pressure of work. The truth was that he couldn't face seeing Karen, so full of life and probably expecting another evening of lovemaking, when he'd just seen Lisa the way he had, with her life over. It wasn't like him to be affected in such a way and the very fact that he was unsettled him.

In order to distract himself he started jotting down notes on a large pad in his neat, spidery writing. Nothing about Lisa's death rang true to Anderson. There was something badly wrong, something out of true that he was missing. Carefully and methodically he went over what he knew already, prior to the post-mortem results.

In the first place, something about Ralph jarred. There was no denying that he was in shock, but a man who'd just killed would be, and a man with enough nerve to kill, call the police and then bluff it out was likely to be in a state of high agitation. Anderson considered that Ralph was capable of doing just that, and that he was enjoying a sense of power as he watched the police scuttle round before coming up with a death by natural causes verdict.

Then there was the mobile phone. If mobile phones were so dangerous to Lisa, Anderson couldn't understand why Lisa had allowed one to be brought into the house. If she'd seen it on the worktop when she'd got back from wherever she'd been, surely she'd have moved it or switched it off?

This suggested to Anderson that it hadn't been there when she'd walked into the kitchen. It had either been brought in afterwards or someone who'd come in with her had brought it with him, or her, but concealed in a pocket or handbag. Even so, he knew that it was unlikely Lisa would have dropped dead at the sight of it. He decided that he needed to know more about her heart condition.

He went over to his bookcase and took down a rarely-used encyclopaedia of health. He thumbed through it until he found cardiac arrhythmia, but it told him little more than John Stevens had already, except for the fact that it was a fairly common condition and that with the right treatment most sufferers could lead relatively normal lives. Anderson recognised that this glossed over the possibility of others dropping dead, but it still didn't get him much further forward.

Lying in bed that night he found himself replaying the scene at the squash club on the Saturday night. He could remember with great clarity the way Lisa had turned pale and complained of feeling tired, also Ralph's mocking comments about a wife whose illness meant she could do the things she wanted to but not the things she didn't. It showed lack of understanding if nothing else, but just as he drifted off to sleep Anderson wondered what Ralph had meant by his wife doing the things she wanted to do.

THREE

The next morning was cooler and there was more cloud. After his run, a shower and then breakfast of espresso and wholemeal toast with sugar-free apricot preserve, Anderson chose a pale fawn wool and mohair suit with a slight sheen to it and a darker stripe running through the fabric. His cotton shirt was a muted rust colour and his tie a rust and gold paisley pattern. He was pleased with the suit; it was new and felt light despite the wool. It also hung well, and when he slipped his notebook into his inside pocket the line of the jacket remained unspoilt. Details like that mattered to him.

On arriving at the police station, Anderson noticed a battered blue Metro parked in the official car park. Chloe's, he assumed: it looked the kind of car she'd drive. He wondered how she was feeling today, and if she was quite so bright-eyed and bushy-tailed about trailing him as she had been before she'd seen Lisa's body.

Walking briskly through the corridors he was greeted by a smiling WPC Kim Baines who had done something different with her dark blonde hair. 'Very nice,' he murmured. She walked on, blushing furiously.

Anderson knew that she fancied him, but the feeling was not reciprocated. She wore far too much make-up and her whole attitude and body language lacked the subtle femininity that attracted him. In any case, he doubted if she was intelligent enough to hold his interest out of bed even supposing they ever got into it. This reminded him that he must ring Karen at some point in the day and arrange another meeting. Some of the previous evening's strange feeling of loss had passed now, and he was beginning to think he'd been mad to cancel, although the thinking he'd done about the Allan case certainly hadn't been a waste of time. Mental puzzles were always enjoyable.

His good mood decreased when he found Chloe Wells sitting in his office waiting for him. She was wearing a fitted floral print dress, had bare legs and the chipped pink nail varnish on her toes showed through the open ends of her sandals. He could see that her colouring and undeniably feminine curves combined with her bubbly enthusiasm might appeal to some men, but he wasn't one of them.

'I thought I'd be early today, in case we get called back to Kingswood,' she said brightly.

'You mean in case I get called back to Kingswood,' he corrected her.

He saw from the expression in her eyes that she was taken aback, but her assumption that they were a team was ridiculous. Since she had Superintendent Parrish's blessing he had no choice but to put up with her, but that didn't mean he had to like it. The one thing that did interest him slightly was how he'd come over in her thesis; he admitted to himself that this was pure vanity on his part.

DS Phil Walker put his head round the door. 'Message from Dr Stevens, sir. He'd like you to ring him when you've got a moment.'

Anderson's pulse quickened. 'Already?'

'Probably to tell you it's not a suspicious death,' Walker replied.

He was almost certainly right, thought Anderson, feeling positively disappointed. He'd looked forward to matching himself against Ralph Allan in a murder hunt. He glanced at Chloe. 'Are you going to have a coffee or something?' Shaking her head she began to scribble in her notebook, forcing Anderson to make the call with her still in the room.

By the time he was put through to John Stevens the roof of his mouth was dry. What he wanted was confirmation that his hunch had been right and that Lisa's death wasn't due to natural causes, whereas he was likely to get the opposite, and with Chloe Wells sitting opposite him to hear her own opinion confirmed.

'Anderson? Good of you to call back so fast. Look, he'll be sending a copy of his report over to you later today but I thought you'd like to know what the pathologist found.'

'Yes, I would,' Anderson said calmly.

'It's a bit of a mess, I'm afraid. You see, the cause of death is definitely heart failure, which could be put down to natural causes given her medical history but – and it's a big but – there was no trace of beta-blockers in her body.'

'Meaning?' Anderson asked sharply.

'Meaning that for some reason her heart wasn't protected in the way it was meant to be. The beta-blockers were vital to her health. She knew that better than anyone, and quite frankly it doesn't make sense, which is why we're going to run a second set of tests.'

'So, was she murdered?' Anderson asked.

'I've no idea,' Stevens said regretfully. 'The pathologist will be able to give you a better idea of that when he's done a second more intensive set of tests. As her GP, though, I'll tell you this, but strictly off the record.'

'Yes,' Anderson said impatiently.

'I think it's very odd.'

'Would you be prepared to tell my superior that you were worried, if he asked?' Anderson queried.

There was a long pause. 'Yes, I suppose so,' Stevens agreed

at last. 'It worries me, and if it worries me then it should worry the police, so that seems fair. Mind you, I'd rather not get involved at this stage because it's an opinion not a fact.'

'It's a fact that there's no trace of beta-blockers though?'

'Oh yes,' Stevens said. 'That's an inexplicable and undisputable fact.'

'Anything interesting?' Chloe asked as Anderson put down the phone.

'Extremely interesting,' he said, smiling with satisfaction. 'I'm going to see Parrish and then with any luck we'll all be on our way to Kingswood to talk to the Allan family.'

'So I lose my bet?'

He nodded. 'Probably, but you should get a better thesis out of it.'

Superintendent Parrish wasn't helpful. He made noises about waiting until the second set of results came through and queried the use of manpower on a case that wasn't definitely murder. It was only when Anderson pointed out that Ralph Allan was very big in the charity world around his area, including the police benevolent fund – information DS Walker had supplied him with earlier – and that as such his local force were anxious that the police should be seen to be doing its job thoroughly that he agreed Anderson could make further enquiries pending the final tests coming through.

'But remember, nothing's certain yet,' he reminded Anderson. 'You can use DS Walker, but apart from that you'll have to manage with the local force until it's been proven one way or the other.'

'I've got Chloe Wells to assist me,' Anderson said smoothly. 'I'm sure her keen unbiased young brain will prove invaluable.'

On the drive to the Allans' house Anderson filled in DS Walker and Chloe Wells on what he'd learnt so far. 'It's not much to go on, sir,' said Walker. 'She might have been the forgetful type. You know what women are like where the Pill's concerned. Except vitamins,' he added. 'My last girlfriend took more vitamins than I'd have thought any human being could digest.'

'A young woman with a heart condition isn't likely to forget to take pills that will keep her alive,' Chloe said from the back of the car. 'She wasn't an airhead was she?'

'Not from what I saw of her,' Anderson said. 'And she was definitely nervous about her health. It doesn't make any sense to me, or to Dr Stevens.'

The front door of The Chilterns was opened by Deborah Allan. She was puffy-eyed from lack of sleep and barely seemed to register Anderson's ID. He could see that she was very like her mother, but with all the added charm of youth.

'I'm sorry to have to trouble you,' he said gently. 'I'm afraid I need to speak to your stepfather urgently, and possibly after that to you and your stepbrother if he's in.'

'We're all here,' Deborah said miserably. 'I'll take you through to Ralph. He's in the games room playing billiards. He can't seem to rest at all. My grandfather was here earlier and that made things even worse.'

Anderson, Walker and Chloe were shown through the dining room into a large games room with a billiard table, pinball machine, bar and darts board. Ralph was aimlessly pushing the balls around the billiard table and seemed almost grateful for the interruption.

'I suppose you've got the post-mortem report,' he said to Anderson.

Anderson nodded. 'If we might have a word in private,' he suggested. Taking the hint, Deborah left, closing the door behind her.

'What's the big secret?' Ralph demanded, looking far more like the man at the squash club dinner dance than the shattered wreck of the previous lunchtime. He'd bounced back quickly, thought Anderson, and glancing at his sergeant he sensed that young Walker was thinking the same.

'There's no secret, sir, but there is a bit of a puzzle that we thought you might be able to help us with.'

'What kind of a puzzle?'

'There were no traces of beta-blockers in your wife's body,' said Anderson, sitting on a hard, armless leather chair by the wall.

Ralph straightened up from the table and glared down at Anderson. 'So what?'

'You're not surprised?' asked Anderson.

'Not particularly; she could be damned stupid at times.'

'In what way, stupid?' Anderson queried.

'You probably don't know this, Chief Inspector, but one of the side-effects of beta-blockers can be a diminished libido. They affected Lisa that way and she found that upsetting to say the least. She was a very sexual young woman, as I'm sure you noticed, and that side of our marriage meant a lot to her, to both of us I should add.'

'It meant a lot to you both,' Anderson repeated.

Ralph stared at Anderson, waiting for him to say something more, but Anderson was too sharp to do any such thing. After a brief silence Ralph couldn't stop himself from carrying on talking. 'Yes, we enjoyed a very full physical relationship in our marriage,' he said, almost smirking at Anderson, whose face was carefully blank. 'Sometimes, although she knew I disapproved, Lisa would miss out a dose so that we could have, shall we say, a more entertaining night.'

'Miss out a dose,' Anderson repeated slowly, before falling silent once more.

'Yes, that's what I said,' Ralph retorted. 'You didn't know Lisa, she could be very obstinate.'

'Obstinate or not, the point is that a total lack of any trace of beta-blockers in her body suggests she missed rather more than one dose. Can you think of any reason why she'd have stopped taking them altogether?'

Ralph looked at Anderson with open dislike. 'I'm

beginning to think there's something personal in this,' he said curtly. 'I saw the way you looked at my wife when you were dancing with her. You wanted her, didn't you? You were jealous of me, and now you're trying to suggest that somehow I was involved in her death. You must be off your bloody head. What would I gain from her death? She meant everything to me,' he added quickly.

'I assure you there's nothing personal in this at all,' Anderson replied stiffly, but he was aware that there was a grain of truth in what Ralph was saying. 'However, if I may remind you, you were the one who called in the police in the first place. We're simply doing our job, which is, I assume, what you wanted when you sent for us.'

'I was expecting Detective Chief Inspector Johnson,' Ralph blurted out. 'He and I know each other well. We golf together. He's a friend and I naturally thought of him the moment I found Lisa.'

'How unfortunate for you that he was tied up with another case,' said Anderson, without a hint of irony. 'I assure you that I shall endeavour to do as well as Chief Inspector Johnson would have done.' And probably a damned sight better, he thought to himself, interested to discover that the phone call had been intended to summon a friend rather than an entire police squad. Ralph Allan must have been somewhat put out, to say the least of it.

'So you can't think of any reason why your wife would have stopped taking her pills?' Anderson persisted.

Ralph's dark eyes met Anderson's squarely and with a hint of triumph. 'As a matter of fact I can. She may well have wanted an even more active libido than I realised, but we'll never know, will we?'

'Meaning what, sir?' Anderson asked evenly.

'Meaning that perhaps she had a boyfriend I knew nothing about. She spent enough time out of the house seeing "friends" when I was working. Perhaps they weren't all female.'

'Do you have any reason to suspect that's the case?'

Ralph suddenly seemed to realise that he was moving into dangerous waters. 'No, no of course not,' he blustered. 'You come up with some wild statement and then expect me to give you an explanation. The truth is I can't, but that one would fit, wouldn't it?'

'Yes, it would fit,' agreed Anderson. 'If she was willing to gamble with her life, that is.'

'She died of natural causes, you cretin!' Ralph shouted, colour suffusing his face as his quick temper finally got the better of him. 'When will you accept that?'

'After the second set of results from the pathologist,' Anderson replied. 'Until then your wife's death is being treated as suspicious. I wonder if I might have a word with your son and stepdaughter while I'm here?'

'I don't suppose I can stop you,' Ralph muttered. 'Tom's in the conservatory. He's the one who makes sure the jungle grows well. Lisa likes –' He stopped and tears filled his eyes for a moment. 'She liked a lot of plants out there,' he finished in a rush.

'We'll find our own way,' said Anderson quietly as they left.

'He was really upset,' said Chloe in a subdued voice. 'It's awful to see strong men cry isn't it?'

'I've seen lots of people cry,' replied Anderson. 'Most of them were very good actors or actresses. Don't be misled, Chloe. Seeing is not believing.'

Chloe had begun to feel antagonistic towards Anderson the day before. She hadn't liked the cold way he'd handled Ralph or the way he'd made DS Walker blush. Although she'd seen a different side of him when he'd smiled at her that morning, she really felt he was cold through and through, and his attitude towards Ralph now infuriated her. 'I don't know what you've got against him,' she hissed as they walked carefully through the sealed-off kitchen and out into the conservatory beyond. 'I think he's nice;

frightened, shocked and a bit loud, but nice underneath.'

'Really?' asked Anderson, with so much scorn in his voice that DS Walker flinched.

Chloe didn't. 'Yes, really,' she retorted.

They found Tom examining the undersides of the leaves of a cheese plant. At six foot one he was about an inch shorter than his father, but where Ralph was heavily built and florid, Tom was quite slim and muscular with a pale complexion and light brown hair that flopped forward over his forehead. His eyes were also light brown and he kept his head slightly bent much of the time, so that he rarely looked anyone directly in the eye.

'Tom Allan?' Anderson asked. The boy turned his head towards the three newcomers and nodded. 'I'm Detective Chief Inspector Anderson. I wondered if we might have a quick word with you about your stepmother, if you've got the time?'

'Sure,' said Tom, flinging himself into one of the cane chairs.

Chloe, who was intrigued by the difference between father and son, thought that Tom looked on edge even though his voice sounded relaxed. She was interested to note that whereas Anderson had been very authoritative with Ralph, he sounded far more paternal when talking to Tom. There was almost a note of warmth in the deep voice.

'I just wanted to know how you got on with your stepmother, and whether or not you realised how serious her heart condition was,' said Anderson softly.

Tom frowned. 'I'll tell you anything you want to know but I'm not sure why you're here. I mean, there's nothing suspicious about her death is there?'

'At the moment we're keeping an open mind,' Anderson said.

'You mean, it might not have been natural causes?' His anxiety level was rising fast now, and he rubbed the palms of his hands together nervously.

'I really can't tell you any more than I have at present. There are still some results to come back from the autopsy,' Anderson explained. 'Right at this moment I'm trying to get a picture of what your stepmother was like and the kind of life she led. This includes the restrictions her heart condition must have brought about.'

Tom shrugged. 'I don't know about restrictions. I mean, she still did most of the things she did before she was ill, but not squash or tennis, and she had to be careful what she did at the gym.'

'Gym?' Anderson asked.

'Yes, she belonged to Fit and Well, which is about ten minutes away from here. She used to go a lot, but mostly I think she swam and used the cycle. We've got one here but she said the one at the gym was better.'

'How did you get on with her?' Anderson asked, switching tack and changing his tone so that the question snapped out abruptly.

'All right,' Tom said warily.

'But you must have missed your mother. You were only what, sixteen, when she died?'

'She killed herself,' Tom said. 'Yes, I did miss her, but that wasn't Lisa's fault.'

'No, but at thirty she must have seemed very young to a boy of sixteen.'

'There was a gap before my father remarried,' Tom pointed out. 'Not a long one, but about a year.'

'Just the same she was young to be your stepmother,' said Anderson, his voice gentle again.

Tom sighed. 'Sure, she was young, but to tell you the truth she never tried to be a stepmother to me. I don't think Lisa had a maternal bone in her body. She found Debs difficult enough. Someone else's child was of no interest to her. Anyway, seventeen's an awkward age isn't it? I was as confused as she was, and we were both horribly moody.'

'Difficult,' Anderson sympathised.

'We managed. After a couple of years it didn't really matter. I was working for Dad, and Lisa and I didn't have that much to do with each other. We worked out a way of coping without quarrelling.'

'How about once she got ill? Did that make her easier or more difficult?'

Tom fidgeted in the chair. 'It doesn't seem right talking about her like this. It must be bloody awful to be so ill when you're relatively young and used to being active. She was very lively before, always the centre of attention at parties and that, which used to piss my Dad off a bit sometimes. I don't know why. Presumably that's why he fancied her in the first place.'

'So she did change?' Anderson said. Chloe wondered why he was so anxious to establish this fact.

'Yeah, she changed. Her mood swings got worse. It might have been the pills. She was always on about herself too. You know, getting pains in her chest, feeling tired, that sort of thing. Well, she's had two convulsions and nearly suffered a cardiac arrest. I suppose anyone would be nervous.'

'Your father must have been worried sick,' Anderson murmured.

Tom laughed. 'That's a joke! Dad's got a lot of virtues, but sensitivity isn't one of them. The more reassurance Lisa needed, the less he gave her. I'd seen it all before with my mother. She had problems, she was at that age or something, and he didn't help her either. I think Lisa kept on about her illness because she wanted his attention. He didn't seem as interested in her in other ways once she was ill, so that was probably her way of keeping him dancing in attendance.'

'How do you mean, in other ways?' Anderson asked.

Tom flushed, which Chloe found rather touching. 'He never used to be able to keep his hands off her, but in the past year or so that changed. Maybe it was because he was getting used to having her as his wife. She still looked gorgeous even if she was ill, but his indifference worried her. They used to have rows about it. They were having one . . .' He hesitated and Anderson's bright eyes watched him carefully. 'Recently,' Tom finished lamely.

Chloe expected Anderson to push Tom on this point, but he didn't. Instead he turned to leave and then turned back to face Tom again. 'I can't quite remember,' he said casually. 'Were you at work when your stepmother was found?'

'Not exactly. I'd been to see a rep for the company who lives near here and when I'd finished with him I came back home for lunch. It's nearer than the office. When I got back Dad had already found Lisa and some police were here, but not you. You came later, I think.'

'If you'd just give the rep's name and address to DS Walker here that will be fine for today,' Anderson said. 'Thank you for your help. I realise it's a difficult time for you right now.'

'It's worse for Debs,' Tom said.

Anderson and Chloe soon discovered what he meant. Although she came down into the front room from her bedroom, Deborah was still close to hysteria. At every mention of her mother's name she started crying and for a moment Anderson considered coming back another day, but then he decided it would be better to press on.

He prided himself on recognising true grief when he saw it, and felt very sorry for the young blonde girl weeping in front of the pair of them. Slowly and gently he managed to coax her out of her tears until at last she became coherent.

'I don't want to upset you more, Deborah,' Anderson explained once she had herself under control, 'but I feel that out of everyone here you're the person who can tell us the most about your mother and what she was really like.'

'I can tell you more about what Ralph's like,' she muttered.

'He isn't nearly as upset as he's pretending to be. I heard him shouting at her on Saturday night. It was one of their big rows too. He called her a tart and said she'd been flirting around at the dinner dance.'

Anderson's face didn't change. No one would have guessed that he knew, as this girl didn't, that he was the man her mother had been flirting with. 'Did they often quarrel?' he asked quietly.

Deborah sniffed and wiped her nose with a tissue. 'They did recently. Once Mummy was ill really. Ralph doesn't believe in illness. He thinks you can keep well if you think positively.'

'But you understood how she was feeling?'

Deborah looked nervously at him before shaking her head. 'Not really. I used to get cross when she was too tired to come and watch me ride. That was horribly selfish I know, but it was difficult to grasp how ill she was. I never thought she'd die. She was meant to be having a special machine fitted so that she could live a more normal life and they made her wait because they said her case wasn't urgent, but they were wrong weren't they?' She started to cry again.

'It looks that way,' Anderson agreed. 'Tell me, Deborah, why was your mother so afraid of mobile phones?'

'Because when she was last in intensive care there were notices everywhere saying that doctors must turn off their mobiles in case they interfered with patients' pacemakers. Mummy said that if the hospital were worried then so should we be.

'We all had to read a booklet about her pacemaker when she came home. That said that in hospital it's all made worse by the different machines that are around, but she did have one of those new pacemakers that isn't set at a fixed pace and they're more sensitive, so we couldn't have a microwave in the house. If they go wrong they can interfere with the pacemaker working properly. Oh yes, and Ralph had to have the burglar alarms taken out. The system he'd got in the house was bad for her.'

Anderson, who'd been sitting back in his chair, leant forward slightly. 'Has he had a new system put in yet?'

Deborah shook her head. 'No, he was trying to find out which would be the best system to use. He's got a friend in the police who was helping him; someone he plays golf with.'

'You were out when your mother died weren't you?' Anderson asked slowly.

Deborah went very white. 'Yes, I was horseriding but I wish I'd never gone. If I'd been here I might have been able to save her. We all knew what to do if she had a fit and I can't bear to think about her knowing she was going to lose consciousness and being all alone. She must have been terrified.' Once again Deborah began to sob hopelessly and as he stood up, Anderson touched her gently on the shoulder.

'You mustn't blame yourself, Deborah. I doubt very much if there was anything you could have done.'

As he and Chloe left the room Ralph went in. He ignored the two of them and going straight over to his sobbing stepdaughter put an arm round her shoulders.

'Come on,' said Anderson quietly. 'Time for us to leave. Where the hell's Walker got to?'

Walker was outside standing by Anderson's BMW. He was feeling rather pleased with himself.

'Where have you been?' Anderson asked.

DS Phil Walker pointed towards the house next door to the Allan's. 'I thought it might be worth having a word with their neighbours, sir. To see if they'd seen or heard anything.'

Anderson raised an eyebrow. 'Really? Do you think Superintendent Parrish would feel this enquiry warrants a house-to-house yet?'

Walker's previously cheerful countenance dropped; he still wasn't used to Anderson's habit of asking unexpected questions. 'I suppose not,' he admitted.

'I think it's a good idea though,' Anderson continued with one of his rare smiles. 'You look as though you heard something interesting. Are you going to let us in on the secret?'

'The woman who lives there's called Sara Cooper and it turns out she was walking her dog at 11.50 a.m. on the day Lisa Allan died. As she was about to turn into her drive she saw Lisa being driven past. She was sitting in the passenger seat of a car driven by a man called Jeff Phillips. Apparently he's the manager of a local health club. Sara Cooper tried to be discreet but I got the distinct impression that it wasn't the first time she'd seen the pair of them together and that in her opinion Lisa Allan and Jeff Phillips knew each other very well.'

'In a carnal sense?' Anderson enquired blandly.

'She didn't say so, sir, but that's what I think she believed.'

'Interesting,' Anderson murmured.

'What now?' Chloe asked.

'Now we go back to Guildford and wait for some test results. Forensics should be able to tell me a bit about the mobile phone by now. Well done, Philip, that's useful information.'

DS Walker felt a glow of pride. He'd heard that Anderson was very sparing with praise and a remark like that was something to be treasured. Actually he was enjoying working with him. He was fast, calm and always gave the impression that he knew what he was doing. Also he wasn't loud, and that made an agreeable change.

Their journey back to Guildford was made in silence, which was the way Anderson liked it.

Almost as soon as Anderson was back in his office he got the call he wanted from Forensics. 'Here's what we've got on the mobile phone,' said the lab technician. 'The only fingerprints on it belong to Ralph Allan, but it isn't his phone. The phone belongs to a Miss Deborah Allan. However, her prints aren't on it.'

'Which means it was wiped clean before Ralph Allan used it,' Anderson murmured.

'Presumably, yes. Also, we've got a note of the calls made from it on the day that interests you. There were only two. At 12.15 a call was made to the speaking clock and at 12.25 a call was made to the local police station. Nothing else, that's everything.'

'It's more than enough,' Anderson said gratefully. After replacing his phone he stared thoughtfully into space. He could vividly remember a large kitchen clock at the Allan's home, and as far as he could remember it was accurate. The call to the speaking clock therefore appeared to be superfluous, but not if it had been made as a method of attacking Lisa Allan by interfering with her pacemaker.

Scribbling down, 'No alarm system in the house' he picked up the phone to ring Karen Raybould. He wanted to see her tonight because he had the feeling that this last piece of information was definitely something to celebrate.

He'd been shaken to learn that Lisa Allan had been having an affair with Jeff Phillips as it meant that his image of Lisa, formed during their brief time together at the dinner dance, appeared to have been a little off beam. Even her daughter's extreme distress was, he suspected, more because she and her mother had not been as close as she wished rather than due to bereavement. He'd pictured Lisa as the victim of a bullying husband and ill health, but it seemed there was rather more to her than that.

However, in his opinion there was now no doubt that she had been murdered and discovering the identity of the killer was going to be a very complex task. He only hoped that the pathologist came up with something that would convince Parrish too.

★

That evening when Chloe arrived back at her parents' house, where she was living while she was working alongside John Anderson, her mother was waiting to talk to her. This was unusual. Respecting the fact that their daughter, at twenty-seven and used to sharing a flat with other students, would find living with them restricting, Susan and George Wells had allowed Chloe to use the annexe to their house on the outskirts of Guildford. The annexe had been occupied by her grandmother until her death the previous year. It was like having her own home, only free, and in general her parents stayed out of her way. She supposed it might seem strange to some people, but as an only child she'd always been independent, and both her parents were professionals. Her father was a headmaster, her mother a special needs teacher, and she'd never been the centre of their universe. The three of them were always there for each other if needed, but without any of the clinging closeness that she'd witnessed among some of her fellow students.

Like Chloe, Susan Wells was a cheerful, outgoing woman. She looked younger than her forty-seven years and was, Chloe suspected, flattered by the amount of attention that she still got from the opposite sex. Not that Chloe thought it ever went beyond flirting, but it kept Susan vibrant and with a greater sense of worldliness than her father, who was very much an introverted academic.

'Hi, Mum,' Chloe said, supressing her surprise because she didn't want her mother to think her visit wasn't welcome. 'Come in and have a cup of tea,' she added, putting her key in the door at the side of the annexe.

Susan Wells smiled. 'That would be nice. Tell me,' she continued as she sat down on the well-worn sofa and watched her daughter plugging in the kettle, 'is this DCI Anderson as attractive as he looks in his photos?'

'What photos?' Chloe asked.

'He's been in the local paper more than once,' her mother replied. 'I noticed him because he was so different from my idea of a policeman. Very handsome in a cultured sort of way, and wonderful dress sense. He's single too.'

'I'm not surprised,' Chloe said shortly. 'He may be handsome, if you like that sort, but he's very detached, and I don't think he likes me one bit.'

'Why's that?' her mother asked with interest.

'Probably because he didn't want to have me trailing along behind him in the first place. I've got a horrible feeling I might have been used by his chief as some kind of punishment. That's the way I'm being treated anyway. He's clearly offended at having someone without any qualifications whatsoever following his every move.'

'He's probably afraid you'll mess up some evidence,' Susan Wells said.

'Mess up his clothes more likely,' Chloe retorted. 'I'd love to know how he manages to keep a linen suit uncreased during a car journey. If he shared that secret with the clothes industry he could make a fortune.'

'No romance, then?' her mother asked in a disappointed voice.

'Definitely not!' Chloe laughed. 'He's probably the kind of man who likes well-organised, compliant females, and even if he weren't he isn't my type, I'm afraid. I prefer them more macho.'

'Yes, I know,' her mother responded dryly. 'I remember where that got you with Grant.'

'No one knew Grant was involved in anything illegal,' Chloe protested. 'Besides, he was only doctoring the mileage on cars and –'

'He went to prison,' her mother reminded her.

'Lucky Anderson doesn't know,' Chloe laughed. 'My stock would fall even further. There is one thing that intrigues me about him, Mum. I'd love to see what kind of a woman he takes out.'

*

At that moment Anderson was collecting Karen Raybould from her home and taking her to see *Ridicule* at a nearby cinema that was showing it in the original French with sub-titles. It starred Fanny Ardant and he'd enjoyed her performance in *La Vie est un Roman*, although the film itself had been too disjointed to gain his full approval. He was pleased that Karen spoke fluent French. It meant they could both enjoy the same films and books, and when he was going out with a woman he always wanted her to appreciate everything that he did. He felt more secure that way, although he never minded if they were slightly less skilled than he was at anything. Teaching them the intricacies of the French language or Italian food was almost as enjoyable as teaching them the delights of slow, leisurely lovemaking and watching their faces as they waited with rising desire for the moment when he allowed them to climax.

It never crossed Anderson's mind that this might be an unusual way of thinking about women. It was the way he was, and the way he'd always been. The one thing he did regret was that Sarah, his ex-wife, hadn't understood this. He still found it impossible to come to terms with the fact that she'd walked away from him, and as far as he was concerned the sooner she went back to America the better. Even knowing she was in the same country as him irritated him. She was a reminder that he'd failed at marriage, and he hated failure.

After the film he and Karen returned to her house and this time they went up to her bedroom, a large and extremely feminine room with frilly curtains, frilled fabric beneath her dressing table and lace-trimmed duvet and pillows. The colours were tasteful, greens and yellows, but it was clear that no man had had a say in the decor.

Anderson had been looking forward to this moment all the evening. He felt that he could encourage Karen to be more adventurous this time, to take her a little further than she was used to going by a mixture of gentle persuasion and firm instructions once she was totally relaxed.

Unfortunately for him Karen had also been anticipating their next sexual encounter, but in rather a different way. The first time they'd made love she knew she'd been nervous, lacking confidence after her divorce, but now she felt more self-assured and during the evening had decided that she would show John Anderson she wasn't such a pathetic creature as she must have appeared last time.

As he stood at the foot of the king-size bed, watching her intently with his amazing navy blue eyes fringed by their ridiculously long lashes, her belly quickened and she moved slowly towards him. 'Let me undress you,' she said, her voice deeper than usual. 'This time I'll make sure you're the one who has the most pleasure.'

Anderson's expression didn't change but inside he felt a twinge of dismay. This wasn't the Karen Raybould he'd thought he knew, the attractively shy, rangy young woman who'd writhed so satisfactorily beneath his touch. In any case, he had no intention of letting her undress him. His Henley-style blazer with the gold buttons that he'd teamed with navy trousers, German-made because in his opinion they suited his shape better than any others, was new. Karen would be bound to fling it on the floor and crease it badly.

As she reached out to unbutton it he clasped her hands between his own, and it was then that desire flared in him again. He loved the feeling of having her trapped, of knowing that she was unable to move until he released her. 'I'd rather you didn't,' he said firmly.

Karen wasn't to be so easily put off. 'You spoilt me last time; this time it's my turn,' she insisted.

Anderson released her hands and had to quench a feeling of irritation. 'Then undress for me,' he said firmly. 'I want to watch you undress. Do it slowly; that will increase the pleasure.' He was grateful that she obeyed because it meant he could undress himself at the same time, and he put his carefully folded clothes on to her bedside chair.

When she was naked she stood proudly before him, cupping the undersides of her breasts with her hands. Anderson moved towards her but she gave a quick smile and nodded towards the bed. 'Lie down there,' she whispered.

Despite the fact that she looked incredibly sexy and attractive, Anderson's desire was waning fast. This was not his idea of a good night's sex. He had to be in control. On the other hand he understood that she was trying her best to please him, and so he had to go along with what she was doing with as good a grace as he could muster.

Once he was lying on his back, his lean but muscular body perfectly still, Karen squatted over him facing his penis, and as she bent to take it into her mouth she lowered her vulva on to him, giving him a teasing genital kiss.

Anderson felt her direct his penis into her mouth and draw it in deeply, moving her mouth in long strokes which she alternated with delicate licking of the glans. As she worked on him she also moved her buttocks until he finally placed his tongue on to her clitoris and heard her quick intake of breath as heat scorched through her lower torso.

Anderson wasn't happy with the entire experience. He was quickly sexually aroused: she was an expert at using her mouth on him, and he was very soon rock hard and on the point of coming, but there had been no slow build-up, no easing into the moment of climax with a long session of foreplay. Even worse, Karen was taking control of her own orgasm, and when he let his tongue drift away from her clitoris and between her sex lips she moved herself into a different position so that he was once again licking her as she liked and not as he wished.

He was relieved when he felt her body start to go rigid as her orgasm approached. She felt it too and quickly increased the rhythm of her mouth on his erection while at the same time moving her hand up and down his shaft.

She was uttering tiny cries of sheer delight now and started to rub herself urgently over his face until she found her favourite position.

Her frantic excitement and the swift movements of her hand and mouth meant that Anderson too lost control and, as he came, in his opinion far too soon, Karen bent her arms and pressed her breasts into his stomach while her body shook and shuddered for several minutes.

Anderson lay absolutely still and silent. As soon as he decently could he'd leave, go back to his penthouse flat and try and put the evening out of his mind. It was unfortunate but he wouldn't see Karen again. She simply wasn't the kind of sexual partner he wanted and there was no way he could explain this to her without hurting her, which was the last thing he wanted to do when she had so plainly planned what she had thought would be a wonderful night for him. It seemed that he'd made an error of judgement where Karen Raybould was concerned and once again he wished that Anna hadn't decided to stay in Plymouth. They had been so compatible sexually that he'd been certain she'd find a way to join him in Surrey. Now it seemed she was destined to become simply a very happy memory.

When Ralph eased his Rover out of his driveway that same evening, he hoped that he wasn't making a mistake, but his need to see Pippa had overridden his natural caution. It had been a horrible shock when John Anderson had turned up from Guildford station. Ralph had been quite certain that Johnson would be on hand to make sure things went smoothly. Now he'd got an over-zealous policeman poking around desperate for something to prove that Lisa's death was murder, and if he looked hard enough he might well end up a happy man. Just the same, given the chronic shortage of manpower within the police force and the knowledge that at this moment Lisa's death was only 'suspicious', Ralph didn't believe there would be anyone tailing him. However, he constantly checked in his mirror and took a very circular route to his rendezvous.

Fearful that Tom or Deborah might hear him, he hadn't phoned her before leaving home, but instead called her on his mobile once he was on the move. To his dismay she didn't answer, but he still pressed on. Sometimes, if she was in the shower or the garden, she didn't hear the phone.

Pippa Wright lived in a terraced house in one of the small backstreets of Croydon, not far from Ralph's factory. She'd come to work at his firm straight from school, and had progressed to becoming his personal secretary three years later, when she was twenty-one. She was now twenty-seven, and had been his mistress as well as PA for the past two years. There'd been times during the past twelve months when Ralph didn't know how he'd have kept going without Pippa.

As usual he parked a couple of streets away from her house, in an NCP car park, and then walked the rest of the way. He was surprised to notice that he was slightly out of breath when he finally rang her doorbell, but knew that it was nerves not fitness that were the trouble. He desperately needed her to be there.

When he heard her footsteps he gave an audible sigh of relief. She opened the door looking tall, slim and elegant in a black dress with an unusual dragon motif on the front, her long legs encased in shining silk stockings and two-strap satin shoes with a buckle and high heels on her feet. For one short moment he wondered what kept her so loyal. This rare moment of self-questioning didn't last long. He knew the reason: it was the strange, mutually satisfying sex life they shared. She'd be lost without it, and he was proud of the fact that he'd made her the creature she was, including the clothes which she certainly couldn't have afforded on a normal PA's salary.

Pippa pushed her long wavy dark hair behind her ears

and her grey-green eyes, which looked Slavic above her high cheekbones, widened in shock. 'What are you doing here?' she whispered. 'Shouldn't you be at home?'

'I had to see you,' said Ralph, pushing past her and walking rapidly through the tiny hall into the small back room. 'I'll go mad if I'm cooped up with Tom and Deborah much longer, quite apart from the horrors of the visiting in-laws.'

Pippa sat down on a stool, wrapped her arms round her knees, and looked up at Ralph as he stood commandingly above her. 'I'm so sorry about Lisa,' she said softly. 'It must have been awful for you. If only you hadn't forgotten those papers that morning then someone else would have found her.' If there was a hidden question in her words, Ralph chose to ignore it. 'Did she have a convulsion?' Pippa continued.

'They don't know yet, there are some more tests to be done,' said Ralph. 'Look, I don't want to talk about that side of things, Pippa. I needed to see you because you're the one person I can trust. You know everything. There isn't anyone else who understands what Lisa's death actually means to me. And I don't want anyone else understanding,' he added, with a hint of menace in his voice. Pippa's eyes darkened and she shivered slightly. Ralph saw this and knew that she wanted him as much as he wanted her. 'Come upstairs,' he said abruptly. 'We'll talk about it more later on.'

Grabbing her by the wrist he pulled her slightly resisting body up the stairs and into the main bedroom. Without waiting for her to undress Ralph pushed her down on to the double bed and with the skill born of long practice kept her pinned there with one hand while with the other he rummaged through a bedside drawer and drew out some chiffon scarves.

Pippa made tiny protesting sounds and twisted beneath his grip, but her eyes were bright with rising desire, and when he fastened her wrists to her iron bedhead with the scarves and then thrust a hand up between her legs he felt the tell-tale damp patch on her silk panties. For a moment he stroked the soft skin at the top of her inner thighs but then without any warning he tore off her stockings and pushed her dress up to her hips while at the same time tweaking one of her nipples hard through the fabric of the dress. Pippa gave a cry of mixed pain and pleasure, and then Ralph was lying over her, his weight on his elbows as he looked down at her.

'You want me, don't you?' he muttered. 'You're as desperate for this as I am, but you're going to have to wait, wait until I let you come. Understand?' Pippa nodded, and as Ralph's hands slid up her slender neck and caressed the side of her face he felt her tremble because she knew what was coming and could hardly bear the excitement.

After tenderly caressing her smooth skin Ralph lowered his head and his teeth closed around the thin skin at the base of her throat. Pippa gave a sudden cry and Ralph covered her mouth with one of his large hands. 'Be quiet,' he ordered her. 'If you make any more noise you'll have to wait longer.'

Pippa's body felt on fire beneath his hands, as though all her nerve endings were closer to the surface of her skin than normal, and he could tell that her orgasm was perilously close. When Ralph's hands started to squeeze roughly at her breasts through her dress she arched her upper torso towards him, as though welcoming the proof that she was still needed and that even in death Lisa had no power to come between them.

Without any preliminaries Ralph then thrust his erection hard into her, moving his hips rapidly as his own climax approached. He loved to watch Pippa's face when this was happening. To see her wide-eyed terror that she'd come before he said and then be punished. The punishments weren't as much fun as this kind of sex, which she adored. As a result she'd learnt incredible control over her body.

He intended that the final few minutes of his thrusting should be pure blissful torture for Pippa, and when he saw her breathing slowly and deeply through slightly parted lips in order to keep that final moment of shattering release at bay he knew that he'd succeeded.

Suddenly with a shout of satisfaction Ralph climaxed, and as his body bucked above hers he looked down into her obedient eyes and with the faintest of smiles on his flashily handsome face he nodded. 'Now you can come, Pippa,' he whispered. One of his hands moved between her parted thighs and a finger touched the very centre of her so that her body arched briefly away and then she was coming and coming, screaming out with delight and her arms were pulling on the scarves so that the muscles were stretched almost to breaking point.

Ralph felt content. Unlike his wife, he could control his mistress, and right now that was vital.

Fifteen minutes later they were both back downstairs sitting in the kitchen and drinking red wine. Leaning across the table Ralph tugged on a strand of Pippa's hair. 'Lovely,' he murmured, but whether he meant the sex or her, Pippa wasn't sure. Her body was still glowing from the wonderful sex, and if he'd given any sign of being keen she'd happily have gone back up to the bedroom for another even more dangerous session, but she could see that tonight Ralph also wanted to talk.

'Have you realised what Lisa's death means?' Ralph asked slowly, watching her intently over the top of his glass.

Pippa nodded, a surge of happiness coursing through her. 'Of course I have. It means we're free to make our relationship public. In due course, naturally.'

Much to her disappointment Ralph didn't seem to want to follow this up. 'I meant from the company's point of view.'

'Of course I do,' she said crisply, reverting to the role of efficient PA, again because she realised that her role as mistress was over for the moment. 'It means that you'll inherit Lisa's money and be able to repay the bank loan at last.'

Ralph nodded. 'Which also means that they won't send in any auditors, our little secret won't come to light and we'll be financially sound for prospective buyers.'

'It couldn't have come at a better time,' Pippa said without thinking, but hearing Ralph's quick intake of breath she realised her mistake. 'I'm sorry, that sounds awful. I didn't mean it like that. I think it's an absolute tragedy that she wouldn't lend you any money when she was alive, just because that stupid mother of hers had told her to keep her money to herself. What's the point of marriage if you won't help your partner when they need it?'

'Lisa never believed I loved her,' Ralph said. 'You know that. She and her bloody mother decided I only wanted her money.'

'But you did love her when you married her, didn't you?' asked Pippa.

Ralph didn't answer. Instead, reaching out his left hand he let his fingers encircle Pippa's right wrist, where there was a red mark caused by the chiffon scarf. 'What I did or didn't feel for Lisa is my business,' he said harshly. 'The less you know the less you can tell people.'

Pippa looked at him in disbelief. 'I'd never discuss your personal affairs with anyone, Ralph. You know that. I love you. You're all that matters to me. That's how it's been from the moment I first set eyes on you.'

Ralph nodded. 'I know, but we're not talking gossip here, Pippa. We're talking police.'

'Police?'

'Listen,' Ralph said impatiently. 'At the moment they're treating Lisa's death as suspicious, and if that bloody John Anderson gets his way it will be turned into a full-scale murder inquiry.'

'It can't be,' Pippa protested. 'Lisa's been ill for over a

year. Everyone knows that. Surely her doctor –'

'Her doctor's the police surgeon and no help at all,' said Ralph shortly. 'The point is that with the way things are going it's quite possible you'll get a visit from our Detective Chief Inspector Anderson in the next few days and if you don't know some things then so much the better.'

'I know a lot,' Pippa said slowly.

Ralph's dark eyes narrowed. 'Meaning?'

Pippa jumped nervously. 'I didn't mean anything, Ralph, I promise. I only meant that there are things about the company that I know, things which wouldn't look good if they came out. What do I do if he starts questioning me about the financial state we're in, or were in before Lisa's death?'

Ralph's face went scarlet. 'You see! Think what that would sound like if you were stupid enough to say it to him. The last thing I want is for Anderson to know I needed the money I'll inherit now Lisa's dead. You'll have to lie, Pippa, and lie convincingly. You know me, I'd never hurt a fly, but Anderson doesn't see me like that. He dislikes me, and if he can pin anything on me over Lisa's death he will.'

Pippa felt totally confused. 'Why does he dislike you?' she asked.

'Because he fancied Lisa,' Ralph said shortly.

Pippa's attitude changed at once. 'I don't know what it was about her,' she said irritably. 'She was blonde and pretty in a fluffy way, but she wasn't exactly a raving beauty. I always thought she didn't appreciate you enough, Ralph.'

'She didn't,' Ralph said softly. 'Not like you, Pippa. You really do appreciate me, don't you? How about another trip upstairs. We'll take the wine with us.'

'Would you use the latex whip this time?' Pippa whispered.

'If you beg me to,' retorted Ralph as they climbed the stairs.

FOUR

Anderson arrived at the station at 8.30 on the Wednesday morning looking immaculate in a light grey linen suit with one of the newly fashionable dark blue shirts and a red and blue tie. The desk sergeant looked up as he passed. 'Someone's been phoning you for the past half hour, a man called Don Mitchell. He's left his number and wants you to ring him back.'

'I've never heard of him,' Anderson said. 'Is Sergeant Walker in?'

'Getting a coffee, I think. This Don Mitchell says he's Lisa Allan's father, does that make sense?'

Anderson felt a moment's excitement. 'Yes, it does. Give me the number. I'll call him right away.'

'And Miss Wells called in. She overslept but should be here by 9.30.'

'How nice for us all,' Anderson said dryly.

He rang Don Mitchell immediately he got to his office and was surprised to hear a rather rough South London voice at the other end. He'd imagined that Lisa's father was a member of the county set, a landowner perhaps.

'You're in charge of the investigation into my daughter's

death, aren't you?' Don Mitchell asked, without any preliminary pleasantries.

'That's right,' Anderson said politely.

'She was murdered,' the other man said flatly.

'Do you have any evidence to support that statement, sir?' asked Anderson, scribbling down what was being said with his free hand.

'I don't need bloody evidence. You want to talk to that husband of hers about his business. Have you done that yet?'

'Right at this moment, Mr Mitchell, your daughter's death is simply being treated as suspicious. We have no proof that she was murdered and until we do there's a limit to what action we can take.'

'Well, you can get off your backsides and look into Ralph's business affairs,' Don Mitchell shouted. 'He's been trying to get his hands on my daughter's money from the day he married her, but he couldn't, not while she was alive.'

'I think we ought to meet, Mr Mitchell. Where are you at the moment?' Anderson asked, signalling for DS Walker, who'd just come into the room, to sit down.

'My wife and I are staying at a country pub in Chipstead. It's called the Mill House. We'll be here for a week or so, until we know exactly what happened. You can come and see us after you've looked into that damned man's business. And if you won't, I know plenty of people high up in New Scotland Yard who'd be only too happy to take over from you.' With that he slammed down the receiver.

'Nice man,' Anderson murmured to himself.

'Who's that, sir?' DS Walker asked.

'Mr Don Mitchell, the late Lisa Allan's father. He doesn't seem to have a very high opinion of his son-in-law, and is very anxious for me to look into the man's business affairs.'

'You don't think very highly of him either, do you, sir?' Walker asked.

Anderson busied himself with some papers on his desk. 'He isn't my type,' he said carefully, 'but that doesn't mean he's a murderer.' When Walker didn't respond Anderson glanced across at him. 'I'd like to know more about his business affairs, and the entire financial set-up in the household,' he admitted. 'The problem is, I need the results of the second set of tests. How long does that damned pathologist at Reigate take? We aren't asking him to rebuild a skeleton in order to identify an unknown victim. This must be as straightforward as it comes.' Even as he spoke, Anderson knew that wasn't true. Lisa's death was very complicated, and if it was murder then the murderer had almost certainly been counting on that fact to help him or her get away with it.

Eventually, at eleven o'clock, Anderson got the call he'd been waiting for from Brian Kent, the pathologist at Reigate. When he heard Kent give a faint sigh his heart sank. 'I'm afraid there's still nothing absolutely conclusive one way or the other,' said the pathologist. 'I've made that very clear in my report.'

'But on balance, what do you think?' asked Anderson, well aware that pathologists hated to tie themselves down to specifics. All he wanted was a pointer in the right direction that he could give to Parrish.

'The cause of death was definitely heart failure, probably brought about by her cardiac arrhythmia. However, there's a total absence of beta-blockers in her body, which means she hadn't taken them for over a week, and there is also faint but definite bruising on the left hand side of her neck and the front of her left shoulder. Given the photos of the position in which she was found this can't be explained by her fall.'

'Her husband had moved her,' Anderson admitted regretfully. 'He put his hands on her shoulders and tried to lift her up. From what he said she was lying on the floor in an almost foetal position.'

'On her back?' Kent asked.

'Yes.'

'Then that still doesn't explain the bruising, and neither could the husband have caused those marks when he moved her. Incidentally there are some older bruises on the insides of both her wrists, but that certainly hasn't got anything to do with her death. They're about four or five days old.'

'What's the likely verdict by the coroner?' asked Anderson.

'Stevens isn't happy. His report will make it clear that he wasn't expecting her to die due to her medical condition. Given that, plus the lack of beta-blockers – very strange in my opinion – and the bruising then I imagine it will be an open verdict.'

'Not misadventure?'

'I'm sorry, Anderson, I'm not psychic. You asked my opinion and I've given you it.'

'Thank you for letting me know so quickly,' Anderson said politely. 'No doubt you'll send the report over today.'

'Of course. What do you intend to do now?'

'Unlike you, I answer to other people,' said Anderson. 'I shall have to give all this to my superior and see what his reaction is. I know what I'm hoping for, and that's a chance to look into the whole affair more thoroughly.'

'If that's what you want, good luck,' said the pathologist. 'I'd have thought there were more important matters for you to deal with. Perhaps things are quieter in Guildford than they are here.'

'Not really, but I pride myself on being thorough,' Anderson said before replacing receiver carefully and quietly when he longed to slam it down. He sometimes wondered what made men become pathologists. They seemed to quickly lose contact with real life. Death became more real to them than anything else.

It was lucky there were people who chose the work, though. They made his job easier, and he wouldn't have wanted to find himself up to his elbows in blood and God knows what else in order to solve a case.

Parrish sat and listened to what Anderson had to say in impassive silence. Anderson guessed that his boss was hoping he'd lose his cool and start overpressing, but after putting all the salient points he'd learnt from Brian Kent he too sat in silence. Finally, as he'd known he must, Parrish spoke.

'You want to treat it as murder, I take it?'

'It seems to me,' Anderson said carefully, 'that there are definite grounds for assuming that death wasn't brought about by natural causes.'

'And you think the husband did it, do you?'

Anderson stared at the older man. 'What makes you say that?'

'I keep my ear to the ground. He isn't your type from what I've heard. How many of us are, I wonder? We can't all be connoisseurs of foreign books, arthouse films and designer label clothes, I'm afraid, but that doesn't make us all murderers.'

Anderson felt a surge of contempt for the overweight, desk-bound man opposite him but none of this showed on his face. 'There are other possibilities,' he said levelly.

Parrish leant back in his chair. 'Glad to hear you haven't closed your mind to every other solution. I'm going to let you work on this for three weeks, but if after that time you can't come up with anything more concrete than the fact that Ralph Allan is a bit of a rough diamond then the case will remain on file. I don't want you to think that I'm doing this because you want me to, either; I'm not. I'm doing it because when Ralph Allan rang his local police station he was expecting to get a man he knew, a golfing friend who understood about his wife's condition and would understand the man's shock but at the same time be anxious to do everything in his power to ascertain there had been no foul play.

'I don't want anyone to think that we at Guildford are

any less skilled at our work than our opposite numbers in Reigate, which is why I'm letting you work on it for three weeks. You can thank Ralph Allan for it rather than the pathologist, who in my opinion doesn't seem convinced himself. As for the doctor, well, you know what GPs are like. He'd hardly want Mrs Allan to have dropped dead from a heart problem that he'd already decided wasn't life threatening would he?'

'I suppose not,' Anderson said. 'Right, if I've only got three weeks I'd better get started.'

As he walked back to his office he smiled at the delicious irony of it all. He was certain Ralph had dialled the police because he wanted his friend, a golf partner as usual – another good reason for disliking the sport – to help keep his name unsullied. As a result Parrish was letting Anderson loose to find out every detail of the man's private affairs, the last thing on earth Ralph Allan would have wanted.

'Come on,' he said to Chloe as he hurried in. 'You, DS Walker and I are going to Croydon.'

'Why Croydon?' Chloe asked, picking up her large canvas bag in which she kept her notebook, pencil, mobile phone and masses of useless junk like cough sweets, peppermints and paracetamols.

'Because that's where Ralph Allan's ladder-making business has its headquarters. I want to talk to him there, and to anyone else who I think might be able to shed a little light on the state of the company. After that we're going to Chipstead, to talk to Lisa's parents. Aren't you a lucky girl? Such feverish activity and all over a case you thought was a natural causes death.'

Chloe flushed. 'I don't much care for being called a girl. Do you always patronise women?'

Anderson looked at her in surprise. 'No, of course not. I meant it as a compliment, but if you prefer "young lady" I'll try and remember.'

★

Ralph Allan's ladder-making factory was on an industrial estate, a grey concrete building with virtually no sign as to what went on there. Even the name, 'ALLAN & SON, INDUSTRIAL LADDER MAKERS' was printed only in small letters over the entrance porch. Chloe could see nothing on the outside walls or the drive-in to the car park, which was shared by two neighbouring companies.

Anderson showed his card to the receptionist and after giving him a worried, wide-eyed look she buzzed through to Ralph Allan. A few minutes later a tall, slim, dark-haired young woman with grey-green eyes came through the swing doors to greet them. She was very elegant and her red pencil skirt was teamed with a cream blouse and a red and green checked lightweight jacket. Chloe could see that she was about her age, but felt worlds apart from her. She didn't much care for women like that, all make-up and smart clothes. She always wondered if there was a real person underneath.

The woman held out her hand politely. 'How do you do, Chief Inspector. I'm Pippa Wright, Mr Allan's personal assistant. If you'd like to follow me, I'll take you to his office.'

'I'd love to follow her,' DS Walker muttered. Chloe pulled a face at him.

Ralph Allan's office was large and plush. Not for him the open-plan, 'everyone's equal' kind of layout. He was the boss and he wanted everyone to know it. Sitting behind his desk and dressed in a business suit, Ralph seemed larger and more imposing than he had straight after his wife's death. Although in his mid-fifties there was no trace of grey in his hair, and today his eyes were alert and sparkled like those of a much younger man. Chloe realised that she quite fancied him, and when he smiled at her she was pleased that she'd decided to wear one of her cotton fit-and-flare dresses today. It was more flattering than some of her other outfits.

'This is a surprise Chief Inspector,' Ralph said, not bothering to get out of his chair but indicating that Anderson should take the seat opposite him. 'Wouldn't a telephone call have sufficed?'

'I could have phoned you,' agreed Anderson, 'but I thought that this was something you should hear in person.'

'Then you'd better tell me,' said Ralph, leaning forward on his desk, his wedding ring glinting in the sun shining through the window at the side of the room.

'We have the second set of test results from the post-mortem,' explained Anderson. 'As a result of those findings we are treating your wife's death as murder and will be making further investigations.'

A little of Ralph's natural colour faded from his cheeks and his jaw tightened. 'You surprise me,' he remarked. 'What exactly led you to this interesting conclusion?'

'Mainly the total absence of beta-blockers and the fact that she had sustained bruises to her neck and shoulder, bruises not consistent with the way she fell.'

'Lisa bruised very easily,' Ralph said.

'So it seems, since she also had fading bruises on the insides of both her wrists. Have you any idea how she came by those?'

'No,' Ralph said flatly.

'Perhaps you wouldn't mind answering one or two questions for us while we're here,' Anderson continued. DS Walker took out his notebook. 'When you arrived back home at lunchtime on Monday, did you check to see if your wife's car had been used recently?' Anderson enquired.

Ralph Allan leant back in his chair and looked at Anderson with some amusement. 'I already knew,' he replied.

'How?'

'Lisa lost her driving licence when she had her first fit. You have to go a year without one before you get it back.'

'But you thought she might be out?'

'As she hadn't answered when I rang home, yes. Although it was possible she'd been resting.'

'Do you know where she'd been, sir?'

'Yes, the gym. One of her friends told me later that dreadful evening that she'd seen her there and that she looked a little pale even then.'

'When you found the body, were you worried that an intruder might still be in the house?' Anderson asked quietly.

Ralph frowned. 'The thought never crossed my mind.'

'And yet you don't have a burglar alarm system installed at the moment, do you? It was taken out because of the type of pacemaker your wife had.'

'But she didn't look as though she'd been murdered! She looked as though she'd collapsed and died. There was no blood, no lump on her head, why should I think about intruders at a time like that? I was in shock. I didn't know what to think or do. I panicked, tried to shake her into consciousness – which probably explains your bruises – and then rang for the police.'

'Yes, the police.' Anderson sounded thoughtful.

Ralph Allan sighed. 'We've been through this before. I have a friend, Detective Chief Inspector Johnson, who works there. I wanted to know what I should do, but he was out. I got some desk sergeant who must have put two and two together and made five. I expect that was my fault. I probably made it sound as though I thought it wasn't a natural death, but I couldn't believe it. All the doctors had said she'd be fine, that her medication and the pacemaker were keeping her going very well.'

'Then it's a great pity she wasn't taking her medication, isn't it?' Anderson pointed out.

'Well, I hardly think a murderer can be held responsible for that. How many times do I have to tell you Lisa could be difficult about her pills?'

'Can you think of anyone who might have wanted to kill your wife?' Anderson asked abruptly.

Ralph stared at him, and it seemed to Chloe that for the first time he was grasping the reality of what he'd just been told. 'No,' he said firmly. 'She wasn't an easy woman, contrary to what you might imagine after one meeting, and she had a habit of making friends and then getting bored with them, but I doubt if anyone would have killed her because they were no longer invited to make up a bridge four.'

Anderson nodded. 'Thank you for your help, Mr Allan. No doubt we'll be talking to you again before very long. In the meantime, if you should think of anything that you feel might help us, any detail no matter how small that you haven't mentioned so far, then please contact me at once. Here's my card; the station can always contact me if I'm not there when you ring.'

'Aren't you going to ask me about my relationship with my wife?' asked Ralph. 'I thought the spouse was always the main suspect.'

'As I said, we'll talk again soon. I don't think that your office is quite the place for a conversation of that kind.'

'I'd rather talk to you here than at home, when the children are around,' said Ralph. 'When you do decide to stop playing cat and mouse and begin asking me the things you really want to know then perhaps you'd make an appointment through my secretary and come here again. I don't like having policemen in and out of my home all the time.'

Anderson didn't answer, but Chloe thought that she saw him smile as he got up and turned towards the door. Having been standing at the back of the room the entire time she'd had a good opportunity to study Ralph Allan and she definitely found him physically attractive. He was her sort, if rather older than she was used to. Not that that meant he was necessarily trustworthy, she realised, thinking of Grant, but she couldn't help wondering what it would be like to go out with a man like him.

'Before we leave I want a word with the secretary,'

Anderson told Walker. 'Set that up, would you. somewhere private.'

'Did you get anything useful from Mr Allan?' Chloe asked him as he waited with her in the corridor.

'He's sharp and knows the way our minds are working but he's confident he's cleverer than we are. That doesn't worry me; quite the opposite in fact. It might well prove his downfall.'

'Assuming he's guilty of anything,' Chloe said.

Anderson ignored the remark. 'Walker and I will join you in the car when we've talked to Miss Wright. Then I'm very anxious to get off to Chipstead and meet Mr Don Mitchell,' was all he said.

Anderson's wish to see Don Mitchell seemed likely to come about fairly speedily. Pippa Wright was so self-contained and loyal that despite his best efforts Anderson failed to make any real headway with her.

After he'd established how long she'd worked for the company and her exact position there she confirmed Ralph's story about phoning home during the morning of Lisa's death. The time she gave for him leaving the office was also consistent with the time he claimed to have arrived back at Kingswood.

'Was Mr Allan worried when his wife didn't answer the phone?' he asked her.

Pippa hesitated. 'I'm not sure you could say worried, but he was put out. He'd expected her to be at home because she'd told him she was tired that morning, and when she was tired she was meant to rest. I suppose if I'm honest he was a little irritated. She wasn't easy, you know,' she added.

'In what way?' Anderson asked.

Pippa clearly regretted making the remark. 'I'm not privy to the intimate details of Mr Allan's marriage, but after her illness began Mrs Allan was often unwell during business dinners or when entertaining his clients. I saw that for myself. I understand too that she used to go out and about with her friends without so many attacks. That was all I meant.'

'Was she involved in the business?' Anderson asked. 'As a partner or an executive director, for example?'

He watched an interesting play of emotions cross Pippa Wright's face. She was an attractive young woman and his type, being intelligent and sophisticated but with an air of vulnerability about her. Until he asked that question he'd found her face interestingly mask-like. Even when her voice was animated, her face wasn't. Now, though, he realised that she was struggling to hide what looked to him like scorn possibly tinged with envy.

'Mrs Allan wasn't in the least interested in the company,' she replied politely. 'Mr Allan will be able to tell you more about that than I can, of course, but she showed no interest whatsoever on the occasions that I met her. She was far more interested in her social life.'

'But it was the business that provided her with that standard of living,' Anderson pointed out.

Pippa opened her mouth, seemed to think better of it, and closed it again. 'That, Inspector, applies to a lot of women where their husband's work is concerned. The majority of them don't have to take an interest in order to be free to enjoy the benefits.'

Anderson smiled at her. 'That's very true, Miss Wright. One more thing before I go. Were you surprised to hear about Mrs Allan's death?'

'Of course I was!' Pippa exclaimed. 'I knew her condition was quite bad, but I never thought it was life-threatening. I mean, the doctors said as much didn't they? She was waiting for a defibrillator and the specialist said it wasn't an emergency. If they'd expected her to die she'd have gone to the top of the list.'

'Was she a National Health patient?' Anderson enquired.

Pippa nodded. 'Yes, she was. Ralph wanted her to go

privately, but she always said that for major things you couldn't beat the National Health and he could hardly force her to join a private scheme, could he?'

'Extraordinary,' Anderson remarked. 'Personally I like the feeling of security private insurance offers.'

'So do I,' Pippa agreed. 'I'm so lucky. It's one of the perks of the job here, once you get to a certain level.'

'Not that it would have mattered of course,' Anderson continued, as though the thought had only just occurred to him.

'What do you mean?' Pippa sounded bewildered.

'We have every reason to believe that Mrs Allan was murdered,' said Anderson quietly. 'Private health insurance doesn't help anyone at a time like that.'

While Ralph Allan's reaction to the news had been far from satisfactory he couldn't have asked for more from the young woman opposite him. If anything the reaction was too extreme. Her mouth literally dropped open with shock. 'But she couldn't have been,' she said stupidly.

'Why do you say that?'

'Because it would be too much of a coincidence. I mean, she was ill, very ill, and when Ralph – Mr Allan – found her she wasn't injured or anything was she? How could it be murder?'

'That's what we have to find out,' Anderson said. 'Thank you for your time, Miss Wright. We'll talk to you again at a future date. Here's my card if you think of anything you'd like to tell me after I've gone.'

'What kind of thing?'

'I've no idea,' Anderson confessed. 'Sometimes when it's a case of murder people see otherwise insignificant things in a different light. Should that happen, please ring me. I assume there are people who can confirm you were here on the morning Mrs Allan died?' he added.

Pippa Wright stared at him with eyes like a startled fawn. 'Yes, of course,' she said weakly. 'Plenty of people.'

'I imagined there would be, but I had to ask,' Anderson said gently.

He returned to his car feeling that at least he'd managed to rattle her composure a little, and he sensed that might be important.

'On to Chipstead,' he remarked, sliding behind the driving wheel.

'Any luck?' Chloe asked.

'Nothing special as yet.'

'I expect she was very loyal. I reckon she's having an affair with her boss. Women can tell,' she added helpfully.

'I doubt it,' said Anderson shortly. 'She's far too sophisticated to fall for that kind of man.'

'A lot of make-up and expensive clothes don't make you sophisticated,' Chloe said sharply. 'Besides, there's something very attractive about him. I rather fancy him myself.'

Anderson was so shocked he couldn't think of anything to say, but once again he wondered what it was that drew intelligent, attractive women to men like Ralph Allan.

Tom Allan stood in the middle of the lounge floor watching his stepsister as she sobbed uncontrollably into the cushions on the sofa. She'd been crying for at least ten minutes now and he had no idea what to do. He'd only come into the room to fetch a book, but seeing her in such distress he'd felt unable to leave even though she didn't appear to have noticed him. Eventually he approached her, and sitting down on the edge of the sofa put a hesitant arm round her shoulders. 'Don't cry like that, Debs. You'll make yourself ill again. Are you taking those pills Dr Stevens gave you?'

Deborah rubbed frantically at her eyes and fished in the pockets of her jeans for a tissue. She hadn't heard Tom come in and didn't want him seeing her like this, but the feel of his arm round her was so wonderful it almost made up for the embarrassment. 'They don't help much,' she sniffed. 'The ones I take at night make me sleep, but the others only make me feel woozy and unreal. I miss Mummy so much, Tom.'

'I know it's awful,' Tom sympathised. 'I can remember when my Mum died, I felt so wretched I wanted to die as well but Lisa wouldn't have wanted to see you like this.' Privately he thought to himself that Lisa wouldn't have wanted to see Deborah full stop. She hadn't had much time for her daughter, and hadn't understood her passion for horses. She had thought it unfeminine, insisting that women who liked horses ended up looking like them.

'I'm glad I've got you, Tom,' Deborah murmured, snuggling up close to his strong young body. 'At least this will bring us closer together. We've got something in common now. You must always have felt left out. I know Mummy wasn't very nice to you.'

'She wasn't very nice to anyone,' Tom said without thinking, and Deborah immediately started crying again, but this time she put her arms round Tom and sobbed into his cotton T-shirt.

'I should have listened to her when she said how ill she felt,' Deborah wailed. 'I never believed her. She was so fussy over things like the mobile phones and microwave ovens in fast food shops that I got fed up, but she really was dangerously ill all the time. Why didn't Dr Stevens tell us?'

Tom tried to unclasp Deborah's arms and put some distance between them without upsetting her. 'Perhaps he did tell Dad. Maybe they kept it from us because they didn't want us to worry. I don't know, but we can't change anything now, Debs. We've got to accept it and move on.'

'How can I?' she cried.

'I don't mean straight away, but in time,' Tom explained, wishing his father was at home or that he'd gone in to work himself instead of making Lisa's death an excuse for staying away.

'I'll cope with your help,' Deborah said softly. 'I know

you'll be there for me, Tom. After all, I've always helped you haven't I?'

Tom stiffened. 'Yes, you have and I'm very grateful but I'm not sure I can offer the kind of support you need,' he said hesitantly. 'I think you should talk to an older woman.'

Deborah stared at him. 'I don't want an older woman. I want you, Tom. I always have, you must have known that.'

Tom squirmed. This was turning into a total nightmare. Deborah was a nice enough girl, but she wasn't for him. 'I know you're fond of me, Debs,' he said carefully, 'and I'm fond of you but only in a brother-and-sister kind of way. I can't fill the role you want me to, I thought you knew that.'

'Why not?' Deborah shouted. 'You were quick enough to borrow money off me when you were short and no one else in the family was interested.'

'You offered it to me, and you always said it was because we were family,' Tom protested. 'I'm grateful and I do care for you, but not in the way you seem to want. Isn't what we've got enough?'

Deborah's face twisted with pain. 'No it isn't!' she shouted. 'You're more like your father than you care to admit, aren't you, Tom Allan? You just use women and move from one to the other without thinking about the pain you're causing.'

'I don't,' Tom protested. 'You've no idea what you're talking about.'

'Yes I have. You're always hanging around that new sixth-form college watching the girls play tennis in their little skirts. You fancy young girls, don't you, like your father prefers younger women.'

Tom flushed. 'Have you been spying on me?'

'No, but I've got friends who know you and they've seen you there.'

'Very sisterly behaviour,' Tom said angrily, getting up and moving away from Deborah, who promptly began to weep again. 'Look,' he added wearily. 'Why don't you talk to your grandparents, or even Pippa Wright if they're too old for you.'

'I wouldn't speak to Pippa Wright if she and I were the last two people left on earth,' Deborah screamed. 'She and your lecherous father have been having an affair for years. Mummy knew, I know she did. That can't have helped her much either.'

'You can't go round saying things like that,' Tom said furiously. 'You don't know it's true. You're only guessing.'

'I heard Mummy mention it during one of their rows.'

'They both said lots of stupid things when they rowed, and then went to bed and made up. Use your common sense, Debs. You'll cause nothing but trouble if you go round talking like this.'

'Perhaps someone ought to tell the police the truth,' Deborah said defiantly. 'Grandpa said the police are investigating your father over Mummy's death. I could be an accessory to murder if I kept this kind of information to myself.'

'Grow up!' Tom snapped. 'You're being hysterical and acting like a silly little girl.'

'Perhaps you fancy me more like that?' Deborah suggested, getting off the sofa at last, much to Tom's relief.

'Where are you going?' he asked.

'I'm ringing Reigate police station. I want to talk to DC Lin Ford. She'll listen to what I have to say, and then my conscience is clear.'

'You're just a trouble-maker. It must run in the family,' Tom muttered.

'It seems we're both chips off the old block,' Deborah retorted, but when Tom had gone she sat down and cried again. This wasn't what she'd wanted at all. All she'd intended to do was get Tom to see her more as a potential lover than a stepsister and now she'd probably alienated him for good. All the same, she made her telephone call.

★

The Mill House in Chipstead Lane was a new but old-world style country pub that also catered for short-term residents. Anderson hated things that weren't what they pretended to be. He liked either genuinely old buildings or aesthetically pleasing modern ones. Fake beams and mock-scruffy brocade armchairs weren't his idea of comfort, but it seemed Don and Mary Mitchell were happy there.

'Nice place,' Lisa's father remarked after Anderson had introduced himself, Chloe and DS Walker. 'Lisa didn't care for it but Ralph booked us in here and we like it. Isn't that right, Mary?' His wife nodded. Where Deborah was the young version of Lisa, Mary Mitchell was what her daughter would almost certainly have looked like had she lived to be fifty-six.

Don Mitchell lacked the looks and the class of his wife and daughter. He was a short, bull-headed man with close-cropped grey hair, piercing dark eyes and a tight downturned mouth that indicated a short temper. Once Anderson and the other two were settled in the lounge part of the Mitchell's suite, Don glared at Anderson.

'Well, have you looked into Ralph's business affairs yet?'

'We've been to visit the premises and talked to some of the staff,' said Anderson. 'I assure you we're looking into everything that we feel may have any bearing on your daughter's death.'

'My daughter's murder you mean,' Don Mitchell snapped. 'I tell you one thing, Andrews –'

'Anderson,' the Chief Inspector said politely.

'Whatever,' Don Mitchell said dismissively. 'I tell you this. If you don't bring my son-in-law to justice then I won't be held responsible for my actions. He only ever married our girl for her money. Oh, he was good-looking enough, and a smooth talker when he wanted to be, but I recognised the type straight away. He'd inherited a business from his father and wanted to expand it, make it into something really big. He knew Lisa was a wealthy young woman, we'd seen to that, and she was beautiful as well and had been to finishing school. What more could a man like him want?'

'If he married her for her money,' Anderson said thoughtfully, 'why should he now kill her for it?'

'I'm afraid that's my fault,' Mary Mitchell said quietly, looking up at Anderson with faded blue eyes. 'You see, I advised her never to let Ralph use her money to make himself rich or she'd end up feeling used and ignored.'

'Why did you think that?' Anderson asked curiously.

Lisa's mother waved her hands awkwardly in the air. 'It's what happens so often, isn't it?'

Anderson had his doubts about that, but having spoken once Mary Mitchell lapsed into resolute silence.

To Anderson's surprise Chloe suddenly stood up. 'I'm very sorry,' she said, looking round the room at everyone. 'It seems terribly hot in here and I feel a bit faint. Do you think I could go outside for some air?'

At once Mary Mitchell got to her feet and put a hand on Chloe's elbow. 'You come with me, my dear. We'll take a little walk in the garden, it's beautiful there and I feel rather claustrophobic myself.'

Anderson watched the two women leave and then settled back in his chair as Don Mitchell proceeded to repeat in even stronger language what he expected Anderson to do and what would happen if he didn't. By the end of the tirade DS Walker had stopped taking notes.

Once out in the garden Chloe took some deep breaths and walked towards a wooden seat. 'Would you mind if we sat down?' she asked the older woman.

Mary Mitchell smiled. 'Whatever you like, dear. Do you feel any better now?'

Chloe nodded. 'I do a little. I'm afraid that as I'm not a trained police officer I find all this rather distressing. I suppose you get used to it when it's your work, but for me it's different. I didn't expect doing my thesis to affect me like this, but Lisa was so young.'

Mary Mitchell's eyes misted but she kept her composure and sat with a very straight back staring out over the garden. Chloe admired her self-control. It was the kind you saw in women who'd been to boarding and finishing schools and were trained to face life stoically. Never complain, never explain was probably the rule she lived by.

'You always want something better for your child than you've had yourself,' she said slowly. Chloe kept very quiet. 'You cherish them when they're tiny, give them all the love and help you can but in the end there's no reason why they shouldn't repeat the same mistakes you've made, is there? And that's what Lisa did.'

'In what way?' Chloe asked softly, aware that the woman was really talking to herself.

'I grew up in Lincolnshire: my father was the high sheriff for five years and I had an idyllic childhood on the estate he'd inherited from his father. Horses, fishing, hunting, swimming, all that kind of thing. I was spoilt I suppose, but we were taught about duty and responsibility too. They don't teach that these days, I'm afraid. I was expected to marry well, of course, and there were plenty of suitable candidates once I got back from France, but then I met Don.

'He wasn't like anyone I'd met before. He seemed so much more masculine, more real than the kind of young man I'd mixed with. My parents were horrified but there was nothing wrong with Don except for the fact that he wasn't our kind of person. In the end I got my way and we married.'

'What did he do for a living?' Chloe asked, anxious to keep the woman talking.

'He hadn't had a very good education, I don't think school interested him, but he had the most incredible energy. He could see opportunities everywhere, all he needed was the money to put his plans into action. When we married he was working as a buyer for a clothing firm, but once the wedding was over he handed in his notice and set up his own company with my money using the knowledge he'd gained from his employer.

'I suspect he was a ruthless businessman, but he prospered. I can't complain that he hasn't kept me in the manner to which I was accustomed because he has. He's a very wealthy man, but I'm not wealthy, not in my own right you see, and I was once. In my day a woman didn't keep her own bank account or think about independence, not if she came from my sort of background.

'After Lisa's birth I lost my figure for a while and got very wrapped up in her. She was frail even then, and so pretty. Don felt ignored I suppose, or maybe he simply wanted a change. Whatever the reason, that was when he had his first affair. There have been others since, of course, but it was the first one that really hurt me. After that I learnt to live with it, but I didn't want the same for Lisa. My mother left Lisa a lot of money when she died, and had she lived she would have inherited everything of ours.

'The moment I set eyes on Ralph I knew that he was the same as Don. Not to look at of course. He was far more handsome, and more sophisticated on the surface because he was older than Don was when I met him, but he was the same under the skin. Perhaps all men are. What do you think?'

'I hope not,' Chloe said sadly.

'So do I, my dear. Anyway, that's why I advised Lisa not to do what I'd done. She knew about her father's affairs and although she worshipped him – well, girls do, it's only natural – she also knew that I'd been very unhappy. She agreed with what I said and made sure that her money stayed her own. She continued to bank where Don and I do and refused to let Ralph use a penny of her money for his business affairs.'

'And was she happy?' Chloe asked.

Mary thought for a moment. 'I think at first she was,' she said slowly. 'It was difficult to tell because naturally Lisa wasn't going to admit to us if she'd been wrong but from what I can remember she looked very happy for the first year or so. Then Ralph started suggesting she put some money into his company. He wanted to expand, the bank was being difficult and to him it seemed a logical step. Lisa came to me and asked me what she should do. I told her that I couldn't tell her, she was a married woman now and must make up her own mind, but I also reminded her of what I'd said before she married. Probably as a result she didn't put any money into the business. Then a few months later she told me that Ralph had managed to get a good loan from the bank after all.'

'But she still wasn't happy?' Chloe asked.

The older woman shook her head. 'Not in the way she had been at first. I blamed myself. Also, she started to tire easily. Ralph said it was because she was burning the candle at both ends. But eventually, after she'd had two blackouts and a convulsion, they discovered her heart condition. That was difficult for all of us to cope with. I don't think Lisa ever did come to terms with it, and Ralph kept trying to push her harder than he should have done. Don used to get very angry.'

'Perhaps Ralph was trying to pretend she wasn't ill,' Chloe suggested. 'It must have been frightening for him too.'

'I suppose it was,' Mary agreed. 'Then Don took him to one side, told him straight out that if he wasn't careful he'd kill . . .' her voice trembled for a moment before she forced herself to continue. 'That he'd kill Lisa with his stupid ideas,' she concluded. 'After that Ralph tried harder to make allowances, but I think Lisa felt she'd failed him. She wasn't the perfect, beautiful, healthy young wife he'd hoped for.'

'What about Deborah?' Chloe asked curiously. 'Had Lisa been married before?'

Mary shook her head. 'That was a terrible time. Lisa was only eighteen when she gave birth to Deborah. We hadn't known she was pregnant until two months before she gave birth. She disguised it very carefully with loose clothes and jokes about getting too curvy. I thought Don would never get over the shock. Luckily, once Deborah arrived he doted on her, just as he'd doted on Lisa.'

'Who was the father?'

Mary sighed. 'A boy who worked for Don. He was nothing special. They'd met at one of the firm's dinners and been dating in secret. Of course he lost his job, and I've no idea what became of him. As soon as Lisa was over the birth we packed her off to France and got a nanny in for Deborah. Once Lisa came back she took over as mother but she wasn't maternal really, and Deborah spent most of her time with her grandpa and me. Lisa was still young, and very popular; we didn't want to spoil her life.'

Privately Chloe thought Lisa had been a hideously spoilt and selfish young woman with no sense of responsibility, but she kept this well hidden. 'Lisa married quite late,' she said at last.

Mary Mitchell got to her feet. 'I think we'd better go in now if you're feeling better,' she suggested. 'Don will wonder where I am.'

'She did marry late, didn't she?'

'I suppose thirty is late, but Don scared a lot of her boyfriends off. If he didn't approve of the ones who stuck around he'd threaten Lisa with the fact that he'd go to the courts and apply to keep Deborah.'

'Wasn't that a little unkind?' Chloe suggested.

'He meant it for the best. He was so worried Lisa would make another mistake.'

'Yes, I see,' Chloe said, deciding that Lisa had inherited her selfish streak from her father.

'But of course despite all his best efforts she did, didn't she?' Mary added sadly. 'We couldn't save her after all.'

'You can't save people from themselves,' Chloe said gently.

Mary Mitchell looked at her in astonishment. 'None of it was Lisa's fault. She trusted people too much, that's all. And she was too pretty. It meant there were always men around her, men who were more interested in her looks and her money than her personality.'

Chloe found it quite difficult to sympathise with any young woman in that position, but she did feel sorry for this brave, grief-stricken woman struggling so hard to make sense of the disaster that had overtaken her.

'Don't worry,' she said gently. 'I know Chief Inspector Anderson will get to the bottom of this. He's very tenacious.'

Mary nodded. 'It doesn't matter, my dear. If he doesn't, Don will find someone else who can. He has a lot of very influential friends, you know.'

'I imagine he has,' Chloe agreed as they rejoined the men inside the hotel.

'What was all that about?' Anderson asked when they finally drove away.

'I thought Mrs Mitchell would talk more freely to a woman,' said Chloe. 'She didn't seem to have a very high opinion of men. I hope you didn't mind?'

'Good thinking,' Anderson said. Glancing in the mirror he noted the look of surprise and pleasure on her face. 'Find out anything?' he added.

Chloe told him all she'd learned. 'Mary Mitchell sounds as though she's had a difficult life,' Anderson said thoughtfully. 'I'm not surprised. Her husband's one of the most difficult and ungracious men I've met in a long time. Strange that a woman like that would marry him in the first place.'

'He was different,' Chloe said. 'She probably doesn't realise it but she was rebelling against all her parents stood for, just as Lisa tried to do time and time again. I imagine that Ralph was the first of her potential husbands who was a match for her father.'

'Or thought he was,' DS Walker remarked. 'His father-in-law is certainly out to nail him now.'

'I don't much like the sound of Lisa Allan,' Chloe admitted. 'She seems to have been almost as difficult as her father, but in a far more subtle way. I loathe manipulative women.'

'You know nothing about her,' Anderson said shortly.

'I think I'm getting a pretty good picture,' said Chloe defensively. 'Apart from her parents no one's exactly made her sound like a paragon of virtue. What about this man from the health club the neighbour saw her with?'

'That's what I need to find out,' Anderson said. 'First though I want to have another word with Stevens. Walker, you'd better check with Forensics that they didn't find any traces of an outsider in the kitchen. That lack of an alarm system means almost anyone could have been lying in wait for Lisa Allan when she went indoors.'

'But who and why?' Walker asked. 'What would be the motive?'

'We now know that Deborah has an unknown father somewhere. We must try and trace him, then when I've talked to Stevens I think we'll call on Jeff Phillips. It's time we learnt more about him, and his relationship with the dead woman.'

'This is getting more fascinating by the minute,' Chloe said. 'I hadn't realised how exciting this kind of work could be.'

'You make it sound like a game,' Anderson said. 'It isn't.'

She couldn't know, but to Anderson it was better than a game. The complexities fascinated him.

FIVE

Jeff Phillips bent over the kitchen sink and scrubbed at the saucepan he'd used to cook the boys' scrambled eggs for their lunch. It had been all right while they'd been chattering round the table, but now they'd gone back to school for the afternoon and it was just him and Liz. Earlier in the day Liz, who was in a lot of pain despite her change in medication, had stayed in bed but the district nurse had come in and got her dressed and downstairs while the boys were eating, which meant that somehow he would have to be as normal as possible and hope that her sharp eyes didn't detect any difference in him.

When the saucepan was so clean that he couldn't think of any possible reason to justify working on it any longer he called through into the tiny lounge. 'Cup of tea, Liz?'

'Only if you want one,' his wife replied despondently.

Jeff's spirits, already low, sank further. It was obviously going to be a bad day. No days were easy, but as Liz's arthritis spread through her body she was becoming more and more bitter and difficult. Her hatred of being dependent on him was obvious, but he couldn't understand it since it wasn't something that bothered him. Illness could strike anyone at any time, just like death. Suddenly he felt cold.

'I was going to have some,' he assured her, plugging in the kettle. When he took two mugs through to the other room Liz's mouth turned down at the corners. 'I don't need a mug, a cup's enough for me. If I drink too much you'll have to keep helping me to the loo and you know I hate that.'

'Drink half then,' Jeff said lightly, resting a hand on the top of his wife's head. She was still a pretty woman with her wavy light brown hair and hazel eyes but nowadays the sparkle had gone from her face, which was etched with lines of pain. Jeff cursed the disease, but never fate: it was just one of those things. He only wished he could help Liz more, but the harder he tried the more she pushed him away. Sometimes he thought she wanted to drive him away for good so that she could say 'I told you so' to her family.

At least she didn't know about any of his affairs, and if he had his way she never would. They were almost a necessity, a way of keeping sane, but they didn't affect his love for Liz. It was just that a man needed sex, and Liz, mostly due to pain, couldn't give him that any more. He felt guilty but justified it as a safety valve. It helped him cope, or had done until Lisa Allan had died. Now he was scared out of his mind.

'You look pale,' Liz said as she sipped her tea, her swollen fingers gripping the handle tightly.

'I told you I don't feel well. That's why I didn't go in today.'

For a moment Liz seemed on the point of saying something more but then she retreated into herself again. Jeff felt that he must make an effort, must try and reassure her that their marriage was safe and he wanted them to fight her disease as a team, not treat each other as enemies.

'Liz,' he said slowly, 'is there something wrong? Something I don't know about?'

She was sitting in an armchair, not her wheelchair, and

that made him feel more comfortable. He could almost pretend that she was well if he didn't look too closely at her hands. She always kept her knees covered with long skirts or trousers.

'Like what?' she asked shortly.

'It's only that you seem annoyed I'm home. I know I'm off-colour, but I still thought you might enjoy having me around on a weekday.'

'Not as much as your girlfriends at the health club,' she said bitterly.

Jeff's stomach lurched. 'Don't be silly,' he said calmly. 'I don't have any girlfriends there. Most of the women are old and overweight, and anyway why would I want a girlfriend when I'm a happily married man?'

'You don't have to pretend,' Liz said, and surprisingly her face looked softer, as though she felt sorry for him. 'I know what this is like for you and you always were popular with women. I had quite a fight to keep you even when we started going out.'

'Once I met you, I knew you were the woman I was going to marry,' Jeff said. It was true, he had.

Liz nodded. 'Maybe you did, but that was me as I was then, not the me you're stuck with now.'

'I still love you, Liz,' Jeff said, reaching out and taking her hands in his. She tried to draw them away, hide them inside her sleeves, but he wouldn't let her and softly stroked her twisted fingers. 'It's true,' he went on, heartened by the fact that she hadn't said anything cutting or turned away. 'You and the boys mean everything to me. We're a family. How could I walk out on you all when you mean so much to me. We'll grow old together, Liz, I promise you.'

'I'll grow old before you do,' said Liz, but without her usual bitterness. 'You still look like a man in his early thirties, no one would guess you're forty. And all that blond hair and those muscles. How could women be expected to keep away from you?'

'I do have a mind of my own you know,' Jeff said with a laugh.

Liz stared at him, stared deep into his eyes. 'Do you, Jeff? Do you really?'

'Yes,' he promised her. 'And once these new pills work and you're feeling a bit better we'll all take a holiday. Go away for a couple of weeks and get a change of air. It will do us the world of good. You spend too much time cooped up in this house on your own Liz. I want that to change.'

Reluctantly, almost fearfully, Liz smiled at him, and at that moment the telephone rang.

Jeff, who had just been about to suggest that he took Liz for a short drive in the car, went and answered it. 'Hello.'

'Jeff Phillips?' asked a woman's voice, but not one he recognised.

'Yes,' he said cautiously, relieved to see that Liz had picked up a magazine and was leafing through it.

'You don't know me, but my name's Sara Cooper; I live next door to the Allans.' Jeff's knees suddenly went weak and he sat down on the telephone stool. 'As you can imagine, I've had the police round,' she went on. 'They wanted to know if I'd seen Lisa on the day she died, and I had to tell them that I had.'

'What's all this got to do with me?' asked Jeff casually, but the palms of his hands were damp with sweat.

'I'm sorry but when I saw Lisa she was sitting in the passenger seat of your car and I saw you swing into her drive. I hope I haven't made things difficult for you, but my husband always says that when you're dealing with the police it's best to be honest, especially when you've nothing to hide.'

'Of course,' said Jeff. 'That's not a problem, but thank you for letting me know.' He put down the receiver with a shaking hand. It was all right for her, whoever she was, with nothing to hide, but hardly the same for him.

'What was that about?' called Liz.

'The swimming pool temperature control's playing up a bit, but it's still within the right limits. I can see to it tomorrow,' he lied.

Liz glanced up from her magazine. 'You really don't look well,' she said sympathetically. 'Why don't you go and have a lie-down for an hour. You'll be busy enough once the boys get back. And Jeff.'

'Yes?'

'You were right, we do have to be more honest with each other. I'll try harder, but you have to do the same.'

'Of course,' he said heartily, then he planted a swift kiss on her mouth before taking her advice and retreating to bed. He didn't sleep at all.

The afternoon wasn't going well for Tom, either. He'd decided to take time off from work for the rest of the week, until the funeral, but when Deborah's grandparents had suddenly turned up talking about some interview they'd had with DCI Anderson he'd left the house. It wasn't much fun knowing that they were both convinced his father had killed his stepmother.

In order to calm himself he'd driven over to the local co-educational sixth-form college and parked in a lay-by near the tennis courts and sports field. Then, half hidden behind some trees, he'd watched as the seventeen and eighteen-year-olds played their mixed doubles.

There was a great deal of fun and messing about, especially on the court that most interested Tom where a small, dark-haired girl and her tall blond partner were playing an auburn-headed girl with very long legs and a dark curly-haired lad. All four of them seemed to know each other very well and Tom watched intently as the blond young man put his arm round the dark-haired girl's shoulders when she netted a volley. The girl looked up at him and he whispered something that made her laugh as she touched the side of his face in an affectionate gesture. Tom felt as though someone had twisted a knife in his stomach and after a while he moved closer to the youngsters, throwing caution to the winds as he watched them from the side of the road.

None of the young people saw him, but a tutor from the college did and walked over towards the wire in order to speak to the lurking stranger. When Tom realised that he'd been spotted he sprinted back to his car and drove away, feeling positively nauseous. He knew he was probably being stupid but jealousy was eating away at him and he couldn't control it. This was his third visit in the past week and if he had any sense he'd stay away from now on. But in this particular case he didn't have any sense.

Deborah's afternoon started well but then went into a steep decline. She was thrilled when Grandpa and Grandma Mitchell arrived at the house, and fussed around them like a proper little hostess. She let her grandmother hold her while she cried a little, and then listened as her grandfather told her about his conversation with DCI Anderson. It was only as he got into the story that she realised he was telling her he knew her stepfather had killed her mother, and suddenly she didn't want to listen any more.

'You shouldn't say things like that, Grandpa,' she protested. 'Ralph's been good to me, and he would never have killed Mummy. I know they had problems, but he wouldn't have murdered her for no reason.'

'Money's always a good reason,' her grandfather said grimly.

Deborah didn't want to listen to this, but she loved both her grandparents and was too much in awe of her grandfather to stand up to him. 'Would you like a whisky, Grandpa?' she suggested in desperation. He nodded, and although she didn't normally drink in the afternoon Deborah decided to have a glass of wine at the same time, in order to relax. After the first glass she felt better than she had for some time as the alcohol combined with the tranquillizers to blur the edges of reality nicely. After a time she found she wasn't even listening to what her grandfather was saying, and the rest of his visit passed agreeably enough.

When they left Deborah suddenly had a desire to see her horse, Moonlight, again. She hadn't been over to the stable since the day her mother died and the mare would be missing her. Without any further delay she jumped into her little Fiesta and sped off towards Tadworth, where the horse was stabled. She was about five minutes away when she heard the sound of a police siren and saw a police car coming up fast behind her. Taking her foot off the accelerator she slowed to allow it to pass, but instead it drew level with her and motioned for her to pull over. It was only then that Deborah remembered the wine she'd been drinking, and when the young policeman put his head through the open window and asked her if she'd mind stepping out and giving a breath test as she'd been doing 80 mph she burst into tears, sobbing not for her mother but for Ralph. Ralph, who always took care of everything for her.

'The Allan family have had a busy afternoon, sir,' said DS Joanna Blackheath as she walked into Anderson's office and placed some papers on his desk. 'Here's the report from Forensics that you asked for. It seems there was no sign of anyone other than the family having been in the kitchen of The Chilterns.'

Anderson looked up at the policewoman. He'd been vaguely aware of her around the station, but she'd joined Guildford while he'd been away in Devon and their paths hadn't crossed professionally since his return. Of medium height and build with her dark gold hair cut in a bob, she gave off the impression of being rather over-enthusiastic, like a puppy, but he'd heard she was very tough when working on a case.

'You make it sound as though you know them,' he said casually, picking up the pages.

'I do a little. After all, I came here from the Reigate force.'

Anderson stared at her. 'Did you? No one told me that.'

'Perhaps you didn't ask, sir.'

'No,' he agreed politely, 'I didn't ask. However, since I'm working on a case that should by rights have been handled by your old force I'm still surprised. You may well have information that could be useful.'

'I thought that,' she agreed.

'But you didn't come and see me?'

'You were assigned DS Walker, and I'm sure he's very competent,' she said brusquely.

'All right, since I know now perhaps you'd tell me if there's anything I should know about the family that might be relevant to the case.'

'Ralph Allan is extremely popular with the Reigate force,' she said admiringly. 'He's very generous and a major contributor to the police fund for widows and orphans. He always gave wonderful raffle prizes for our charity dinners and supported local neighbourhood watch schemes and that kind of thing.'

'An extremely public-spirited man,' Anderson said.

'We thought so, sir.' DS Blackheath's tone made it clear that she'd already heard Anderson didn't feel the same about him.

'And that's the sum total of it?'

He could have sworn she hesitated for a moment before replying. 'Yes, sir,' she said at last.

'Then tell me what they've been up to that's important enough to be passed on to me. I only spoke to Tom and Deborah yesterday, and I saw Ralph Allan this morning.'

'There's been a complaint from the local sixth-form college that a young man answering to Tom Allan's description has been seen twice this week hanging around the tennis courts watching the youngsters play, and the second incident took place this afternoon. A little later, at 15.40 hours to be precise, Deborah Allan was booked for speeding while under the influence of drink. She's still at Reigate station. The officer who breathalysed her says she couldn't stop crying and kept asking for her stepfather.'

'Did she indeed,' said Anderson thoughtfully. 'Thank you Sergeant Blackheath, both for the information and for finally letting me know that you come from the Reigate division. Incidentally, where's Sergeant Walker?'

'He's gone off to interview a Mrs Sara Cooper, sir. He asked me to tell you he won't be long.'

Anderson was just about to go and ask Parrish what the hell he was up to not telling him that Joanna Blackheath was from Reigate when his call from Dr Stevens came through.

'Hi, John Stevens here,' he said cheerfully. 'I gather you've been trying to contact me. Presumably it's about Lisa Allan.'

'Yes,' said Anderson. 'I won't quote you on this but, off the record, what in your professional opinion was the worst thing for her heart condition?'

'The worst thing?' the doctor queried, sounding puzzled.

Anderson tried to curb his impatience. 'Yes. The point is, would a mobile phone have meant instant death if used near her? Or was she more likely to die by standing in front of a faulty microwave? Or by overdoing it at her local health club? I'm in the dark here and I must have more information.'

'As you've probably guessed, I can't give you a definitive answer,' the doctor responded. 'The truth of the matter is that none of the things you mentioned were what I consider life threatening, and yet at the same time with a heart condition like Mrs Allan's there's always the possibility of sudden death if the rhythm of the heart is upset and the pacemaker can't cope. That's why she was going to have the defibrillator fitted.'

'I know all that,' persisted Anderson patiently. 'But surely there was one thing that you'd have warned her about above all others.'

'Yes, of course,' Stevens said cheerfully. 'It's the curse of modern day living, stress.'

'Stress?' This wasn't at all what Anderson had been expecting to hear.

'That's right. People who do have defibrillators fitted and then feel them kick in, and believe me you can't miss that, frequently report that at the time it happened they were under extreme physical or mental stress.'

'So a shock could do it?' Anderson queried. 'Suppose someone Mrs Allan hadn't seen for a very long time literally jumped out at her in her own home, might that have been sufficient to kill her?'

'It might have been, but the key word is might. Why? Have you anyone in mind?'

'No,' Anderson said, remembering the latest report from Forensics. 'I'm simply trying to build up a better picture of her overall condition and thought you were the person to ask.'

'I'm as bewildered by her death as you are,' the doctor admitted.

'I'm sure the phone's important,' Anderson said thoughtfully. 'Otherwise, why was it there when Lisa Allan resolutely refused to have them in the house?'

'Luckily I don't have to answer that,' Dr Stevens said. 'I'm just a doctor. You're the detective. Don't hesitate to call again if there's anything else you want to know.'

'Thanks,' Anderson said, but when he put down the phone he was even more puzzled than before he'd taken the call.

'What did you discover?' Anderson asked DS Walker when he finally returned from talking to Sara Cooper.

Opening his notebook, Walker sat down opposite his

Chief Inspector. 'Mrs Cooper is not by nature a gossip, and she refused to say any more about Mrs Allan and Jeff Phillips although I'm quite sure she believes the pair were having an affair. What she did say, and this is interesting, is that only two days before she died Lisa wasn't sure whether or not she should go to the health club as she'd mislaid her beta-blockers and wasn't certain if it was all right to exercise without them.'

'She'd mislaid them?' Anderson asked incredulously. 'Why on earth didn't she ring her doctor and ask for some more?'

'According to Mrs Cooper, Ralph Allan could be very difficult and cutting where his wife was concerned. Lisa didn't dare tell her husband what had happened because she hated it when he called her a dumb blonde. She knew they were in the house somewhere and told Sara Cooper she'd have a thorough search when everyone was out of the house. Mrs Cooper assumed she'd found them.

'I tried to get more information on the husband and Mrs Cooper said that while she was friendly with Lisa, she and her husband didn't mix socially with the Allans because Ralph would make scenes in public. She didn't enlarge on that statement, but it was clear she and her husband aren't the kind of people who would put up with that.'

'Anything else? You're looking suspiciously pleased with yourself,' Anderson said.

DS Walker wished his chief's eyes weren't so sharp. He'd been looking forward to springing this final piece of information on the man, especially after his remark to Chloe, whom Walker fancied. 'There was one more thing,' he admitted. 'Sara Cooper says that Ralph Allan and his secretary Pippa Wright were lovers and that Lisa knew about this. She'd even talked about divorce a year or so ago, but my guess is that instead she decided what was sauce for the goose was sauce for the gander.'

'That's a distinct possibility,' Anderson admitted. 'We also have to take into account the fact that the goose may not have seen this reciprocal behaviour in quite the same way.' DS Walker looked blank. 'Ralph Allan is probably one of those men who believe there are two sets of rules, one for men and the other for women. It still happens, even in these days of sexual equality, believe it or not.'

'Most men play around,' Walker protested. 'It's different with women, especially wives.'

Anderson looked at him in disbelief. 'I think I'll pretend I didn't hear that. The women at this station would string you up, and quite a lot of the men, myself included, might feel insulted to be included in such a Neanderthal blanket assessment of your own sex.'

'Yes, sir,' Walker muttered. He found it hard to follow what Anderson was talking about and in any case was more interested in working out whether or not he had a chance with Chloe Wells.

'Tomorrow morning,' continued Anderson, 'we'll call on Jeff Phillips at the health club. I checked and he was at home ill today. Since his wife's apparently an invalid I didn't think it fair to turn up there and start asking questions about his relationship with another woman, but the clock's ticking away and I need some proof that this was murder or Parrish is going to pull us all off the case. The medication they give you for an ulcer doesn't appear to improve the patient's disposition,' he added sardonically.

'Perhaps Superintendent Parrish is in pain, sir,' Walker suggested.

In the silence that followed he realised that Anderson probably hoped he was right.

'Where are you going?' Deborah asked as Ralph came down the stairs shrugging on a crumpled lightweight summer jacket.

'Out,' Ralph said shortly. Then, remembering Deborah's run-in with the police earlier in the day, he put an arm round her. 'Cheer up, sweetie. It's not the end of the world.

We'll get Laurenson onto it. You're on tranquillizers, and you've just lost your mother, they're hardly going to sling the book at you. He's a good solicitor.'

'He would be,' Tom said, watching the scene from the kitchen doorway. 'Nothing but the best for you, Dad, is it?'

Ralph looked at his son. 'You can keep Deborah company while I'm out.'

'I can't, I'm going out.'

'Got a date, have you?' Ralph sneered.

'As a matter of fact, yes.'

There was a tangible sense of hostility between the two of them and Deborah looked isolated and bewildered. 'I don't want to spoil anything for Tom,' she said uncertainly.

'You won't,' Ralph said decisively. 'Tom's far too nice to leave you alone feeling the way you are.'

'Why can't she have her grandparents over? They were here half the afternoon,' Tom muttered.

Ralph's eyes narrowed. 'Is that true, Debs?'

She nodded. 'I forgot to tell you with everything that happened later. That's why I'd been drinking.'

'Your grandfather is enough to drive anyone to drink,' Ralph agreed. 'All right, see if they'll come over then. They might as well make themselves useful while they're here. The sooner the coroner releases Lisa's body for cremation the better. I can't wait for that damned man to go back to London and leave me alone.'

'I love him,' Deborah protested, flinching at the mention of her mother's body.

'Let's hope he loves you enough to come over then,' Tom said as he followed his father out of the house.

Ralph drove quickly but carefully to Croydon. He didn't want another member of the family to be booked by the police today. Once again he parked in the car park and then walked the last few hundred yards to Pippa's house. This time he knew that she was in. He'd set up the meeting earlier in the day, and had seen by her face how excited she was at the prospect of an evening together.

When Pippa opened the door to him she was wearing a floor-length aquamarine kimono and her hair was hanging loose, softly framing her face. He guessed that beneath the garment she was naked apart from a garter. He loved garters and she'd quickly learnt how to please him. He was certainly going to miss her, and had half a mind to have her one more time before he told her, but he couldn't behave that badly. It wasn't her fault that the affair had to end.

'Do you want a drink, or shall we go straight up?' she asked, pulling the front door closed behind him.

'I need a drink,' he said shortly, letting her kiss him but not responding. Pippa accepted this without comment, as he'd known she would. She spent her life trying to keep him happy.

'Here you are, your favourite.' She smiled and handed him a double malt.

'Aren't you having anything?' Ralph asked.

'I prefer to drink after, or even during,' she said, her eyes gleaming with excitement. 'I don't mind if I don't use a glass either.'

Ralph took a deep breath. Christ, this was harder than he'd expected, and the worst thing of all was that he still wanted her. 'Pippa, there's something I have to tell you. You won't like it, but it's got to be said.' Her eyes widened but she didn't speak. Ralph hurried on.

'I can't see you any more,' he blurted out, unable to think of a better way of telling her. Pippa went pale but she didn't say a word. 'It isn't that I don't want to,' he continued, talking rapidly now, anxious to get the whole thing over with before she burst into tears. 'It's because of Lisa.'

'But she's dead,' Pippa said. 'Surely if there was a time when we should have stopped it was while she was alive.'

Ralph wondered how she could be so stupid. 'It didn't matter to the police while she was alive,' he snapped. 'Now that she's dead and they suspect she was murdered, I'm their prime suspect. Husbands and wives always are. How do you think it will look if they find out about us?'

'But she hasn't been killed,' Pippa protested. 'That's just a theory. You know how ill she was, and anyway who would have wanted to kill her?'

'Me?' suggested Ralph.

Pippa stared at him. 'You didn't, did you?' she asked, her voice barely audible.

Ralph wondered what she'd do if he shouted 'Yes!' at her. 'Don't be stupid, of course not, but I can't prove it. I was there straight after it happened, and once they begin poking into my business affairs they'll soon learn how badly I needed money. Money that Lisa wouldn't give me but that I'll inherit now she's dead.'

'They'll never find that out,' Pippa said firmly. 'They haven't got the right to pry into your financial affairs at this stage, not when it isn't definitely a murder. No bank manager would help them.'

'Of course he would,' Ralph said irritably. 'There's nothing I can do to stop that, but at least I can show that Lisa's death affected me so much that I gave up my mistress.'

Pippa shook her head in protest. 'I'm more than that, Ralph, aren't I? We're lovers, friends, closer than you and Lisa ever were. I understand you, and I know how to make you happy. Once all this blows over we can get married. It's what we've always wanted. I suppose we could stop seeing each other for a time, but later on we can get back together again and it will all be in the open. Is that what you mean?'

Ralph was not, and never had been, a tactful man. 'No, it isn't what I mean,' he said shortly. 'You've been an incredible mistress, Pippa. I couldn't have asked for anyone better. We've had a great time, and as far as sex goes you'll take some beating – in more ways than one – but that's all it ever was. I never mentioned marriage; I had no idea it was on your mind. When we talked about the future it was just the way you do when you've had sex with someone. It didn't mean anything, I thought you knew the rules of the game too well to assume it did. As for becoming my wife, it's out of the question.'

'Why?' Pippa asked, obviously fighting to keep back tears.

'Because you're not the kind of wife I need,' he said bluntly. 'I need someone to add some class to my life. You're self-made, the same as I am. We're two of a kind, and that's not what I want from a wife. Lisa had years of breeding behind her on her mother's side, and that counted for something. She opened doors for me, got me accepted in clubs where I'd been shunned before I met her. She had class, style too.'

'But the pair of you didn't love each other,' Pippa protested. 'I'd have died for you.'

'You sound like something out of a cheap romance,' snapped Ralph, who wanted to get out of the house as quickly as possible now he'd said what he'd come to say.

'I know a lot about the company,' Pippa said suddenly as Ralph turned towards the door.

His head twisted round and his dark eyes were cold. 'Meaning what?'

Pippa opened her mouth to speak, but then Ralph saw a flicker of fear in her eyes. 'Nothing,' she said quickly. 'I'd never talk about what I know, I promise.'

'It doesn't matter if you do,' he lied. 'None of it has any bearing on Lisa's death, but for a woman who claims to have been willing to die for me you don't sound very friendly all of a sudden.'

Before he could get out of the door Pippa hurled herself across the room and threw her arms round him. 'Don't go, Ralph. Please, please don't leave me. I love you so much. You're everything to me. I haven't been out with another man since the first time we slept together. If you leave me now I've nothing, nothing at all. And how can I carry on working with you? I won't be able to bear it.'

'In that case,' he said, pushing her off quite forcefully, 'you'd better start looking for another job. I'll give you excellent references, in the office and the bedroom!'

Suddenly Pippa lost control and before Ralph knew what was happening she'd drawn back her arm and slapped him hard on his left cheek. Without thinking, Ralph hit her back and the force of the blow sent her half way across the room. For a few moments he stood frozen in fear as she lay motionless, but then she started to sit up, and as tears ran down her face and she began to sob he hurried out of the house and back to his car.

During the drive back he realised that he was shaking from head to toe and before arriving home he stopped off at a pub for a swift half to steady his nerves. The last thing he wanted was to arrive back home looking as though anything was wrong, especially if his bloody father-in-law was still there with Deborah.

It had been a horrible scene, and he wished that the affair could have ended better, but at least it was over now. No matter what the police discovered he could truthfully tell them that as far as Pippa was concerned it was finished. He was also, he realised with a rush of pleasure, a free man.

Ralph Allan would have been very surprised to learn that his *bête noire*, DCI John Anderson, was having a very similar if less dramatic evening of his own.

Karen Raybould had been leaving messages on his answerphone for the past two nights, and realising that he couldn't ignore the situation Anderson finally drove over to see her. He'd phoned in advance to say he was coming but that he couldn't stop.

'Come in,' Karen said calmly, and Anderson was relieved by her tone. He sensed that she already knew what he was going to say, and that she would handle it well. He only wished the pair of them had proved more compatible sexually because in other ways she suited him very well.

Karen brought him ground coffee in a bone china cup and then sat opposite him with her long legs crossed so that the skirt of her pale blue silk shift dress rose up revealing taut silk-covered thighs. 'How's work?' she asked politely.

'I'm very busy,' explained Anderson, looking directly into her eyes and seeing the way they darkened as the impact of what he was saying sank in. 'I'm sorry, but it means I have very little free time.'

'And the free time that you do have, you don't want to spend with me. Is that right?' she asked quietly.

Anderson was taken aback by the question, but admired her direct approach. 'I don't think it would work out,' he explained, putting his cup down on a tiny lacquered table. 'I did at first, but last time we slept together I realised that it wouldn't.'

'Was it something I did?' Karen enquired.

There was no way that Anderson was going to admit that it had been; that her desire to please him and take the initiative had been a turn-off for him and that he could only get satisfaction from a sexual relationship where he was in control the whole time. It was true, but not a facet of his personality that he wished to analyse too closely.

'Of course not,' he assured her. 'I had a very intense relationship with someone in the winter. It's over now, chiefly for geographical reasons if the truth be known, and I thought that I was ready to begin again, but I'm not. You're a very attractive woman, Karen, and I like you too much. If we were less well suited, if the relationship had been more casual then it might have been all right, but from the first time I slept with you I realised that it was going to be more than that and once I was proved right I realised I wasn't ready to handle it. I apologise. I never intended to mislead you.'

He could see from the expression in her eyes that she was hurt, and also that she didn't totally believe his explanation.

'Don't worry about it, John,' she said with a strained smile. 'We're both adults, we know things can't always go the way we hope or plan. I enjoyed the time we did have, however brief, and I hope we'll remain friends. We make a very good team at the squash club.'

Anderson relaxed and some of the tension drained out of him. Karen wasn't going to make a scene and she'd accepted his explanation. He admired her all the more now, especially for the dignified way she was taking her rejection, because however well he'd wrapped it up that was what it was.

'Of course we'll remain friends,' he said smoothly. 'As for the squash, let's wait and see how much time I have before we commit ourselves to any competitions.'

'Of course,' Karen agreed.

Much to his relief she got to her feet. Now he'd said his piece, Anderson wanted to leave as quickly as possible.

At the front door they kissed briefly, more of a social kiss than one of ex-lovers, and then he drove away in his silver BMW aware that they wouldn't remain friends in the way she'd meant it because he wasn't the kind of man who had friends. It occurred to him that, if he wasn't careful, he might spend most of his life in isolation, unable to commit himself fully and equally to any relationship. It was a disquieting thought, but one that he was able to push aside quite quickly.

He hoped that he'd done a little to give Karen the confidence to pick herself up and get on with her life. He must work out his own private demons for himself.

SIX

The following morning, as Anderson stepped from his shower after his early morning run, he thought about what the day ahead involved. It was now three days since Lisa Allan had been found dead. The inquest would be the following Monday, and once the coroner had given his verdict the body would be released for burial. Don Mitchell had already made clear his displeasure at the delay, and had managed to offend Dr Stevens, the pathologist and the coroner in the process. Anderson didn't like the man, but he could understand his distress. A funeral was an official goodbye, and in the absence of any official arrest for what Don Mitchell considered a murder he needed to experience that formal farewell.

As he glanced through his morning paper and ate his croissants Anderson mentally sifted through his list of suspects. Top of the list was still Ralph Allan, and later that day he would be interviewing him again, along with his secretary now that an affair between them had been confirmed. DS Walker had so far heard nothing to indicate that Ralph's business was in trouble, but there had been rumours that the man wanted to sell. If he needed an injection of Lisa's cash in order to make the business a good proposition and she'd refused him any then he had a very good motive, coupled with the fact that she was possibly having an affair with Jeff Phillips.

This brought Anderson to his second suspect. So far he knew very little about the man, except for the fact that if he was innocent he was almost certainly the last person to see Lisa Allan alive apart from the murderer, and that he had an invalid wife. As soon as he'd checked in at the station Anderson intended to go to the health club and talk to Jeff Phillips. After that he'd have a better idea of whether or not he seemed a likely suspect.

Then there were Tom and Deborah Allan to consider. If either of them was responsible it had to be for psychological reasons, some severe form of family dysfunction, and it seemed to him that the Allans were a pretty dysfunctional unit. All the same both of them were a very long shot unless something more came up on either of them, and both had alibis. Deborah's grief and the drink-driving charge coupled with her swings in attitude towards her stepfather were fascinating but not necessarily relevant. He made a mental note to ask Chloe what she thought of the girl.

Tom had obviously inherited his father's liking for younger females. If he had been the man hanging around the sixth-form college then that would provide a good excuse for talking to him again, but like his stepsister it was difficult to think why he would have killed his stepmother or to imagine him doing it. Of all the family Anderson felt that he had the least backbone. Not that that excluded him. Weak people could kill if pushed too far, but there would have to be a reason. If Ralph were the victim rather than Lisa, Tom would figure higher on Anderson's list of suspects because he felt that father and son had little in common, and it was clear that Tom didn't share his father's enthusiasm for the ladder-making business.

Finally, if you excluded a random killing, and given the

complexity of the murder Anderson had already ruled that out, there was the unknown father of Deborah. Don Mitchell had clearly ruthlessly cut the unfortunate young man off from his girlfriend and baby daughter without any compunction, losing him his job at the same time. There was always the possibility too that Lisa had stayed in contact without letting her father know and that the relationship had got into difficulties for some reason. He decided to make sure he mentioned her natural father to Deborah when he next interviewed her.

By the time he was shaved, dressed and on his way to the station, Anderson had his day planned out, keenly aware that this was a race against time, a race that he had to win, especially if he wanted Parrish's job when it came up. Lisa's death was murder, he knew it, but in order to prove it he might well have to arrest the killer without any further help from Forensics or the medical profession.

'DC Lin Ford rang you, from Reigate station,' called the duty sergeant as Anderson walked in the door. 'She asked you to call back urgently.' Anderson felt a surge of excitement and hurried to his office, but the information she gave him was disappointing.

'You're telling me that Deborah Allan called you and said her stepfather had been having an affair with his secretary, is that it?' he asked after speaking to the policewoman.

'That's right, sir.'

'We already knew that,' he said heavily. 'All the same, it's interesting that his stepdaughter decided to tell you about it. When did she call?'

'Thirty-six hours ago,' Lin Ford admitted.

'In future,' Anderson said slowly, 'I would appreciate it if information was passed to me a little quicker than that. We are meant to be liaising over this murder and thirty-six hours is a disgraceful time lapse.'

'I'm sorry, sir,' apologised the DC 'My chief doesn't feel

that it is a murder case and although I jotted it down to call you the same day it slipped my mind when I had to do something else.'

'If your chief wants to run the enquiry perhaps he'd like to tell Superintendent Parrish,' Anderson suggested before he hung up. No wonder Ralph Allan had called the Reigate police, he thought to himself as he went to find Chloe and DS Walker. They would have let him get away with it without any trouble. Well, he would find that John Anderson was more than a match for him.

Anderson found Chloe Wells and DS Walker sitting together in the canteen. 'Chloe might be free to spend her time here, but there's always work for you, Phil,' he remarked. 'For a start I want you to pay a visit to the bank that handles Ralph Allan's business affairs and find out exactly how healthy a situation the company's really in.'

Turning a delicate shade of pink, DS Walker jumped to his feet. 'Right away, sir,' he said quickly.

'When you've done that, drive over to Croydon and wait in the slip road near his office. Chloe and I will join you there after we've been to see Jeff Phillips. I'll take DS Blackheath with me too. Apparently she's free and she might know something about him as she comes from that area.'

'Won't Mr Phillips be overwhelmed by so many women?' enquired Chloe sweetly as she and Anderson made their way to the car.

'No,' Anderson said with a smile. 'You'll be looking round the health club while DS Blackheath and I are talking to him. Somehow I don't think she'll create too much of a flutter in his possibly over-susceptible breast. You, on the other hand, might if DS Walker is anything to go by.'

Anderson was amused by the slight pink flush that suffused Chloe's cheeks at his words. He'd noticed Phil Walker's interest in her from the start, and although he personally didn't find her at all appealing he could see that she had a certain kind of charm that might attract someone like Sergeant Walker. He wasn't quite so certain what Chloe thought of her admirer and was awaiting the outcome of Walker's efforts with interest. It was possible to learn a lot about his men by studying them at moments when they thought they were unobserved, and Anderson always filed the information away in his head for future reference.

As they drove to the health club he glanced in his mirror and realised that Chloe was studying Joanna Blackheath with interest. That was understandable. As he understood it, Joanna was something of an enigma to everyone at the station, and no doubt Chloe wanted to get to know her better for her thesis, which he suspected would spend more time on personalities than was necessary. As far as he was concerned all that mattered about Joanna Blackheath was that she did her job well. If she didn't want to give anything away about her private life then that was her business, and it certainly didn't mean, as he'd heard some of his men say, that she was frigid or stuck-up. He had no doubt that there were a lot of rumours about him too, but no one had ever been unwise enough to repeat any of them to him.

All Anderson wanted was to do his job well and solve crimes. That was the whole point of being a police officer. The force might do better if it had more Joanna Blackheaths in it and fewer Phil Walkers. It would cut down on the laddish cult that he found intensely distasteful.

'Do you know Jeff Phillips?' Anderson asked Joanna as they approached the health club.

Joanna shook her head. 'Only by reputation. He was said to be quite a ladies' man, but more the kind that chats women up and makes them feel good than the type who has lots of affairs. At least that's what I heard. It's probably why he got the job. There are a lot of rich, bored women there; an attractive man like him with a good line in chat will help keep the numbers up.'

'Now's the time to find out if he did more than just chat to them,' said Anderson, parking the car swiftly and expertly in a small space outside the main entrance. 'Chloe, you go off and have a look round. If anyone stops you, say you're thinking of becoming a member. And keep your ears open. Gossip is something I'm very interested in at the moment.'

Chloe disappeared into reception and Anderson and DS Blackheath waited a few minutes before following her through the main doors. At the desk Anderson showed his ID and asked to see Jeff Phillips.

'He's in the gym, second door on the right down that corridor,' the receptionist said, giving Anderson a warm smile but ignoring Joanna. He wondered if she minded; it had sometimes annoyed Pat Fielding when she was his sergeant, but if it did nothing showed on Joanna's face. Anderson was pleased. Being able to conceal your emotions was a great advantage for a police officer of any rank.

Jeff Phillips was checking out an exercise bike when Anderson and DS Blackheath walked in. He turned at the sound of the doors opening, and when Anderson took out his ID all the colour drained from his face. 'I wondered how soon it would be before you came to see me,' he said nervously. 'For some reason I imagined it would be at home.'

'Normally I would have called at your home,' Anderson agreed. 'However, in view of your wife's health and the somewhat delicate nature of our enquiry I felt that it was better to come here. I have no wish to distress your wife if that can be avoided.'

The other man bit on his lower lip and let out a small sigh. 'I wish to God I'd never met Lisa Allan,' he said softly.

'I'm sure you do,' Anderson agreed as the DS took out her notebook. 'Perhaps you'd care to tell me the exact nature of your relationship with her?'

Jeff Phillips hesitated, only briefly. 'We were lovers,' he admitted.

'And how long had the affair been going on?'

'About six months I think. I can't remember exactly

when it began. We'd been friendly for some time before that, chatting and so on when she came in. Also, I had to help design a programme for her in the gym because of her heart condition; that was how we first got to know each other well.'

'Do you remember when you last saw her?' Anderson asked, watching the other man keenly as he waited for his answer.

'Of course, it was on the Monday morning, just before she died. I drove her back home from here about twelve o'clock.' Anderson was surprised at how readily Jeff Phillips was offering this information. 'That's when Sara Cooper saw me,' he added.

Anderson's heart sank. 'How do you know Mrs Cooper saw you?' he asked.

'She rang me at home to tell me. She was worried that she might have put me in a difficult position, which in a way she had, but it could have been made worse by her ringing me at home.'

Anderson cursed Sara Cooper's honesty. Since Jeff Phillips had already known that the police were aware he'd taken Lisa home then his honesty meant nothing and they couldn't use the information to shock anything out of him. 'I take it you'd brought her here as well then,' he said.

Jeff nodded. 'Lisa had lost her driving licence due to her illness. Sometimes she took a taxi here, and now and again she even used the bike Ralph bought her when her GP said cycling on level ground was good exercise, but on Monday she wasn't feeling well and asked me to pick her up.'

'Yet, despite not feeling well she wanted to come to the club and work out?'

'Not to work out. She wanted to talk to me about our future,' replied the other man, lowering his voice as a club member came in. 'Look, could we talk in the staff room?' he added. 'This is getting a bit difficult.'

Anderson and DS Blackheath followed him to a small,

surprisingly dingy room and all three of them sat down on wooden chairs more suitable for a playgroup than a staff room. 'Were the two of you planning a future together?' asked Anderson when Jeff Phillips showed no sign of continuing.

'No! I'll be honest with you, Chief Inspector, Lisa had begun to want more from the affair than I did. She wasn't happy in her marriage, her husband was a philandering bully and she wanted out. I'd had affairs before, she wasn't the first, but I don't think she had. I didn't realise that or I'd never have started it. You see, although my wife's ill and things aren't perfect at home, I'd never leave. I've got two sons and a wife who needs me. My affairs are just a bit of fun, a sexual thing not a deep meaningful relationship.

'I told Lisa this right at the start, but somehow things got a bit out of control. I was terrified Liz, that's my wife, would get to hear of it because Lisa spent so much time here and people gossip. Liz has already got depression, it's a combination of her condition and the drugs she takes for it. The last thing I want to do is make that worse.'

'What exactly is wrong with your wife, Mr Phillips?' Anderson asked.

'Rheumatoid arthritis. They're bringing out new drugs all the time, I keep telling her that, but at the moment she's bad. It's spread to her knees and ankles as well as her hands and shoulders. Sometimes I wonder how she puts up with it as well as she does.'

'And Mrs Allan came here on Monday to talk about your future together, is that right?' Anderson asked quietly, trying to get Jeff Phillips back on track.

'Yes. She wanted to know what I thought about the pair of us going off together. I said it was out of the question. I'd never leave Liz, and anyway I couldn't afford it. Lisa was used to a very high standard of living. I don't earn that much here.'

'What did she say to that?'

'She said money wasn't a problem. Apparently she was a rich woman in her own right and she said she'd support me, but I wouldn't have wanted that. It isn't the right way round, is it?'

Anderson thought that Ralph Allan would probably have a fit if he knew that his wife had offered to share her money with another man while refusing it to her husband. 'It's more common than it used to be,' he said carefully. 'Tell me, how did Mrs Allan take your rejection?'

'Naturally she was pretty upset at first. But I reminded her that I'd always said I couldn't leave Liz, and besides we weren't suited for a long-term relationship. She was from a different background, out of my class really. It would never have worked.'

'And Mrs Allan accepted that?' Anderson allowed his surprise to show in his voice.

'Yes, yes she did,' Jeff Phillips assured him. 'Being ill herself she thought that it was wonderful that I still cared for Liz. She said she wished Ralph was the same. I don't think he ever took much notice of her heart condition.'

'So, let me make sure I've got this right,' Anderson said calmly. 'Mrs Allan came here to talk about the possibility of the pair of you sharing the rest of your lives together. You told her that was out of the question and that you wanted to stay with your wife, and then she happily agreed this was for the best and let you drive her home. Correct?'

Jeff Phillips looked uncomfortable. 'When you put it like that it sounds pretty unlikely, and it wasn't as clear cut as that, but the end result was the same. I did think she might prefer to take a taxi home, but she said she wanted one last ride with me.'

'Which is precisely what she got,' Anderson remarked.

The health club manager stared at him. 'I didn't kill her!' he exclaimed. 'Surely you don't think that?'

'Why else would we be here? To check your driving licence is in order?' DS Blackheath snapped abruptly.

Anderson concealed his surprise at her interruption, although he wasn't best pleased. The interview had been going along nicely with Jeff Phillips falling over himself to co-operate. At times like that a person often gave away more than they realised but now it was clear from his shocked expression that he would treat them far more warily.

'I thought you wanted to know how she was, and whether I saw anyone at the house, that sort of thing,' he muttered, keeping his eyes averted instead of looking Anderson full in the face as he had been doing.

'Naturally we're interested in what you saw at the house,' said Anderson smoothly. 'Was there anyone else at home when you and Lisa went in?'

'I didn't go into the house,' Phillips said quickly. 'To be honest I didn't want to prolong the goodbye. I waited in the car until Lisa was inside and then drove off.'

'Which door did she go in, the front or the back?' Anderson asked.

'The front, that was the one she always used. She said the back door was for tradesmen.'

'And you didn't see any other cars or people hanging around the house as you drove away?' Anderson asked. Jeff shook his head. 'In that case we don't need to trouble you any further at the moment, but we will want a full statement from you in the near future. One of my officers will ring and arrange a convenient time for you to go to the station in order for that to be done. And don't worry, we'll make sure your wife doesn't learn about any of this from us.'

'May I ask a question?' Jeff Phillips said suddenly. Anderson nodded. 'I don't understand about Lisa's pills.'

Anderson felt the hairs on the back of his neck rise. 'Understand what, Mr Phillips?'

'Why they didn't keep her alive.'

'Beta-blockers aren't a safeguard against murder,' Anderson pointed out.

'It isn't definitely murder, is it?' Phillips said defiantly.

'I believe that it is,' Anderson replied.

'But, what makes you say that? I mean, how can you tell? I heard that she'd simply collapsed, which was something she was always afraid of happening when she was alone. I feel pretty guilty that I didn't go in with her. If I had I might have been able to help her.'

'In that respect your conscience can be quite clear,' Anderson assured him. 'If you'd gone in, you might have been murdered too.'

Leaving Phillips to mull over that statement, Anderson and Joanna returned to the BMW, where they waited for Chloe.

'What did you make of him?' Anderson asked.

'Hard to tell in such a short time,' said the DS. 'He's one of those men who likes to make out that he never does anything wrong, but all the time he's cheating on his wife and probably misleading his lady friends too. He didn't seem violent or malicious, but that's not really the kind of thing you can tell as he's obviously a very smooth talker and would hardly give himself away to us.'

'In other words you didn't like him but you're not sure he's the stuff that murderers are made of,' Anderson remarked with a smile.

'I'm not certain Lisa Allan was murdered at all,' Joanna said shortly. 'From what I've heard, Jeff Phillips may be right and she simply had a convulsion followed by total heart block.'

'Bruising herself on her front shoulder and the side of her neck as she fell onto her back?' asked Anderson.

'Well . . .'

'And why wasn't there any trace of beta-blockers in her body? I was interested to hear Mr Phillips mention the drug. Either he's a better actor than I'd have expected or he didn't know she wasn't taking them any more. That puts him a little lower down the list of suspects in my book because I think that the lack of beta-blockers is all part of the killing.'

'I heard she'd mislaid them herself. That's what DS Walker told me.'

'She thought she had,' Anderson said. 'But it's always possible someone else concealed them, or even threw them away, knowing that she'd be reluctant to admit she'd lost them. She didn't like the fact that she could be forgetful and her loving husband used to call her a blonde bimbo.'

'If you ask me she had pretty poor taste in men. Neither her husband nor her lover seem to be up to much,' Joanna said shortly.

'If it's true that all girls subconsciously marry their fathers I'm not surprised,' Anderson said. 'You should meet Don Mitchell; he's formidable.'

'Where's your shadow?' Joanna asked. 'She's taking a long time. Perhaps they've offered her a free swim as an introductory offer.'

'While we wait,' said Anderson, 'I'd like to know why you chose to leap in during my conversation with Jeff Phillips and turn him from a co-operative witness into a defensive one.'

'We weren't getting anywhere. I thought a change of tactics might be useful,' she explained, for the first time looking slightly unsure of herself.

'In future,' Anderson said quietly, 'I'd prefer it if you waited for my signal before doing something like that.'

'Very good, sir,' Joanna said stiffly.

Anderson could tell that she was annoyed, and felt a momentary sense of disappointment. Not so much because she'd come in too hard and spoilt the interview, although she had, but because it looked as though she wasn't quite as logical and unemotional as he'd thought.

He hoped that she'd soon get over her annoyance. No one liked criticism, but if he and she were going to work together again she had to learn that he didn't expect her to interrupt him unless this was something they'd discussed together in advance.

At that moment, Chloe emerged from the health club and waved cheerfully at the waiting couple. 'She seems to have forgotten she's working undercover,' Joanna said crossly.

'When she climbs in the car with us that cover will be blown anyway,' Anderson pointed out with amusement. He was beginning to find Chloe's cheerful approach to life and her boundless enthusiasm for things quite refreshing. She was like a puppy, but a puppy that needed more training.

'Sorry to have kept you,' Chloe said. 'I bumped into what has to be the club's biggest gossip, and as luck would have it she was here on Monday morning. She had plenty to tell me about what she'd "accidentally" overheard going on between Jeff Phillips and Lisa Allan.'

'Well done,' Anderson said briefly. He saw a slight shadow cross Joanna Blackheath's face and realised that for some reason she disliked him praising Chloe. Well, if she wanted any praise from him herself she'd have to do better than she had during their interview with Jeff Phillips. 'You can tell us about it as we drive to Croydon,' he continued, climbing into the driving seat.

'Apparently,' Chloe said, unable to wait until they'd gone more than a few metres, 'Jeff and Lisa had a furious argument in the car park. It was very heated, went on for over ten minutes and this woman said that she was surprised by the language Lisa was using.'

'So much for her taking the news of being dumped well,' remarked Joanna.

'Is that what Jeff Phillips told you?' Chloe asked. 'It certainly didn't sound that way from what I've been hearing. It also seems that everyone here knew the pair of them were an item, and that Lisa was the keener of the two. It seems that Jeff Phillips is famous for his close friendships with some of the more attractive lady members, but this affair with Lisa was different. She wasn't, in my informant's view, discreet enough and she pursued him relentlessly. She even joined exercise classes that were too strenuous for her and then she'd sit them out watching him from the side of the room.'

'A woman obsessed,' Anderson said thoughtfully.

'So it appears. I asked if she was married, and I was told that she had a lovely husband who deserved better. I took that to mean that the lady in question had seen Ralph Allan and fancied him. Not unreasonable since I do too!'

'He seems to have something that escapes me,' Anderson murmured. 'You said you knew him, Joanna. What's your opinion of his manly charms?'

'He isn't really my type, but I can see the attraction. He's very much in control. You get the feeling he'd be able to protect you and take care of everything.'

'He certainly took care of his wife,' Anderson said dryly. The two women in the car obviously thought it wiser not to dispute the statement, and they drove on in silence.

'So now we know Jeff Phillips is a liar,' Chloe said as they approached the lay-by where DS Walker was waiting for them.

'If you'd been there when we interviewed him you'd have worked that out already,' Anderson said. 'I wouldn't have expected anything different. He'd have to be very stupid indeed to say that they'd quarrelled furiously when he knows we're looking for the person who killed her only half an hour or so later, don't you think?'

'Except he claimed to believe it was death by natural causes,' said Joanna.

'I didn't believe that either. He knows the police don't waste this much time unless they're certain.'

'Superintendent Parrish probably doesn't share your view,' Joanna said.

'Why should he? He never gets off his chair to find out the truth about anything, but even he's willing for us to spend three weeks on the case.'

'We've nearly completed one of them,' Chloe said rather unhelpfully.

'I'm well aware of that.' Anderson's tone was icy as he pulled into the lay-by. 'All the more reason to start increasing the pressure. Joanna, you'd better drive Philip's car back to Guildford. Allan is used to seeing me with him and Chloe. I don't want anything to change. Besides, you know him from Reigate, and a friendly face is the last thing I want him to see this morning.'

'Very good, sir,' Joanna said.

'How did you get on at the bank?' Anderson asked Walker as they got out of the car a few minutes later.

'The company took out quite a big loan nearly a year ago, then borrowed some more last month. The bank manager said there was no problem as the loan was well covered by the stock and the wood, most of which, surprisingly, is imported from America.'

'Is that relevant?'

Walker looked sheepish. 'Of course not, but I thought it was interesting.'

'Not as interesting as the second loan only a month before Lisa Allan died.'

'Also,' Walker added as they crossed the car park, 'the bank were going to send their auditors in soon because loan repayments have fallen behind. They won't have to now though because Ralph Allan has told them he'll be repaying in full prior to selling the company.'

'With his dead wife's money I assume,' Anderson murmured. 'Fascinating.'

The first thing that struck Anderson as they walked into Ralph Allan's business premises was that the atmosphere had changed. The young girl behind the reception desk looked at his card in silence, there was no welcoming smile, and when she rang through to his secretary her voice was subdued.

The changes in the receptionist were subtle, but the changes in Pippa Wright were not, and Anderson heard Chloe's sharp intake of breath, indicating that she too was shocked by the other woman's appearance. Pippa was still made up, but far too heavily, as though trying to disguise the ravages of what was either a very heavy night or a night spent crying. From the puffiness of her eyelids Anderson suspected the latter.

Her hair was scraped back off her face, with no regard to how she looked, and held in place by a plain gilt slide. Instead of her sharp business suit she was wearing a knee-length skirt with pleats and a white overblouse, more suited to the behind-the-scenes manageress of a small hotel than a glamorous PA, which was how she'd presented herself before.

Despite this, Anderson thought that she was still a very attractive woman and when she looked at him she gave out such a desperate air of sadness that he felt he should physically move towards her and attempt to protect her from whatever it was that had caused the change. He was reluctant to admit to himself that this caused him any sexual excitement, but it did. Her sad eyes and air of defeat were intensely arousing.

'Is Mr Allan in?' DS Walker asked.

'Of course. I'll take you through,' Pippa replied. As they followed her Anderson noticed that even her walk had changed. The slight swing of the hips, the subdued but definite hint of sexuality was missing now.

Inside his office, sitting comfortably behind his desk, Ralph Allan looked exactly the same. He smiled at them all, stood up and held out a hand to Anderson, who pretended not to notice. 'I should have mentioned to you last time, Mr Allan, that Miss Chloe Wells is not a policewoman but a postgraduate student who is working on a thesis connected to the police force. In connection with this she is accompanying me to work for six weeks. If you would prefer her not to be present at this interview then please say so.'

'Perhaps I should complain that you didn't tell me that last time,' said Ralph with a grin. 'I won't though. Miss Wells is far too pretty for me to object to her presence. Anyway, you told my father-in-law, so I knew already. Enjoying yourself, Miss Wells?'

'It's very interesting, Mr Allan, but murder isn't proving very enjoyable.'

Ralph's smile faded. 'What can I do for you, Chief Inspector?'

'There are some points that I'd like to go over again if you don't mind, sir. Firstly, have you had time to think any more about the fact that your wife's body contained no trace of beta-blockers?'

Ralph nodded. 'I've had lots of time to think about it, but apart from the answer I gave you last time there's no explanation.'

'And you haven't found the tablets since she died?'

'No,' Ralph said blandly. 'Your men didn't find them either, so they must be well hidden.'

'Why would your wife wish to hide them?'

'So that I couldn't insist she took them I suppose. How the hell should I know? Lisa did what she liked.'

'She told a friend that she'd lost them but was afraid to tell you,' said Anderson.

'Bloody ridiculous. Why not just ring for a repeat prescription?'

'Because she would have had difficulty in getting one. How was she to explain the fact that she'd used up a month's supply in one week, which according to Dr Stevens is what it would have been.'

'Not if she'd told them she'd lost them.'

'Doctors are sceptical about patients losing drugs.'

'I think you'll find that's only when the drugs are addictive. Beta-blockers aren't.'

'Yet she didn't ask you to help her find them, did she?'

'No, she didn't,' Ralph agreed. 'That's probably because she didn't really want to find them. Perhaps it was one of those accidentally-on-purpose kind of things. Without them she was undoubtedly feeling sexier.'

'Presumably you're the best judge of that,' Anderson said.

For the first time Ralph seemed slightly thrown. 'Not necessarily,' he admitted. 'She might have had a lover. She had enough time on her hands, and she'd certainly lost interest in me.'

'Had you lost interest in her?' Anderson suggested.

Ralph shook his head. 'Hardly! You saw her, Anderson. You fancied her yourself, I could see it all over your face. Most men wanted my wife. She gave off a very strong suggestion of sexuality.'

Anderson knew that both Chloe and DS Walker were very interested in what they'd heard, but neither of them gave any sign of this, which was wise of them.

'Then you were a faithful husband, were you Mr Allan?' asked Anderson, watching the other man closely.

Ralph stared at the detective, looking deep into his eyes as he decided how to answer the question. 'No, not all the time,' he admitted at last.

'Would you care to expand on that answer, sir?'

'No,' Ralph said bluntly.

'Generally speaking it's better to cooperate with the police, you know,' DS Walker said. 'We're very discreet and when people hide things from us it makes us suspicious and means we have to start digging around a little.'

'Your chief inspector's been suspicious of me from the moment he found my wife dead,' Ralph retorted. 'He's been digging around in my affairs ever since then. If he wants me to answer every question then he'd better charge me with an offence and take me to the station. My extramarital affairs have nothing to do with Lisa's death.'

'How do you know?' Anderson enquired.

'Well if they are, prove it,' Ralph said belligerently.

Anderson kept silent. Usually this had the effect of making suspects speak, but Ralph didn't. The room remained silent until Anderson was forced to try his last card. 'As I understand it, your wife wasn't interested in the business, Mr Allan, but she was a wealthy woman in her own right. Would this money have been useful to your company?'

Ralph's eyes narrowed. 'That sounds to me like the kind of question I need a solicitor to advise me on.'

'You don't have to answer any of my questions,' Anderson reminded him.

Ralph gave a harsh bark of laughter. 'But if I don't, I make things look pretty bad don't I? Well, for what it's worth I'll tell you this. Yes, I could have done with some money from Lisa, but more a year or so ago than now. The bank have been very co-operative and business is booming. Obviously I'd rather not have had the interest to repay, but probably Lisa was right. If she'd started putting money into the company she'd have felt obliged to study all the accounts and so on. That would then have caused her stress, because she didn't have a head for business.'

'Was stress bad for her?' Anderson asked blandly.

'Yes, or so she claimed the doctor said. Personally I thrive on it, but then as far as I know there's nothing wrong with my ticker . . .'

Next to Anderson DS Walker shifted in his chair, pencil poised. Anderson had the annoying feeling that he wasn't going to get anywhere with Ralph Allan by pursuing his questioning and this frustrated him. 'Perhaps we could arrange a convenient time for you to come to the station and make a statement about all this,' he suggested.

'I've made a statement about the morning I found my wife. I fail to see why you need another one. If you want me to come to the station again then charge me with something,' said Ralph.

'There's no question of that,' Anderson said politely. 'I

simply wanted to clarify things, but if you'd rather not make another visit to the station that's your right.'

'Too fucking right,' Ralph said, suddenly angry. 'You're so damned supercilious and blinkered. In your mind I killed my wife, and that's the only line of enquiry that interests you, isn't it?'

Anderson shook his head, pleased that he'd finally rattled the man. 'Not at all, sir. We're pursuing a number of lines of enquiry.'

'Including Jeff Phillips, the manager of the so-called health club?'

'We have spoken to Mr Phillips,' Anderson replied carefully.

'Fine. Well, I've nothing more to say to you so I'd be grateful if you'd leave my office now. If you want to interview me again you can invite me to the station and I'll bring my solicitor with me. You're treading a very fine line here, Chief Inspector. There is such a thing as harrassment.'

'Your wife was murdered,' Anderson reminded him. 'You found her, and you called in the police. I'm sure you're as anxious as we are to find out what really happened that Monday morning, but if you feel you're being persecuted I apologise. However, should you complain you'll find you haven't been interviewed any more or less frequently than other people closely connected to your late wife.'

Ralph leant back in his chair and looked directly at the chief inspector. 'I've met your sort before, Anderson. You're so proud of your own intelligence, so certain that everyone else is inferior, but underneath you're no different from the rest of us. In fact, I bet that you've got quite an interesting private life. Men like you often do have. This poncing around in posh suits and playing the intellectual can be a veneer for all kinds of surprising things. Did you know that, Sergeant?' he asked Phil Walker.

DS Walker closed his notebook without answering and Anderson stood up. 'If that's all, Mr Allan then I'd like a word with your secretary before I leave. If you'd rather I didn't talk to her here, I'll arrange to interview her at another time.'

'Talk to her all you like, she barely knew Lisa. I doubt if she'll want your Girl Friday with you though. She's a man's woman.'

'I'll wait in the car,' said Chloe quickly.

Ralph switched his gaze to her. 'Why not let me show you round the place?' he suggested. 'It might give you something interesting to put in your thesis other than the colour of the chief inspector's shirts. What do you know about ladder-making?'

'Nothing at all!' laughed Chloe.

'Then I'll remedy that. With your permission, Anderson?'

Anderson nodded. He just hoped that with Chloe, Ralph Allan might let his guard down and give away something useful. At least she should get an idea of whether the place looked busy and thriving or not.

As Ralph guided Chloe towards the warehouse he tapped on Pippa Wright's door before pushing it open. His PA was sitting with her chin in her hands staring out of the window at the car park and gave a start of surprise. 'Not busy, Pippa? What on earth will the chief inspector think of us? He'd like a quick word with you,' added her boss before departing with Chloe at his heels.

'Please, sit down Inspector and you too, Sergeant,' Pippa said wearily. 'Would you like some coffee? I can get the girl to make it.'

Anderson shook his head. 'It doesn't matter, Miss Wright. We won't take up much of your time. You look as though you've got a touch of this summer flu going around. Do you feel up to talking to us?'

'I'm a little tired, that's all,' she murmured, but she didn't look at Anderson as she spoke and she kept twisting round a diamond and sapphire eternity ring on the second finger of her right hand.

'You've worked here a long time, haven't you?' Anderson

said quietly. 'Perhaps you could tell me how you feel the company's doing now compared with when you started here?'

He fully expected Pippa Wright to say she had no idea or it wasn't her place to say but instead she lifted her head and for the first time allowed their eyes to meet. 'It's seen better days,' she stated flatly.

Anderson hid his surprise at her confession. 'Would you say the company is in trouble?'

'Not exactly trouble, but there is a large loan from the bank outstanding and the repayments were becoming difficult to meet.'

'Were?' he queried.

Pippa nodded. 'I gather that won't be a problem for much longer,' she said discreetly.

Anderson took in her meaning but let the full implications pass. If he could reach her on a personal level then he was quite certain that the distressed young woman in front of him knew a lot of Ralph Allan's secrets, and that for some reason she was now ready to share them with him.

'When we last spoke you told me that you had no inside knowledge of Mr Allan's marriage but knew from personal experience that Mrs Allan could be difficult. Is there anything that you'd like to add to that statement now?'

His voice was low and gentle, and his eyes full of sympathy. Suddenly tears filled Pippa's eyes and Anderson watched her as she blinked hard to clear her vision. 'I –' She stopped, sobs choking her words. Anderson pushed an immaculately ironed linen handkerchief across the desk to her. Picking it up she dabbed at her eyes. 'I'm so sorry. What must you think of me. This isn't like me, but I've had a terrible shock. It's personal, nothing to do with the company but –'

'This is no time for you to be answering questions,' said Anderson quietly. 'Why don't you take the rest of the day off? I'm sure Mr Allan is an understanding boss. You'd be better off resting.' As soon as he mentioned Ralph's name, Pippa's tears flowed even faster. 'Perhaps you could give me your home address,' added Anderson. 'I'll call on you there tomorrow evening when you've had time to get over your trauma. In the meantime, you have my card, don't you?' Pippa nodded. 'Then please remember that you can ring me any time. No matter how trivial the reason may seem to you it might have considerable significance to us. Things work like that in investigations, so don't be afraid to come forward with any piece of information at all.'

Pippa nodded and went to return his handkerchief, but Anderson gently pushed her hand back. 'It's all right. I'll collect it when I next see you.'

Pippa Wright looked up at him. Seeing her eyes filled with a mixture of despair and need, Anderson was catapulted abruptly back in time to Plymouth and the memory of Anna Ferreira's dark, soulful eyes. Something of this must have shown on his face because Pippa's expression changed too, and Anderson knew then that there was a possibility of the pair of them getting together. It was an exciting thought. He felt certain she would be a revelation in bed with the right man, and the right man was more likely to be him than the insensitive Ralph Allan.

'That's all,' he said quietly, and DS Walker shot him a look of surprise which Anderson ignored. As they walked outside the sergeant couldn't keep quiet any longer. 'You hardly asked her anything,' he protested. 'She was anxious to talk this time. Why didn't you push her a bit?'

'There's no point in pushing a woman who's emotionally disturbed, which Miss Wright certainly was today. Far better to wait until she's regained her composure. In my opinion she's had a major shock, and she's going to find it hard to come to terms with it.'

'What kind of a shock, sir?'

'I imagine she's been dumped by a very nervous Ralph Allan.'

Anderson and Walker waited another fifteen minutes in the car before Chloe joined them, and when she did she looked like a cat who'd got the cream.

'I've got a date,' she announced proudly.

'With whom?' Anderson asked.

'With Ralph Allan of course. We're going out for a drink tonight. He's quite a charmer you know, and very sweet under that macho exterior.'

'So sweet he's taking you out before his dead wife's even been buried,' Anderson pointed out.

Chloe shrugged. 'It's only a drink. Anyway, I thought you'd like to have someone on the inside.'

'Just as long as you don't end up in a crumpled heap in the corner of your kitchen you can do what you like,' Anderson said shortly, privately shocked that Chloe would risk a date with a man she knew to be at the top of his list of suspects. Clearly she didn't feel the same, but he would have expected her to take some notice of an experienced police officer. He considered whether he had the authority to instruct her not to socialise with a suspect, and decided that on balance he probably didn't. Would Parrish hear of it? How would he react? It was just something else to worry about.

'Did you notice anything about the warehouse, apart from the charms of its owner?' he enquired as they drove back to Guildford.

'Yes, it's positively humming. People working hard, lots of orders being made up and piles of wood from the States in the yard. In other words they're busy, and they've got a lot of orders coming in all the time. I saw them myself.'

'You haven't ever done a thesis on business studies I suppose?' asked Anderson.

'No, but I think I recognise a thriving business when I see one.'

'Let's hope you recognise a murderer as swiftly,' Anderson said dryly.

SEVEN

It was the first weekend following Lisa Allan's death. A week of the three-week investigation had gone, and Anderson knew that he had to start putting together a strong case against Ralph Allan if he was going to get him down to the station and interview him properly. The man was never going to give himself away during normal routine enquiries, but in custody Anderson knew the other man would be no match for him.

Slowly it was all coming together: Ralph's resentment over his wife's refusal to put money into his business, jealousy over a possible lover, and his own affair. But there had to be something that had provided the final trigger. Even if the bank had been planning to send in auditors, Chloe made it sound as though there was plenty of stock there to cover the loan, and unless the bank manager confirmed that they had told Ralph they were going to recall the loan why should he suddenly have decided that his wife had to die? The date Anderson was looking for must have been at least a week before the murder because of the lack of beta-blockers in Lisa's body.

Deciding against the squash club as a means of working

off some of his frustration – he had no wish to see Karen Raybould again yet – Anderson settled instead for an extra long run and then spending the afternoon browsing through art galleries and antique shops. He already knew what he intended to do in the evening: visit Pippa Wright under the guise of concern for her health.

While Anderson enjoyed his meticulously planned day, Jeff Phillips was enduring an unplanned scene at home. He'd woken up in a bad mood because on Friday the owner of the health club, Grant West, had given him a written warning for being late several times in the past month. He hadn't been able to give an excuse since the reason for his lateness was that Lisa had taken to writing anonymous letters to Liz, the first of which he'd intercepted purely by chance when he recognised the writing, and after that he'd hung around waiting for the postman every morning.

He tried to conceal his mood from Liz, and the presence of the boys helped, but it quickly became apparent that she wasn't happy either. Nothing he or the boys did suited her and after she'd complained about the noise young Ben was making Jeff said he'd take both the children out for a game of cricket on some nearby waste ground.

'That's right,' Liz complained. 'You all go off and leave me. I'll be all right. I'm used to being alone. Why should I expect anything different at weekends?'

Normally Jeff would have ignored her, but this time his temper exploded. 'All you do is bloody complain,' he shouted as the boys watched in wide-eyed surprise. 'Either the kids are too noisy for you or they're not. If you like company then don't moan the moment they start playing around. They're only children you know. We're all human, and that includes me. I do my best, what else can I do? It's not my fault you're ill, but God knows it's me you're punishing.'

Liz glared at him in white-faced fury. 'I'm not punishing

you because I'm ill,' she hissed. 'I'm punishing you for that Allan woman.'

Jeff turned to the boys. 'Go upstairs and play on your Sega. It's what you always want to do when you're meant to be getting ready for school.' Without any argument the boys went.

'What's this about the Allan woman?' Jeff demanded.

'I'm just being honest, like you wanted,' said Liz bitterly. 'Did you really think you could stop her contacting me? I used to watch you hanging around here waiting for the postman and I wanted to laugh. She was pretty determined to have you, wasn't she Jeff? Once she realised her letters weren't getting through she'd come and post them here herself. She gave me long descriptions of what the pair of you used to do. I had no idea you were so inventive in bed. You must have been practising a lot.'

Jeff felt himself start to shake and he sank down into a chair, staring at his wife in disbelief. 'How long have you known?'

'Over a month now. What happened? Did she push you too far? Is that why she's dead? No, on second thoughts don't answer that. I don't want to know, but I'll tell you one thing. I'm glad she's dead, really glad, and if it wasn't you that killed her then the murderer deserves a medal. She was a thoroughly nasty little rich bitch and how you were taken in by her I can't imagine.'

'I'm sorry,' Jeff whispered. 'I never thought you'd know. I didn't want to hurt you. I promise I'd never have left you for her, or for anyone. She was a diversion, I suppose, that's all.'

'And that's supposed to make me feel better?' Liz asked bitterly. 'Sorry, Jeff, but it doesn't. Whenever you touch me now I remember what she told me about the way you used to touch her and I want to vomit. How's that for total honesty?'

Jeff couldn't think of any reply. He wondered how he and Liz could carry on now, and cursed the day he'd first slept with Lisa. Despite her death it seemed she'd still managed to ruin his life.

At eight o'clock that evening, just as Chloe set off from her parents' house to meet Ralph, John Anderson arrived at Pippa Wright's home in Croydon. Dressed in cream linen slacks with an Augusta green jacket worn over a cream shirt and a green and orange patterned silk tie he looked smart but casual. It was important that Pippa felt it was a social call as much as a professional one, and also important to him on a personal level that she found him attractive. In any case, this was as casual as he ever got when it came to clothes.

Pippa answered the door wearing an ankle-length dark rose-coloured crinkle-cut dress with a scoop neck. She looked younger than her twenty-seven years and was wearing far less make-up than she wore for the office, having used it mainly to accentuate her eyes and cheekbones. When she saw Anderson standing outside her house she was clearly surprised, but opened the door immediately. 'You'd better come in,' she said, a hint of nervousness in her voice.

'Are you sure it's convenient?' Anderson asked softly. 'I only called round to see how you were. You looked so ill yesterday I was worried about you.'

She gave a small smile. 'That's very sweet of you, and it's quite convenient. I don't get many visitors at weekends.'

Anderson stepped inside the house. He was pleased to see that it was immaculately tidy, and everything about it suggested good taste and quality. Like his home it gave off a sense of space, which couldn't have been easy given the small dimensions of the rooms.

'Would you like a drink?' Pippa asked, taking him through into the front room. 'Or isn't that allowed?'

He gave her one of his warmest smiles and saw a slight tremor run through her. Her grey-green eyes reminded him of his ex-wife. When he took a step towards her he saw her pupils widen and he knew that she found him attractive, but behind the attraction he also sensed fear. The mixture of emotions she was giving off started to arouse him as well. 'I'm not on duty, and I'd love a drink,' he replied.

'I've got a good claret; do you like wine?' Anderson nodded, and watched as she half-filled a large wine glass giving the wine enough room to breathe and allowing him to savour the bouquet.

'You look a little better now,' he remarked, raising his glass, 'so I'll toast your continuing good health.'

Pippa took a sip from her glass and then wrapped her arms round her knees as she sat in the chair opposite Anderson, who kept his dark eyes fixed hypnotically on her face. 'I wasn't ill yesterday,' she confessed. 'I'd had a trauma in my personal life which meant I hadn't slept.'

'I'm sorry,' Anderson said politely, but then he fell silent.

'I'd like to talk to you about it,' Pippa said suddenly.

'That might help you, especially if you haven't been able to share it with any family or friends yet.'

'My family live in Cornwall and I lost touch with all my friends about two years ago,' she said sadly. 'I gave them up for a man, the same man who –' She broke off, and Anderson realised she was struggling for composure. He kept his expression sympathetic and after a pause she carried on. 'I've been this man's mistress for the past two years,' she said in a rush. 'He was everything to me. He meant more than my friends, my family or even my own happiness. All I wanted was to make him happy and just when I thought I could, when it looked as though I'd be able to be more than a mistress, he dumped me.'

'Do you know why?' Anderson asked softly.

Pippa nodded, and now the tears were trickling down her cheeks. 'What's the point in pretending,' she said brokenly. 'It was Ralph Allan, you probably know that already, and he said that we had to stop seeing each other because otherwise you'd think he killed his wife.'

'Because he was sleeping with you?' Anderson asked in apparent surprise. 'That doesn't seem very logical.'

'That's what I told him. I mean, we'd been having an affair for two years so why should that affect anything now? Anyway, Lisa wasn't murdered, she died of natural causes, I'm sure of that. Ralph wouldn't hurt a fly.'

Anderson stood up and walked over to her chair, reaching out a hand to touch her gently on her left cheekbone. 'Is that true, Pippa? This looks like a well-concealed bruise to me.' His lean fingers brushed away a stray tear from her face as they caressed the place where Ralph had hit her after she'd slapped him. 'I hit him first,' she admitted.

'I doubt if he's got a bruise,' Anderson commented, allowing his fingers to continue stroking her cheek for a few seconds longer before moving away and pouring himself more wine.

'He'd never hit me before,' Pippa said, and then she blushed. Anderson watched her curiously, but he stayed silent, sensing this was the best way to keep her talking. 'Our sex life was quite rough,' she confessed, lowering her eyes. 'That was something Ralph taught me, and I didn't mind. I enjoyed it too. Lisa didn't you see, which frustrated him. But that's not the same as hitting people out of anger, is it?'

Anderson realised that this was something that had been worrying her. 'No,' he assured her. 'It isn't the same thing.'

Pippa looked up at him, and Anderson sat on the arm of her chair with his left arm resting along its back. 'How often did you see Ralph out of the office?' he asked.

'Twice a week, I suppose. He always came here in the week because Lisa used to go out to the gym or to play bridge and he'd have a few hours to spare. At weekends it was more difficult, but sometimes we'd manage to meet up for an hour or so at Headley Common. It was an easy drive for Ralph and not too far for me. It sounds horrible and dirty talking about it now, but it wasn't. We were in love, and any chance to be together was worth taking.'

Anderson realised that this was another case of obsession. Clearly Pippa would have done anything in order to spend time with Ralph, but by ditching her so brutally he'd almost certainly turned her into an enemy. Love and hate were very closely linked. Indifference was impossible where strong emotions had been involved.

'I never thought he'd do this to me,' she continued, passing her empty glass to Anderson who refilled it for her. 'I believed I meant as much to him as he did to me; but even if I didn't, he was taking a terrible risk. I know so much about the company, the problems we've had and the things he's had to do to keep it afloat. You'd think he'd have considered that wouldn't you?'

Anderson murmured something non-committal. He wanted to hear about the company, that was part of the reason for his visit, but he was also increasingly aware of his sexual arousal as he smelt the scent of Pippa's perfume and felt the warmth coming off her body. Leaning back, Pippa gave a quiet sigh. 'I expect that's really why you're here isn't it? To hear about the company.'

'If I wanted to ask you about the company I'd do it during an official police interview,' Anderson said. 'I came here today because I liked you and I was worried about you. Now that I know you're all right I can leave if you like. You don't need to feel obliged to tell me anything at all.'

Standing up he placed his wine glass on the sideboard and turned towards the door. Suddenly Pippa jumped up and he felt her hand grab his arm. 'Don't go,' she begged him. 'I like you too, and I need company. I've been going mad sitting here on my own going over and over the past two years. Please, don't leave yet.'

Anderson put his hands on her shoulders to reassure her, and to his surprise felt her shrink away as her eyes widened with apparent fear. 'I know, I've behaved badly haven't I?' she asked him softly. 'I've been bad. Ralph was always telling me that I was bad, that I needed to be punished and he was right. Is that why you're here? To punish me?'

It took a few moments for Anderson to realise what was happening. That Pippa was actually sending out sexual signals, and that her desire for him matched his for her but she needed to dress it up so that it seemed by allowing him to give her pleasure she was really letting him punish her for imagined sins.

This realisation fuelled his own desire and to his surprise he found himself grabbing hold of her wrists and pulling her towards him so that her body was resting against him. 'Is that what you want?' he asked, and when she didn't answer he lowered his head and covered her mouth with his, his tongue invading the soft moistness of her mouth, forcing its way between her teeth in rapid darting movements and then softly caressing the insides of her lips.

When he finally stopped kissing her, her knees seemed to buckle and she half-fell against him. 'Take me upstairs,' she begged him. 'Quickly. You can do anything you like with me.'

Anderson had never intended the evening to go like this. He'd expected to spend it seducing her slowly so that in the next few days they'd end up in bed together, but never in his wildest dreams had he expected her to come on to him so strongly.

On the other hand, he was as aroused as she was, and the realisation that she half-wanted to be punished and was expecting him to take charge proved an irresistible temptation. He half-dragged her up the stairs behind him, and although Pippa had to show him which door led to the bedroom that was the only time she took the lead.

Once inside Anderson released her hands and then stood back from her. She was pale, but the pupils of her eyes were dilated with arousal and her lips were moist. She was breathing rapidly and kept glancing at Anderson with an anxious expression that almost drove him out of his mind with need.

'Take off your clothes,' he said softly. 'I want to see you naked.'

She obeyed without demur, peeling the dress up over her head and letting it fall to the floor. Beneath it she was naked apart from a white G-string which she quickly removed as well before standing by the side of the bed awaiting his next order.

She had a marvellous figure, slim and yet full breasted, and Anderson's erection was already rock hard. He motioned for her to come over to him and then pushed on the top of her head. He didn't need to speak. Pippa fell obediently to her knees, unzipped his slacks and taking out his swollen penis enfolded the glans between her lips and sucked lightly on it until the first tell-tale tingles in the tip told him that if he wanted the evening to last she had to stop. Without thinking he tugged hard on her long hair and her head jerked back as she looked pleadingly up at him, obviously longing to continue.

'Not yet,' said Anderson harshly. 'There are other things I want us to do before it all comes to an end.'

Pippa nodded. 'You're right,' she whispered. 'I need a proper punishment.' For a second Anderson wondered if he was out of his depth, but it was too late to back out now and as he took off his clothes Pippa opened her bedside drawer.

Trembling with excitement she pulled out two silk scarves and handed them to Anderson, and when he automatically reached out for them she lay down on the bed stretching her arms above her head so that her wrists were close to the wrought-iron bedhead. Her eyes were dark with longing and Anderson felt his excitement reaching a new peak as he bent over her and swiftly bound her wrists. Once she was tied he jerked on the ends of the scarves with unnecessary force to check that they were secure, and immediately Pippa's nipples swelled as she pulled against the bonds.

'I don't even remember your Christian name,' she whispered suddenly.

Anderson felt a surge of power. 'It's John, but I don't want you to speak.' She seemed surprised and opened her mouth to protest, but having pitched Anderson into the world she'd learnt from Ralph, Pippa had lost him to it. Placing his right hand over her mouth he stared down at her. 'In fact, I don't want you to make a sound until it's all over. The only way I'll know you've come is by what your body tells me. If you make a noise, any noise, then I shall stop.'

He watched as Pippa shivered with delight. She'd probably never expected him to enter into the game so well, he thought, but then she didn't know about Anna, or how much he missed her and the strange dark side of him that she'd started to bring to the surface. Occasionally now he wondered if Anna had manipulated him. If that was so he was going to make quite sure that Pippa Wright didn't do the same thing.

His sensitive hands cupped the undersides of her breasts and then he moved his mouth from one hard nipple to the next, grazing them gently with his teeth at first, but then as Pippa squirmed beneath him he suddenly bit her left nipple hard and her lower body arched off the bed as a muffled groan of sheer delight emerged from between her lips.

Emboldened by this, and secure in the knowledge that he was in total control of the situation, Anderson's fingers pinched at the tender flesh over her hip bones and then he stroked the resulting marks with gentle caresses. He followed this pattern in everything that he did, nipping and biting at her soft skin before licking the same areas with long sweeps of his tongue as he moved his way down her body until finally he parted her thighs and lowered his head between them.

As his tongue darted into her vagina he pressed the heel of his left hand down hard above her pubic bone, and the resulting streaks of searing pleasure caused Pippa to gasp with gratitude. At once Anderson lifted his head and the pressure of his hand relaxed. Pippa raised her head. 'Don't stop, please don't stop!' she begged him.

'Then keep quiet,' ordered Anderson. Pippa gave a whimper of frustration that only added to the excitement for both of them. Once she'd obeyed he moved his head back between her thighs but this time he used his tongue to encircle the hard clitoris, which he proceeded to draw into his mouth and then imprison lightly between his teeth as he flicked the backs of his fingers against her belly in a swift stinging motion that caused the skin to redden. He knew that she was totally in his power, unable to speak or move for fear of pain or deprivation of the climax that was steadily building inside her, as her head turned from side to side on the pillows and her body became flushed and damp.

Anderson's own body was responding swiftly too, and once he could wait no longer he lifted his head, slid up her body and then positioned himself above her as he allowed the head of his penis to slide into her.

Pippa tightened her muscles around him, but Anderson immediately withdrew. Tears of frustration filled her eyes, and Anderson gently kissed the corner of her mouth. 'You're not to do anything,' he said firmly in his rich baritone voice, and Pippa's eyes acknowledged the command.

Anderson played with her for twenty minutes like this, entering her, bringing them both to the point of no return and then withdrawing, until Pippa's hair was streaked with sweat and her eyes were beseeching him with increasing desperation, a desperation that his own body felt, but the sheer ecstasy of the session was more than compensation for the delay in final release.

When he felt that neither of them could bear it much

longer, Anderson untied Pippa and roughly turned her on to her face, pulling upwards on her waist until she was crouched on all fours with her back to him. Then he pressed between her shoulder blades, so that she lowered her upper torso, before gripping her round the hips and thrusting into her. 'Now massage your clitoris,' he gasped as he felt his own climax approaching. 'Quickly, I want to feel you come before I do. I want your muscles to trigger my release, do you understand?'

Pippa nodded and slid her right hand beneath her body, her fingers parting her sex lips until they located the moist swollen bud that was aching with need for stimulation. Within seconds she'd found the rhythm that she needed and as the fiendishly delayed climax finally swept over her body her internal muscles gripped Anderson tightly, the contractions of her powerful orgasm milking him mercilessly. She was unable to remain silent and at the final moment uttered a tiny groan of relief. Anderson heard her and after he'd climaxed he swiftly withdrew and manhandled Pippa on to her back again. He quickly found her clitoris, still exposed and vulnerable, and using Pippa's own moisture to lubricate his fingers he rubbed the stem of the mass of jangling nerve endings.

He ignored Pippa's tiny cry of protest, knowing that it was part of the sexual scenario, and continued to stimulate her until he finally wrenched yet another explosion from her, watching intently as her body writhed helplessly in the throes of intense sexual release.

When Anderson saw Pippa's belly stop contracting and realised that this time she'd managed to stay silent he kissed her on the forehead and stroked her damp hair out of her eyes. He was breathing as heavily as she was, but it had been a glorious moment of revelation for him when he'd forced her to climax again against her will and seen for himself that if anything she'd got even more pleasure the second time.

Exhausted, he lay on his back, and Pippa lay beside him, her head resting in the hollow of his neck. 'Thank you,' she whispered. Anderson didn't reply, he was still replaying the entire episode, remembering every response and facial expression of Pippa's. 'I expect you have to go now,' she added. 'I'll make some coffee first if you like.'

Anderson turned his head and knew that although she was offering him the chance to go she was terrified of being left alone so soon after he'd finished making love to her. 'I don't have to go,' he said easily. 'In fact, I can stay overnight if you like.' At his words she relaxed against him, and within a few minutes she was fast asleep, worn out by all the complex emotions of the past few days. Later, Anderson too slept.

The next morning, as it began to get light, he was woken by the sound of Pippa's voice. At first he thought she was talking in her sleep but then he realised she was talking to him, without knowing whether he was awake or not. Within seconds his mind was alert, and as he made out what she was saying he realised that she would never want to know if he'd heard or not. That way she wouldn't feel she'd betrayed her ex-lover; she would always be able to pretend that she'd thought Anderson was asleep and she'd been talking to herself.

'Sometimes I think I really am bad,' she was saying softly, her breath warm against his back. 'I've helped Ralph overvalue his stock for so long now I don't even think about it, but it's illegal and if the bank ever found out then I'd be as guilty as him.' She stopped, and Anderson kept his breathing even. She must know he was awake, but he would never confront her with what she'd told him unless it was unavoidable.

'It's easy,' she confessed, her voice still a whisper. 'The price of the wood we import from America varies so much according to the value of the dollar. We just alter the invoices in our favour. There's no way anyone would find out unless they were looking for something like that, but once Ralph wanted to sell the business I got scared. Then, when the bank threatened to send in their auditors because they wanted to call in the loan I was terrified. Ralph said I was an accessory, and I suppose I was, but I never really understood what I was doing. He was the one who set it all up, I just did as he said.'

Anderson curled himself into a ball and allowed a soft sigh to escape from his mouth before settling back down into the bed. Pippa kept quiet until he was still again, but he guessed that his movement had assured her she was getting through to him.

'I'm afraid now,' she said, her voice so low he could hardly catch it. 'I know he wanted Lisa to put money in, to cover us in case the bank carried out its threat, but she wouldn't. She refused again the week before she died, he told me all about it. They had a huge row. Now he'll get the money and it seems such a coincidence. And why has he finished with me? Is it because I know too much? And if I do, does that mean I'm in danger as well? I always knew I'd be punished one day, but I'd never have done it if I hadn't loved him and believed he loved me. The dreadful thing is, I thought I'd never find another man who could satisfy me in bed like he did, but that wasn't true. You can, John. Tonight was bliss for me, and so perhaps I've wasted two years of my life and broken the law for nothing at all. I ought to tell people, I know that, but I'm afraid. That's my trouble, I always want to please everyone, but in the end I can hardly live with myself.'

Suddenly she fell silent. Turning over, Anderson put an arm round her, keeping his eyes closed as he did so, until finally he knew by her breathing that Pippa had gone back to sleep. Anderson, however, did not. She'd given him a lot to think about.

Much to Pippa's surprise, Anderson didn't hurry away after

breakfast that morning. She'd become used to being a clandestine mistress, and when he suggested that they went to Sheffield Park in Sussex and spent the rest of the day looking round the gardens there, she realised that in some ways Ralph's rejection had released her. She was now free to go out and about with a man, and it felt wonderful.

Anderson was equally delighted at the pleasure Pippa took in the gardens, and her knowledge at the wide variety of trees and shrubs. When he finally dropped her back home he felt more content than he had for some time. Quite apart from the information she'd given him, which had been an unexpected bonus, Pippa had been the perfect lover for him and a well-informed and cheerful companion during the day. He only wished that he could go to bed with her again, but with the inquest on Lisa Allan the following morning he needed to have all his notes up to date just in case Parrish tried to curtail the original three weeks he'd allowed for the investigation into her death.

Ralph and Chloe had gone to a quiet country club for their Saturday night out, and the evening had sped by. Ralph was as good a listener as he was a talker and after a few drinks Chloe had talked to him about her past relationships, most of them disastrous, while he talked with considerable sadness about his second marriage and Lisa's illness.

Ralph found Chloe extremely attractive, and knew that the feeling was reciprocated. However, he was far too wise to try and take things any further than putting an affectionate arm round her in the pub and kissing her goodnight in the car when he finally drove her back to her annexe in the early hours of the morning.

When she lingered in his car he smiled at her and stroked the side of her face. 'I've had a great time,' he assured her. 'When things have settled down more we'll go out again, if you'd like to that is.'

'I would,' Chloe said eagerly.

'Then that's settled,' Ralph said with satisfaction, pleased that his tactics had payed off and already looking forward to their next meeting. 'Now I must go. I promised the family I wouldn't be late.'

He watched Chloe go in through her front door and then drove far too fast back to The Chilterns, but despite his good intentions it was gone 2 a.m. when he finally got in. Don and Mary Mitchell had left, but Tom – who'd been out with a group of friends himself – informed his father that they were coming back the next day.

'Why?' Ralph demanded. 'Don't they go to church on a Sunday? I'd have thought Mother Mary would have been a regular attender.'

'They want to talk about the inquest,' Tom said over his shoulder. 'You can't really blame them; she was their only child.'

'She was my wife!' Ralph shouted, incensed by Tom's tone. 'Doesn't anyone remember that?'

'We all do,' Tom retorted. 'Did the woman you were with tonight remember as well? Or is she too besotted to care that you haven't yet bothered to bury the second Mrs Allan before you start testing prospective candidates for the post of Mrs Allan Mark III?'

'You're in no position to lecture me on morals,' Ralph snarled.

'I wouldn't dream of it; I'm sure Lisa's parents will do far better than I could anyway,' Tom said, disappearing up the stairs.

As a result, while Anderson and Pippa were enjoying themselves strolling round Sheffield Park in the warm June sunshine, Ralph, Tom and Deborah Allan were sitting round the dining-room table with Don and Mary Mitchell. The atmosphere was strained, but Mary and Deborah tried valiantly to keep some kind of conversation going, drawing the men in now and again and hurrying to smooth out potential areas of trouble before they erupted into argument.

It was only during coffee, when they were all sitting in the conservatory that Lisa had adored, that Don Mitchell finally came out with what had been on his mind the entire visit.

'What verdict are you expecting tomorrow?' he asked his son-in-law.

Ralph shrugged. 'I'm not sure what to expect any more. Chief Inspector Anderson seems convinced it's murder –'

'So am I,' Don snapped.

'But I can't see any way the coroner will uphold that,' Ralph continued. 'Most reasonable people assume Lisa died due to her heart condition, and that it was a tragic accident. Unluckily, since even her doctor has an axe to grind here because he's in danger of seeming incompetent for not insisting on the defibrillator operation earlier, it will probably be death by misadventure.'

Don Mitchell glared at him. 'I don't believe a fucking word you're saying,' he snarled.

Mary Mitchell made a small sound of protest and touched her husband on the arm but he ignored her. 'What about the mobile phone? And the fact that she didn't have any of those pills inside her?' he demanded. 'How do you explain that? Someone killed my little girl, and that someone's sitting right here today.'

Ralph turned to his son. 'Did you hear that, Tom? I hope Don isn't accusing you of killing your stepmother.'

Tom ignored his father, but Deborah made a sound of protest. 'Don't Ralph, that's a horrible thing to say.'

'More horrible than being accused myself?' Ralph shouted. 'Listen Don, this is my house, it's my wife who died and you're sitting here eating my food, drinking my wine and then accusing me of murdering your daughter. I don't see why I should put up with that, and unless you can give me a very good reason for what you've suggested I think you should leave now, before I get –'

'Violent?' Don suggested, with a satisfied smile. 'That's

your answer to everything isn't it? And it was your answer when Lisa wouldn't put money into your tinpot little business too. You killed her for the same reason you married her, in order to get your hands on her money and if the law doesn't make you pay for what you did I'll find someone who will. Don't worry, Mary and I are leaving now and we won't be coming back. Deborah, in future you'll have to come and visit us. After the funeral I don't ever want to set eyes on your stepfather again. I just wish to God Lisa had never met him, then she'd still be with us.'

As he and his wife left, Don had tears in his eyes, and Mary hugged their granddaughter tightly. 'It's a difficult time for everyone, darling,' she said soothingly. 'Try not to get too upset. It will get better in time.'

Deborah watched them drive away and then ran upstairs to her bedroom, tears streaming down her face. She knew that it would never get better, and right now she wished that she was dead too.

EIGHT

On the Monday morning Pippa awoke in turmoil. Her weekend with John Anderson had been one of the most enjoyable she'd had for two years. She found him very attractive and the sex had been marvellous, but she still couldn't believe that her affair with Ralph was over. Before she committed herself fully to a new relationship she felt she had to make sure that there really wasn't any future for the pair of them.

Aware that today was the day of the inquest into Lisa's death and that he wouldn't be going in to work, Pippa rang Ralph at home at eight o'clock, knowing that he was an early riser when he had things on his mind. Unfortunately for her, Deborah had got up early as well. She answered the phone.

'Is Ralph there, Deborah?' Pippa asked in her most efficient tone, hoping Deborah would assume the call was about work.

'Can't you leave him alone even on a day like this?' Deborah asked before going off to fetch her stepfather. Pippa felt bad, but she also felt totally justified. Ralph had led her to believe so many things that were now turning out to be untrue and both her mind and her emotions were unwilling to accept that she'd been taken in by a professional seducer.

'Pippa? What on earth do *you* want?' Ralph asked when he came to the phone.

Pippa's heart sank. It wasn't the most encouraging of starts. 'I had to speak to you, Ralph. When you left me last I could believe everything was finished. Now there's the prospect of someone new in my life. I like him, but I had to speak to you because I need to hear you say it again.'

'Say what?' Ralph was clearly irritated.

'That it's all over between us,' Pippa said tremulously.

Ralph sighed heavily. 'Today is the day they hold the inquest into my wife's death. Don't you think I've got more on my mind than your little problems, Pippa?'

'They're not little!' she shouted, incensed at his tone. 'I gave up everything for you, and you told me no one had ever loved you like I did. Now you're trying to push me away. I can understand you feel guilty, but –'

'What have I got to feel guilty about?' he asked softly.

'Only the affair,' Pippa said quickly. 'I didn't mean anything else. But that didn't have anything to do with –'

'Look, I've told you before but since you don't seem to have taken it in I'll tell you again,' Ralph said slowly. 'You and I are finished. The whole thing's over. To be frank, I was beginning to get bored anyway. We had some great times, Pippa. Let it go at that, and don't call me here again.'

'What about work?' she asked in a strangely dull voice.

'I think you ought to start looking for another job. Take time off. Don't worry about that. I can get temps in to cover, and as I said you'll get excellent references.'

'Haven't you ever heard of the dangers of a woman scorned?' Pippa asked him.

'Don't even think of talking to me about danger, Pippa. When it comes to being dangerous you're a novice compared to me. Be a good girl, slip away quietly and I'll make it worth your while. Make things difficult for me and I'll make sure everyone in the firm and all your family know exactly what turns you on in bed. Then there's always the little matter of your collusion over business affairs, remember? You're not lily-white, Pippa, and you're in no position to make trouble for me.'

'This has nothing to do with Lisa's death has it?' Pippa demanded. 'You've used that as an excuse to drop me because you were already tired of the affair. Isn't that true?'

'Partly,' he admitted. 'Come on, you say you've got someone new, well concentrate on him. He's probably a much nicer bloke than I am. You deserve a husband and a family. I'm too old to give you that. It's not what I want from life any more. Now I've got to go.'

'I wish I'd never met you,' Pippa sobbed. 'I used to envy Lisa, now I pity her.' Her voice suddenly cracked and Ralph slammed down the phone.

The inquest was held at 10.30 a.m. Ralph, Tom and Deborah attended, and so did Don and Mary Mitchell although they sat apart from the Allans. The pathologist went through his findings at the postmortem and Dr Stevens was on the stand for a long time explaining the intricacies of Lisa's condition and the importance of the lack of beta-blockers in her body.

'In your opinion, doctor,' asked the coroner, 'was the deceased likely to have deliberately stopped taking her medication because of the side-effects, such as loss of libido, as has been suggested by her husband?'

'In my professional opinion that's most unlikely. If anything Mrs Allan was over-cautious about her condition and terrified of having another blackout. She accepted the side-effects of her medication as a small price to pay for peace of mind.'

As evidence was given, Anderson sat with Chloe at the

back of the room, listening intently. As he watched the back of Ralph Allan's head Anderson felt a strong physical yearning to put his hands round the man's throat and shake the truth out of him, he was becoming so frustrated by his lack of progress on the case.

When the time came for the coroner to deliver his verdict, Anderson realised that all his muscles were tense, and he forced himself to breathe slowly and deeply until he relaxed. He could tell Chloe was equally nervous, but suspected it was for Ralph, not the sake of the investigation.

The coroner explained at length the difficult situation in which he was placed given the medical evidence of Lisa's fragile state of health before her death and the results of the postmortem. In the end he said that taking into account the presence of a mobile phone, the recorded call to the speaking clock and the lack of beta-blockers in her body, he found himself unable to reach a definite conclusion and would reluctantly have to record an open verdict.

'What does that mean?' Chloe whispered to a tight-lipped Anderson.

'It means that he can't say whether she died of natural causes or was murdered,' Anderson explained, getting up and hurrying out of the courtroom. 'It also means that no one will be happy. Not the supposedly grieving husband, the enraged parents or Superintendent Parrish.'

'Will the murder enquiry be called off?' she asked eagerly.

Anderson looked at her in surprise. 'Is that what you want? Aren't you interested in how Lisa Allan died? Doesn't justice enter this thesis of yours?'

Chloe flushed. 'Of course it does, but I'm not sure –' At that moment the Allan family walked past them, and Ralph glanced sideways at Chloe causing her cheeks to turn pink.

'Of course, I forgot,' Anderson said with heavy irony. 'You and the widower were going to become better acquainted. I assume that explains your desire for the investigation to stop.'

'No it doesn't,' Chloe snapped. 'But it has made me realise how determined you are to pin the so-called murder on him, and I can't for the life of me think why.'

As Anderson had feared, the local press were waiting outside. Thanks to years of practice he managed to evade them as he knew that it would be Parrish who issued the official statement about the verdict, but the Allans and the Mitchells both had things to say.

'I can appreciate why the coroner was forced to this conclusion,' Ralph told the reporters. 'Unfortunately it means that for me and my family there is no conclusion. I only hope that in time my wife's death will be accepted as the tragic accident that we, her family, know it was. I'd also be grateful if we could now be left alone to make arrangements for her funeral service.'

'What about the rumours she was having an affair?' shouted one reporter.

Ralph shook his head. 'I don't know anything about that. We were a very happy couple and still deeply in love.'

'Is it true your first wife killed herself?' called another reporter.

For the first time Ralph's composure slipped. 'That's none of your damned business,' he snapped, and pushing Tom and Deborah into the car he sped off.

Don Mitchell didn't manage even a veneer of self-control. 'My wife and I both believe that our daughter was murdered,' he told the local press angrily. 'We hope and pray that the police don't now scale down their investigation and that they soon find Lisa's killer and bring him to justice.'

'How do you know it's a man?' shouted a voice.

Mary Mitchell put her arm through her husband's. 'We don't, of course. My husband and I simply want the killer found, whatever their sex.'

'What about the business with the mobile phone? Did you know about that before you came to the court?' asked a woman's voice.

'The police have kept us well informed,' said Mary Mitchell courteously, and then she hurried her husband away before he could say anything slanderous about Ralph.

Once he got back to the station, Anderson went straight to Parrish's room. The superintendent had just taken a phone call and signalled for his DCI to sit down. 'That was Don Mitchell. He's as obsessed as you are with the fact that Ralph Allan killed his wife. I had to warn him about the laws of libel and slander. I hope he listened to me.'

'What are you going to say to the press?' Anderson asked bluntly.

'I shall tell them that at the moment enquiries into her death are still continuing, and that we are following up several lines of enquiry. I'd like to think that's true, but from what I've read of your reports you're still concentrating on the husband.'

'And Jeff Phillips.'

'To a lesser degree,' Parrish conceded. 'Well, my advice to you is either you show me enough evidence to get him down to the station to help with enquiries or you start looking more closely at other possibilities.'

'Like who?' demanded Anderson, who deeply resented this interference.

Parrish smiled thinly. 'I've no idea. You're the one who thinks it's a murder, not me.'

Anderson spent the rest of the morning chasing up his officers over the alibis of Tom and Deborah Allan. Parrish's remark had stung, because he knew he'd neglected some of the other people closely related to Lisa.

He wasn't pleased to learn that neither of the youngsters' alibis had yet been verified. The owner of the stables where Deborah kept her horse had been abroad taking part in a competition and buying more horses. She wasn't expected back for another day or so. In addition, the rep Tom had been visiting was on holiday and not due back until the middle of the week.

'Why wasn't I told?' Anderson asked DS Walker.

'It didn't seem that important,' Walker replied. 'From what we'd heard I thought that after the husband the lover was the next most likely suspect.'

'Yes, he is,' Anderson agreed. 'That doesn't mean I don't expect you to follow up on everything else.'

'I don't see what we could do about it. We can't drag someone back from the holiday of a lifetime in the Caribbean, or interrupt an international horse show for something relatively trivial.'

'Where is the horse show?' Anderson demanded.

'Austria, which is why we thought it could wait.'

'Just make sure I'm told as soon as the alibis are confirmed. Parrish is breathing heavily down my neck over this one, suggesting personal bias. I don't want him to have any grounds to prove that, understood?'

'Of course, sir,' Walker agreed.

After lunch, which Anderson ate on his own at his favourite sandwich bar in the centre of Guildford, he returned to his office to learn that Pippa Wright had been calling him from work. Hastily he rang her back.

'I'm sorry to disturb you at work, John,' she said quietly, 'but I'd like to come and see you. I want to make a statement.'

'A statement?'

'Yes.' Her voice was firm. 'I've been thinking things over and I realise that I've been very selfish. It's my duty to help as much as I can over Lisa's death, and there are things I know which might be important.'

'When would you like to come?' Anderson enquired, wondering what had brought about this change of heart.

'As soon as possible. Now, if you like.'

'I'll be waiting,' Anderson assured her, and within the hour she was seated in one of the interview rooms opposite Anderson and DS Joanna Blackheath, who explained the statement procedure to her despite Pippa's obvious impatience. A police constable sat in the corner of the room, pad and pencil poised.

Suddenly Pippa looked nervous and Anderson gave her an encouraging smile. 'Take your time, Miss Wright. Simply tell us in your own words whatever it is that you want to say, then we'll type it up for you and get you to sign and date it.'

'There are two things that I really want to say,' Pippa began nervously. 'The first concerns the company, Allan & Son. For over a year now, Ralph Allan and I have been overvaluing the company's stock to keep the bank loan going. Without that the business would have folded. We did this by changing the value of the wood, which is imported from America, on the invoices. We used the varying exchange rates of the dollar in our favour. If the bank had ever sent in auditors, as Mr Allan told me recently he thought they were about to do, then they would quickly have worked out what had been going on. At the time I did this I didn't realise that I was assisting in a criminal offence, but I do now. Ralph Allan desperately needed an injection of cash from some other source in order to repay some of the loan and keep the bank off his back and he approached his wife, Lisa, about three weeks ago. He told me that she refused to give him any money saying that she wasn't going to be like her mother and support a man who wasn't even faithful to her.

'When he was telling me about this argument, Ralph said that Lisa had become very worked up and that she'd had to take one of her tablets. I asked him what kind of tablet and he said that it was a beta-blocker. He said that although they had been prescribed for her she used them as a kind of security blanket and panicked if she missed even one dose. I'd heard that beta-blockers could have a number of unpleasant side-effects and asked him if Lisa had suffered any. He said that she had, but that she didn't mind. The only thing that mattered to her was that her heart kept going and she didn't suffer any more blackouts.'

Listening to the words tumbling out of Pippa's mouth Anderson felt a mixture of triumph and compassion. Triumph because here at last was the hard evidence he'd been looking for that Ralph had consistently lied to them, but compassion for Pippa who had been so betrayed that she was willing to put her own deceit on record in order to help bring her ex-lover to justice. Something had happened since the previous day to bring about the change, and he wondered what it was.

'Is that all?' he asked gently. Pippa nodded. 'In that case we'll get it typed up for you, and once you've read it through you sign it and the witness statement. After that you can leave. And thank you for your co-operation.'

'Quite a breakthrough,' Joanna said as they left the room.

Anderson nodded in satisfaction. 'I'll take this to Parrish, but I doubt if even he will deny me a warrant after this. With any luck I'll get it tomorrow.'

'I wonder why she suddenly decided to talk?' Joanna mused.

Anderson didn't answer, but when he saw Pippa driving away from the station in her white Carina half an hour later he wondered if her change of heart had come about as a result of their weekend together. Maybe it had made her realise Ralph wasn't as special as she'd imagined. His pride hoped that was the reason.

Much to his annoyance he wasn't able to see Superintendent Parrish until the following morning. Under the circumstances he decided it was better not to return the call from Pippa that he found waiting on his answerphone when he got back to the flat. His priority now lay in getting a warrant for Ralph Allan's arrest.

Before he could sit down to eat he got a call from the desk sergeant at the station saying that Mary Mitchell was anxious to speak to him. Remembering her husband's face at the inquest that morning Anderson didn't delay in ringing her. She sounded exhausted, and he wondered how she was managing to cope with both her husband's anger and her own grief.

'I'm sorry to bother you,' she said nervously, 'but my husband keeps on asking if anything is going to be done about Ralph and I wondered if you could help. Do you know if he's definitely under suspicion? Or is the investigation being wound down now?'

Anderson wished he could tell her the truth, but as he hadn't yet spoken to Parrish he couldn't possibly say that at this very moment he was hoping to get an arrest warrant.

'There's no question of the investigation being wound down,' he promised her. 'We're pursuing several lines of enquiry and although the matter may take some time yet I'm confident that in the end we will apprehend your daughter's killer.'

'But why is it taking so long?' she asked despairingly. 'Only Ralph had anything to gain by Lisa's death and he's never even been taken to the police station. My husband doesn't believe you've looked into Ralph's business affairs properly.'

Anderson could hear Don Mitchell shouting at his wife as she was talking, telling her the questions he wanted asked.

'Please, Mrs Mitchell, you and your husband must believe me when I say that we are doing absolutely everything necessary in order to solve this crime,' he said gently. 'Unfortunately it's complicated and if we rush things solely in order to make an arrest there's always the possibility of the killer getting off, either on a technicality or due to lack of evidence. Once that happens he or she can't be tried again. Neither of you would want that to happen, would you?'

'Tell him if he's not up to the job I'll find someone who is,' shouted Don Mitchell in the background.

'Of course not Chief Inspector,' said his wife. 'We

understand the logic behind it all, but it's hard for us . . .' Her voice tailed off as she struggled for composure.

'As soon as we make any progress you'll be the first to know,' promised Anderson. 'Your daughter's been dead only a week. Many far more straightforward murder enquiries take months to solve, but we do get there in the end.'

When he finally did sit down to eat he wondered why it was that the nicest women always ended up married to the most unpleasant men. In his heart he was sure that Lisa had basically been a nice girl, but that her marriage to Ralph had changed her. Perhaps her parents had spoilt her in some ways, but she'd been forced to give up a boyfriend and her baby daughter, for the first vital years of her life, by a domineering father. Tragically she'd finally found refuge with an equally domineering husband. It was no wonder she'd looked for comfort and affection elsewhere, especially with the added problems of her health.

The next morning he walked briskly into the station trying hard to conceal his feeling of excited anticipation. He even smiled at Chloe, who met him on the station steps.

'You look very cheerful,' she commented.

He nodded. 'I feel cheerful. Today may well be the day when Ralph Allan finally gets his come-uppance. I'm off to see the superintendent. Wait for me in the canteen. When I've got what I need I'll come and collect you.'

Chloe went white and swiftly vanished in the direction of the canteen. Only then did Anderson remember she'd been out with Ralph Allan. He sighed to himself. If she'd listened to him in the first place then she wouldn't have got hurt.

Unfortunately for Anderson, Parrish wasn't as impressed by Pippa's statement as he was. 'Why has she come up with all this now?' he asked. 'I suppose she's been given the push and this is her way of paying him back.'

'I've no idea,' Anderson lied smoothly, wishing that Parrish had retired on the grounds of ill health as soon as his ulcer was diagnosed.

'And all this business about doctoring invoices for the bank, is there any independent proof of that? Have you had auditors in to see if it's true?'

'I hardly think she'd incriminate herself in a business fraud if it wasn't true,' Anderson said tightly.

'Women will do anything to punish a man who's rejected them,' said Parrish, making Anderson wonder how the hell such an overweight, lazy and unattractive man would have any idea about women, apart from his own wife.

'There's a lot of information in that statement,' he persisted. 'Mr Allan told us he thought Mrs Allan had stopped taking the pills because they ruined her libido, but he told his PA she was overdependent on them.'

'Perhaps he was lying to his PA, trying to make out that his wife was more neurotic than she was in order to get some sympathy. It means he lied, but how do we know he lied to you rather than her?'

'You're saying you don't think we can bring him in, is that it?' asked Anderson, barely able to control himself but remembering how important it was that he didn't mess up where relations with other officers were concerned if he was going to get Parrish's job.

'I'm saying no one is going to give us a warrant based on the flimsy evidence you've gathered together and this statement. The only thing it means is that you can bring him down to the station and question him closely under interview conditions, but make bloody sure you caution him first, in case he says something that incriminates him, and tell him he isn't obliged to remain here if he wishes to leave.'

Anderson went white with fury. 'I think I know the correct procedure for bringing someone in to help with enquiries after all these years,' he snapped.

Parrish smiled with satisfaction. 'I'm sure you know the

correct procedure, John. It's just that in this particular instance I'm a little worried your belief in the man's guilt could lead to a breach of rules which might, if you were right, get him off.'

'I shall be extra vigilant where Mr Allan is concerned,' said Anderson, realising with amusement that if he were a physical rather than a cerebral man Parrish would probably have received a swift blow to the jaw by now. Satisfying certainly, but hardly conducive to maintaining a career in the police force, let alone gaining promotion.

'Have I amused you, John?' Parrish sounded surprised, and Anderson wondered if a smile of satisfaction had actually crossed his face.

'Not at all, sir. I'm always grateful for any assistance you're able to give me,' he replied.

He watched as Parrish hesitated, his dislike for Anderson showing briefly on his face before he appeared to decide to take the remark as a compliment.

'That's what I'll do then,' continued Anderson, fully aware now that Parrish would never recommend him as his successor. 'With your permission of course?'

'It's your case, you must do as you think best. Just don't mess it up, because you can't afford any more mistakes,' snapped Parrish.

Anderson was well aware of this. Back in his office he went through all the papers on the case from the moment the first officer arrived at the scene of crime. He studied all the forensic reports and every statement, searching behind all the words for anything he might have missed in his quest for the truth behind Lisa Allan's complicated death. To his relief he still came up with the same answer. No one but Ralph Allan stood to gain anything from Lisa's death, and he was probably the person best placed to hide her beta-blockers, aware that after years of marriage to him she lacked the confidence to confess what she would think of as her own stupidity to anyone as she searched for them.

Given his added anger over her affair with Jeff Phillips he had an excellent motive, and no alibi other than the fact that he was on his way home when she died. Since she could hardly have been dead longer than ten minutes given the time difference between the call to the speaking clock and Ralph's other – and in Anderson's view, second – call to the Reigate police, this could hardly be considered an alibi.

At 12.30, content in his mind that he was right and that he could outwit Ralph Allan, Anderson rang for DS Walker and then got up from his desk. He wouldn't take Chloe with them. It wouldn't be fair on her and could be highly embarrassing for everyone if she or Ralph blurted out anything about their evening out. She would have to wait until they brought him back before she learnt the news, news that she must already be half-expecting.

DS Walker put his head round the door. 'You wanted me, sir?'

'Yes, we're going to Croydon to invite Mr Allan to accompany us to the station in order to assist us with enquiries into his wife's death. No arrest, no warrant, nothing like that. We just want to have a friendly talk with him, but I'm sure he won't refuse.'

'I think he might. Last time we spoke to him he said he wouldn't talk to us again without having a solicitor present.'

'In that case his refusal to assist us will be noted,' Anderson remarked. 'He knows that. He may be many things but he isn't a fool. In fact, he's quite clever, but not as clever as he thinks he is.'

DS Walker cleared his throat. 'Sir?'

'What?' Anderson asked, in a hurry to be off.

'You don't think this might look a bit like a personal vendetta, do you?'

'No, I don't,' Anderson retorted, ignoring the look of doubt on the sergeant's face. 'Come on, I don't want to waste any more time.'

They were actually at the station doors when Joanna Blackheath came rushing towards them. 'Sir, would you wait a moment, something's come up.'

'And what's that?' Anderson asked, disguising his impatience.

Joanna was out of breath and it was a few seconds before she could speak. Anderson stood waiting impassively, his expression cool. 'We've just had a call from the Reigate police, sir. Ralph Allan's been found dead on Headley Common.'

Anderson couldn't believe his ears. 'Dead? You mean he's killed himself?'

'Not by the sound of it, sir. The officer I spoke to said he'd been murdered. He wouldn't give any further details. I said you'd be there as soon as possible.'

'We're on our way,' Anderson said.

'Where are you going?' called Chloe, materialising at the worst possible moment from the corridor.

'Out,' Anderson said curtly, unable to meet her eyes.

As Anderson drove they were given directions to the exact spot where the body had been found over the car radio. On arrival, Anderson ducked under the yellow tape and walked briskly towards a group of officers who were assembled near Ralph's familiar Rover. As he approached them he was stopped by a young constable and quickly showed his ID.

'They're expecting you, sir,' said the constable. 'DS Kirby is officer in charge.'

Anderson recognised the detective sergeant from their meeting at the Allan's house on the morning of Lisa's death. 'What happened?' he asked.

DS Kirby stepped to one side, allowing Anderson an uninterrupted view of the scene. It was a grisly sight. Ralph was lying slumped in the driving seat of his car. There was a gaping hole clearly visible on his forehead and the back of his seat was covered in a mixture of blood and brains, some of which had run down over the victim's shoulders and chest. Blood had also splattered onto the rear window.

'No sign of a weapon?' asked Anderson, noting the empty-eyed stare of the dead man.

'None at all. It's not suicide. His car window was open. Presumably someone came along, he wound down his window to speak to them and they shot him through the head.'

'No sign of violence? Nothing suggesting a struggle?'

'It was all as you see it now. The forensic team are on their way but I doubt if they'll be able to tell us much more than we can see for ourselves. Except the make of the gun. The bullet must be buried in the car. They'll dig that out for us.'

'I don't imagine the murderer still has the gun in their possession,' Anderson remarked. 'You'd better start searching the common for it, and look for anything else that might help. It's a pity we've had such a dry spring and summer. This ground isn't going to tell us anything. Has anyone informed the next of kin yet?'

'No sir.'

'Then keep this under wraps. I'll let them know myself.'

'Right, and I'll get Forensics to call you as soon as they've finished,' Kirby promised.

'Please do. I suppose there weren't any witnesses? No one who saw Ralph Allan arrive here, or knows if he had a passenger with him?'

'It's a pretty remote spot as you can see. People don't just pass by. In fact, I'd say it's the perfect spot for a murder.'

'Kirby's right, but we have to assume Ralph Allan drove himself here,' Anderson said to Walker as they went back to the BMW. 'He would hardly have come happily to a rendezvous with death.'

'Good spot for a lover's meeting,' Walker pointed out.

'Yes,' Anderson said heavily. 'I'd already thought of that.

What I'm interested in now is the reaction of people close to him over this. Where possible I want to break the news myself. Lin Ford can help us tell the Allan youngsters and the Mitchells. I'll take DS Blackheath when I see Pippa Wright.'

'Looks as though he didn't kill his wife after all,' DS Walker said, climbing back into the car. Anderson didn't reply.

When they got back to the station he told Walker to arrange for DC Lin Ford to meet them in the road outside the Allan's house in forty minutes. In the meantime he knew that he would have to break the news about Ralph's death to Chloe himself. He didn't relish the task, but wouldn't have dreamt of delegating it to anyone else.

He found Chloe sitting scribbling in her notebook in the canteen. She looked up as he approached her table. 'It's Ralph, isn't it?' she asked. 'You've arrested him over the murder of Lisa. You're wrong you know. He isn't that kind of a man. He'd never have –'

'Chloe,' Anderson said gently. 'Come into my office. We have to talk.'

Thrown by his kindness, Chloe followed him meekly out of the room, past the interested gaze of DS Walker and into his office. 'You'd better sit down,' he said quietly. 'This is going to come as a nasty shock to you, but I'd rather you heard it from me than anyone else.'

Her mouth tightened. 'You're going to try and tell me he's confessed aren't you? Well, I don't believe you. You've never liked him. I suppose it's because he's so different from you, but that doesn't mean there's anything wrong with him. You might be astonished to know that not everyone's bowled over by your personal charm. Most human beings have weaknesses. You're the weird one, not Ralph.'

Anderson waited until her outburst had finished and

then went over to the window so that he was half-looking away from her. 'I'm afraid what I've got to tell you is worse than that, Chloe. Ralph's been murdered.'

He didn't know what he expected, tears probably or hysterical screams, but it certainly wasn't the total silence that suddenly filled the room. Quickly he turned to face her and realised immediately that she'd gone into a state of shock. Her face was totally without colour and she was staring at him as though she'd seen a ghost, while her entire body trembled.

Anderson picked up the phone and ordered tea, strong and sweet, before walking over and putting an arm round her shoulders. 'I'm sorry,' he said quietly. 'I do know how much this must hurt, but there was no easy way of breaking the news.'

'You were wrong, weren't you?' she muttered, through chattering teeth. 'He didn't kill Lisa, but because you thought he had you let the real killer get away and now Ralph's been murdered too. I hate you, and I'll never forgive you. Nor will anyone else who's been working with you. He was a genuinely nice man, and now I'll never see him again thanks to you and your prejudices.'

Her pain was so raw that Anderson wished he could do something to ease it, but there was no time. After she'd drunk her tea he'd send her home for the rest of the day; after that it was up to her if she came back or not. Her thesis wasn't his responsibility, but there was now the nagging suspicion at the back of his mind that Ralph's death might have been.

Even before Chloe's tea arrived he was summoned to Superintendent Parrish's office. His superior officer was not a happy man. 'I understand you're intending to break the news of Ralph Allan's death to his family yourself,' he said shortly. Anderson nodded. 'It's probably the least you can do. Thank God they don't know you were on your way to bring him in for questioning. I told you no one in their right mind would have issued a warrant.'

'There's always the possibility we're looking for two killers,' said Anderson. 'That's one of my lines of enquiry.'

Parrish's face went red. 'Is it really? What a surprise. I suppose it hasn't occurred to you that you might have been wrong, and that whoever killed Lisa Allan has now struck again?'

'Yes, it has,' Anderson said calmly. He had no intention of losing his temper at this vital moment. 'It's probably the most likely solution and the one I intend to follow up first.'

'Then you'd better get your team assembled and start working from square one immediately. I'm not looking forward to meeting with my superiors about this. Ralph Allan was a highly respected member of his community. First you had him as your prime suspect and now he's dead. I imagine the Reigate force are wishing they'd never asked for our help. I want this solved, Anderson, and I want it solved fast before the entire Allan family are wiped out.'

'Who does he think did it, the cleaning woman?' Anderson demanded of DS Walker as they drove towards The Chilterns. 'It has to be someone close, or at least someone involved with them both.'

'Like Jeff Phillips?' Walker suggested helpfully.

'Yes, like Jeff Phillips.'

He swung the car into Mile Road and saw a police car parked on the bend with DC Lin Ford waiting by its side.

'Any idea who's at home?' Anderson asked her as she came over and got into the back of his BMW.

'Deborah Allan is, that's certain. She rang me about half an hour before you did saying she'd found something that she'd like me to look at. I tried to contact you, but of course you were already on your way to Headley Common.'

'So she'll be expecting you, but not us,' mused Anderson.

Lin Ford rang the front doorbell while Anderson and

Walker stood behind her. Deborah opened it with a look of excitement on her face, but when she saw Anderson lurking in the background her expression changed. 'Why did you bring him? I asked for you.'

'I'm sorry Deborah, but I'm here about something else,' explained Anderson quietly. 'Perhaps we could come through for a moment? Is your brother in?'

'No, he's at work.'

'Call and get someone to fetch him back quickly,' Anderson ordered.

'Why? What do you need to see Tom for? I'm the one who's got something to show you,' Deborah said.

'Deborah, Chief Inspector Anderson has something to tell you,' said Lin softly. 'I'm afraid it isn't good news either.'

The girl stared at the three police officers in bewilderment. 'I don't understand. What's happened now?'

Anderson never found this part of a murder investigation easy, but because Deborah reminded him so strongly of her mother and her blue eyes were full of anxiety and fear it was even worse this time. 'It's your stepfather,' he explained, knowing that it was best to get it over with quickly. 'I'm afraid he's dead.'

Deborah shook her head in denial. 'No! He can't be! That doesn't make sense. Why would anyone want to kill Ralph? You're lying. This is some kind of trick isn't it? A way of making me tell you things.'

Anderson listened with interest, part of him hurting for the girl's sake and part of him listening keenly to what she was saying as a result of her shock and confusion.

'The police would never do anything like that, Deborah,' Lin Ford was saying softly. 'I'm afraid it's true. Your stepfather is dead.'

'How? What happened? Did he kill himself, is that it?'

'No,' Anderson said firmly. 'He was murdered.'

It was then that Deborah started screaming, and she continued screaming while Walker rang for Dr Stevens.

Lin Ford tried her best to comfort her, but it was useless and her hysteria was shattering for all of them. By the time Dr Stevens had got to the house, examined the girl and given her a strong sedative, Tom had arrived back. Hurrying in he confronted Anderson immediately.

'What the hell's going on here?' he demanded. 'Why's Dr Stevens' car parked out there? And where's my father? I went to tell him you'd sent for me and he wasn't at work. What's going on? Is he under arrest?'

'I think you'd better sit down,' Anderson said, getting to his feet.

Tom hesitated for a moment, but then something in the police officer's face seemed to convince him that he'd be sensible to obey. He sat on the edge of the nearest chair and looked up at Anderson. 'Right, I'm sitting. What is it?'

'I regret to have to tell you that your father was found dead on Headley Common at approximately twelve o'clock this morning. He'd been shot through the head at close range,' said Anderson, determined not to go through the suicide routine again.

Like his stepsister, Tom shook his head in total confusion. 'That doesn't make sense. I thought . . . Are you sure he didn't kill himself?'

'Quite sure,' Anderson said, intrigued by the fact that both the Allan youngsters were more willing to believe that Ralph had killed himself than that he'd been murdered.

'Which means that my stepmother probably was murdered too,' Tom continued. 'I never believed that you know,' he added, glancing up at Anderson. 'I thought you were wrong, but now . . . This can't be a coincidence, can it.'

It was a statement, not a question, and Anderson shook his head. 'I doubt it. Can you think of anyone who'd want your father and stepmother dead?'

'No, of course I can't. I can't think of anything right now. It's like a nightmare. He was at work today, I talked to him mid-morning. He never said anything about going out. We were due to have a meeting at one o'clock. If he was found at Headley Common at mid-day he was going to be late for the meeting, but he never even told me he was leaving the building. None of this makes sense.'

Although deeply shocked, Tom was in a better condition than his sister and Anderson tried one last question. 'Was Pippa Wright at work today?'

'No. Dad told me she was having a few days off to look for another job. I think there'd been a falling out between them and they felt it was less awkward if they weren't together professionally any more.'

'I see.'

Tom glared at him. 'No you don't. Pippa would never have killed my father. She loved him, and she'd have defended him against anyone. Besides, she hardly knew my stepmother. How could she have got into the house and killed her?'

'I never suggested that she did,' Anderson said. 'Before Dr Stevens leaves I think he'd better check you over. Your stepsister has been put to bed under sedation. Is there anyone who can come and stay with you both for a few days?'

'Deborah's grandparents I suppose,' Tom said reluctantly. 'They said they weren't ever setting foot in the house again, but that was only while my father was –' It was then that his composure broke and Anderson left him to Dr Stevens.

'Where to now, sir?' Walker asked once they were back in the car.

'Reigate station,' Anderson replied. 'I think it's time we got ourselves organised.'

NINE

The small room that had been set aside for Anderson at Reigate station was crowded. Apart from DS Walker and DC Lin Ford there was DS Luke Kirby with two of his detective constables and DS Joanna Blackheath had joined them from Guildford. Walker had set up a picture board and Anderson used this to illustrate exactly why he wanted to pursue the lines of enquiry he did.

'As you can see,' he said crisply, 'at the top of the board we have a photo of Lisa Allan, which is where all this began. Despite initial doubt from several quarters it's now accepted that she was murdered. I believed this to be the case right from the start, and my prime suspect was her husband Ralph Allan, for the reasons set out on the board.

'I don't suppose it's any secret that at the time he died, I was on my way to invite Mr Allan to Guildford station to assist me with my enquiries. His death poses two questions. One, was it a revenge killing by someone who knew he'd killed his wife? Two, was he killed by the same person who killed his wife?

'With the revenge theory we have to take into account Don Mitchell's almost unendurable anguish at his daughter's death, which he was sure was at the hands of his son-in-law, and the fact that he kept telling me that if I didn't hurry up and arrest Ralph he'd find someone who could deal with the affair better. This means that we need to know exactly where Don Mitchell was this morning.

'Also going with the revenge theory there's the possibility that Jeff Phillips might have killed a man who he believed to have killed his mistress, but I'm a little doubtful about that. He wanted to end the affair, and if anything would have been grateful for her death. In my opinion Jeff Phillips is more a candidate if it's a double murder.

'We still haven't been able to check out the alibis for either of the Allen youngsters, and I need to interview both of them once they're over the initial shock of Ralph Allan's death. I believe that both of them are hiding things. This doesn't mean they're killers, but they certainly know more than they're letting on.

'Finally, we come to Miss Pippa Wright. If it's a double murder then I believe she's our main suspect, although she appeared to have an alibi for Lisa Allan's murder. We spoke to people at the company who'd seen her there during the time Lisa was being killed, so we must go back and check that out again. It's easy to make mistakes over time and we're not talking about huge time differences here, they're relatively small. Did she have time to go to Kingswood and murder Lisa? If she did, she had to fit it in between Lisa being dropped off by Jeff Phillips and Ralph arriving home.'

'Unless Ralph saw her and decided not to say anything,' suggested DS Kirby.

'Good point,' Anderson agreed. 'If that's the case, then she had a very strong motive to get rid of him too, quite apart from the fact that she was, as the superintendent is fond of saying, a woman scorned. Now, I want DS Kirby to check out Don Mitchell while Walker and I go and see Miss Wright. Has she been informed of Ralph's death?'

'Yes, sir,' said Joanna. 'I thought someone should tell her

before it was put out on the local TV news.'

'Fine, then she's had time to get over the shock, if there was any, and we should be able to talk to her. Tomorrow, Walker and I will talk to Tom and Deborah again. Any questions?'

There were none.

As they arrived at Pippa Wright's house in the middle of the afternoon, Anderson remembered with hideous clarity the last time he'd been there and what had happened in the double bedroom. He'd been contemptuous and shocked by Chloe's seeming willingness to bed a suspect, but now it looked as though he'd unwittingly done the very same thing himself, and not for the first time. It took a lot to shake Anderson's self-confidence, but where women were concerned he was beginning to wonder if he understood them at all. His judgement certainly seemed flawed.

Pippa let him and DS Walker in without a word. She appeared stunned by what had happened, and there was no doubt that she'd been crying. Her eyes were almost as puffy as the time Anderson had talked to her after Ralph had ended their affair. If she was his killer then she was suffering a severe reaction, but that would be understandable. If she was a double killer then possibly the tears and shock were an act, but they were a good one.

'I'll make some tea, or would you prefer coffee?' she asked Anderson with a shy but intimate look. His heart sank. Surely she realised that there could be no question of any relationship between them now. She must understand that she was a suspect, and in that case her natural intelligence would tell her that he wouldn't be able to continue their affair. However, from the way she fussed about him, despite her distress, he had the distinct impression that she hadn't yet grasped that vital fact.

'I understand you've been told about Mr Allan's death?' he said, his voice stiff and formal.

Pippa looked surprised by his tone, but she nodded. 'Yes, a policewoman told me. She said she didn't want me to hear it on the news. I suppose that was you, John. Thank you, I appreciate it.'

Anderson stiffened. Walker wasn't showing any signs of surprise, but he knew that Pippa's use of his Christian name would intrigue the detective sergeant. 'Have you any idea who might have wanted Ralph dead?' he continued.

'None at all,' said Pippa. 'I've been thinking about it ever since I heard. The only thing that makes any sense is that Ralph had got himself involved with some shady characters when he was trying to find a way of bailing the company out of trouble. Perhaps he borrowed money off them without telling me and they got tired of waiting for the repayments. Or maybe it's got something to do with the fact that we've had people looking round with a view to buying the company. A couple of the prospective buyers were foreign you know.'

'But why would they want to kill him?' Walker asked.

'I don't know,' Pippa admitted feebly. 'But it's the best I could come up with.'

'And Mrs Allan?' Anderson asked. Pippa's face went blank. 'Do you believe men like that would have wanted to kill Ralph's wife as well?'

'No! Surely you don't think the two deaths are connected, John? I've always told you that Lisa's death was an accident. You should have listened to me, then you wouldn't be trying to tie the two in together. By doing that you'll probably miss the killer.'

'I think you can leave that to me, Miss Wright,' Anderson said formally and at last she seemed to realise that things had changed between them because he heard her catch her breath and for a moment tears filled her eyes, tears which she quickly covered by leaving the room to make the tea.

When she returned, Anderson tried another tack. 'What

does Ralph's death mean as far as his business is concerned?' he asked.

Pippa handed him and Walker bone china cups of Earl Grey tea. 'It means that Tom inherits it all, but I've no doubt he'll sell it as soon as possible and then everyone will be looking for another job. Still, at least it will be the end of Tom's financial problems.'

'I didn't know he had any,' Anderson remarked in surprise. 'He drives a nice car, works for his father and presumably earns a good salary.'

'Did you know that Tom's mother was an alcoholic?' asked Pippa.

'No.'

'Oh she was; that came out at her inquest. I think that Tom inherited her weakness, only with him it took a different form. Ralph had to give Tom quite a lot of money twice about a year ago. He told me it was to settle some gambling debts. Addiction's a dreadful thing, it ruins lives, and Ralph was very worried about Tom.'

'You say this was a year ago; has he lent him money since?' asked Walker.

'Not as far as I know, but then he probably wouldn't have done. After he'd settled Tom's second lot of debts he told him that he was now on his own. He wasn't a bottomless pit of money, but they all took from him. He was so generous you see, not like that wife of his who kept it all for herself.

'Do you know, Ralph even paid Deborah's monthly allowance, a ridiculously generous one, and she wasn't his daughter. I told him he was silly, that Lisa was taking advantage of him but he said Deborah had had a difficult start in life and he wanted her to think of him as a father.'

'It sounds as though he might have been trying to buy her love,' Anderson remarked.

Pippa looked angry. 'What if he was? I don't blame him. He wanted to be loved, we all do, and despite his manner he was very insecure underneath. He knew that Lisa's family thought he wasn't good enough for her, that he was only after her money, and he spent a fortune on Lisa to try and show it wasn't true. Not that it made any difference; he ended up virtually bankrupt as a result. It was ridiculous. He even paid for Deborah's horse. And were any of them grateful? No. The more he gave the more they expected.'

Anderson decided to leave it at that for the moment. 'Thank you Miss Wright,' he said levelly. 'We'll be in touch again. Before we go, could you just tell us where you were this morning?'

'Here,' Pippa said. 'I'd started to look for another job and spent most of the time ringing round contacts.'

'And you never left the house?'

She looked him straight in the eye, pleading for some sign of their previous intimacy but Anderson kept his face expressionless. 'No, not once,' she murmured at last.

'Perhaps you could give my sergeant a list of the people you phoned at some time. That way we can check the timings of the calls, and then you'll have your alibi.'

'But I wasn't on the phone all the time. I mean, I didn't know I'd need an alibi did I?' Suddenly she laughed with apparent relief. 'If I'd killed Ralph I would have known, and I'd have made sure I had one, don't you see?'

'That's one way of looking at it,' Anderson admitted as he turned to go.

'John,' Pippa said urgently, 'ring me tonight please. I need to talk to you. It's personal.'

DS Walker vanished tactfully out of the front door. 'I can't,' said Anderson, and Pippa could tell the regret in his voice was genuine. 'Everything's changed now. I'm sorry, but that's the way it has to be.'

Anderson walked towards the car, knowing that inside the flat Pippa was already crying her heart out.

Going to the station the following morning was the hardest thing that Chloe had ever had to do. She'd spent most of the previous afternoon and evening trying to come to terms with Ralph's death. Although they'd only been out once she'd felt that her feelings for him had been strong and she'd looked forward to the relationship developing. Now she would never see him again. It was the first time in her relatively young life that she'd had to cope with losing someone due to sudden, violent death. Dying of old age was a very different matter. The main thing that forced her to return to work was the knowledge that Anderson had been totally wrong about Ralph, and she wanted to watch him as he tried to repair the damage his bias had done to the investigation. It would make her thesis very interesting.

Driven by her dislike for Anderson, it was something of a shock when he greeted her with unusual warmth and a smile that even she realised held genuine compassion. It was a side of him she hadn't expected to see and as a result nearly reduced her to tears.

Anderson quickly became brisk again. 'I'm taking DC Lin Ford to The Chilterns. Deborah and Tom are expecting us and there are quite a few questions I need to ask them. Do you want to come with us or would you rather go with DS Walker? He's off to interview Don Mitchell.'

'I'd rather come to The Chilterns,' said Chloe. 'The house is really the centre of all this, don't you think?'

'Not literally, but I agree in principle. I believe that there was a lot more going on in that household than we've managed to uncover. I can't afford to waste any more time, so we have to find out what the family secrets are, and quickly.'

'I suppose all families have secrets,' Chloe remarked as they drove towards the Allan home.

She knew that Anderson normally preferred silence when he was driving, but he seemed to understand her need to talk. 'Of course, but once the police become involved then however embarrassing it may be it's always better for the family to be open from the beginning.'

'It must be horrible having strangers invade your privacy,' Lin mused. 'I know we think of ourselves as special, but to the families we're not are we? We're simply intruders, prying into things that don't concern us.'

'We're not interested in them out of prurience,' Anderson said patiently. 'If something isn't relevant then we discard it.'

'Agreed, but you can't discard the knowledge, can you?' Chloe asked. 'What I'm trying to say is, once you've spilled your secrets to the police you know that other people now share in what used to be a private matter. It must feel horrible.'

Anderson agreed and Chloe thought that a man who kept such a firm barrier around himself would probably understand other people's need for privacy.

'One thing,' said Lin as they drew up outside The Chilterns. 'I learnt this morning that Deborah's alibi doesn't hold up. Her riding lesson was earlier than she told us.'

When Deborah answered the door she looked apprehensive. Anderson hoped that the presence of the two other women might help her. 'Where's Tom?' he asked, following Deborah through into the large kitchen where only eight days earlier they'd seen the body of her mother on the floor.

'He's sorry but he was called in to work for a couple of hours. It's pretty chaotic there as you can imagine. He'll be back as soon as he can.'

'I did ask him to wait here,' Anderson said, mentally noting that Tom appeared to be braver now his father was dead.

Deborah sat down at the kitchen table. 'I hope you don't mind being here, but I feel closer to Mummy,' she explained. 'The rest of the house is horrible now, like a big empty museum.'

Anderson, who would much have preferred the comfort of one of the other rooms, sat down on a kitchen chair. 'Deborah, do you feel well enough to answer some questions today?' She nodded and Anderson sprang his shock question. 'What do you know about your real father?'

Deborah looked at him in astonishment. 'My father? He's dead. He died before he and Mummy could get married.'

'Who told you that?'

'Grandpa. I was quite small. It was when Mummy was out a lot and he explained that she was trying to get over her grief. My father was very rich, like Grandpa and Grandma, and he had a sports car that he adored. One night he took a bend too fast, spun off the road and was killed outright. Mummy was only two months pregnant; he didn't even know about me.'

Anderson was surprised by this. He wouldn't have thought Don Mitchell capable of guilt, but clearly he'd lacked the guts to tell his granddaughter that he was the man who'd cut her and her mother off from her natural father and also sacked the young man for good measure.

'Did ever discuss him with your mother?'

'Yes, but only once. She got quite upset. She said that thinking about him still broke her heart and she'd rather I didn't bring it up again, so I didn't.'

'And you never saw a photograph?' DC Ford asked.

'No, I don't think Mummy had any. I looked so much like her I wasn't that curious, and I suppose because Grandpa was so good to me I never felt that I lacked a father figure. Later on there was Ralph, and he was wonderful. He couldn't have been nicer if he had been my father.'

'DC Ford tells me that before we learnt of your father's death yesterday you'd already rung asking her to come out because you'd got something to show her,' said Anderson quickly, anxious to prevent any tears. 'Now that you're feeling better, perhaps you'd care to show it to us all.'

'It's upstairs,' Deborah said eagerly. 'I'll go and fetch it.'

'What do you make of all that?' Anderson asked Chloe and Lin.

'She seemed to be telling the truth,' said the DC. 'I don't think her natural father has ever been of interest to her.'

'So much the worse for him if he's interested in her,' Chloe pointed out.

'I agree,' said Anderson. 'The problem is, we don't have any evidence that points towards a stranger being involved in Lisa's death.'

'But we've no idea who killed Ralph,' said Lin.

'In my view there are two main contenders for his death,' Anderson said quietly. 'The first is Pippa Wright. We know she used to meet Ralph on Headley Common for secret assignations when they were lovers.'

'We do?' interrupted his DC.

'Yes,' Anderson said brusquely. 'She told me so herself. And if she killed Ralph the chances are that she killed Lisa as well. Ralph either died because he didn't do what she expected and offer to make an honest woman of her after his wife's death, or he died because he'd seen her driving away from the house when he got back that Monday morning. Until we've re-checked her alibi we can't be sure about the first killing, but she's the strongest suspect.'

'What about the second?' Chloe asked. 'Is it Jeff Phillips?'

Anderson shook his head. 'He has to come third. For the killing of Lisa he would have been top of my list, but there's no evidence he ever came into this room. With regard to Ralph's death I can't find a good enough motive, although I'm working on it. No, the second choice has to be Don Mitchell, who wanted revenge for his daughter's death at all costs.'

'I hope you're wrong,' said Chloe. 'I don't think Deborah could cope with the loss of her grandfather as well.'

'Here it is,' said Deborah, coming into the room with a small bottle clutched in her right hand. 'These are my mother's pills, the beta-blockers that she'd stopped taking. I found them in the bottom of her wardrobe when I was turning out some of her clothes. I think they must have fallen out of one of her pockets and rolled under her shoes. It's horrible to think she wouldn't mention it. We all used to tell her it wasn't the end of the world if she missed a dose, and that she'd become obsessed with her health, so I can understand why she kept quiet, but when I think that that's why she died I can hardly bear it. We're all to blame aren't we? None of us wanted to believe she was as ill as she was.'

She started to cry, and Chloe put an arm round the young girl while Anderson put the bottle into a plastic bag and sealed it. Now Deborah had an excuse for having her fingerprints on the bottle in addition to Lisa's, and he wondered how on earth his men could have failed to find them if they really were in such an accessible place. Come to that, how could Lisa have missed them? Logically her wardrobe would have been one of the first places she'd have checked.

'Deborah,' he said softly. 'I know this is all very painful for you, but the best thing you can do for your mother now is tell us the truth about everything. That way, maybe we can catch her killer. Right?' Deborah nodded. 'Fine. For a start, you say that Ralph was like a real father to you. I take it that includes giving you an allowance, helping out with the cost of your horse and so on. Am I right?'

'Yes,' Deborah sniffed, still sitting close to Chloe. 'He was always very generous. Mummy wasn't, you see. She used to say that we should love her for herself, not her money, but I didn't love Ralph because he gave me things. I loved him because he treated me like his own family, and this was the first proper family I'd had.'

'Exactly how generous was he?' Anderson persisted, unmoved by her emotional words.

'He gave me a thousand pounds a month as an allowance,' Deborah muttered.

Anderson saw the stunned expressions on the faces of Chloe and Lin. 'That's quite a lot,' he remarked. 'I suppose keeping a horse is expensive.'

'Yes, and clothes. I'm a shopaholic.'

Anderson laughed. 'I pity your future husband! You know, that surprises me a bit, Deborah. You always look very nice, but I had the impression that it was horses that interested you more than clothes. Are you into designer labels, that sort of thing?'

'Yes, sometimes,' Deborah conceded, but she was starting to look uncomfortable.

'I'd love to see some of them,' said Chloe. 'Would you let me have a look before we go? I've been a student for so many years now I've forgotten what expensive clothes look like!'

Deborah moved away from Chloe and shifted uneasily in her seat. 'I haven't got a lot here. I get bored with them quite quickly and sell them off at the "Nearly New" shop in Banstead. It's the shopping I enjoy.'

'Not all of them surely!' Chloe laughed. 'At least let me look at your latest ones.'

'I've just taken a load and sold them. It was a way of starting afresh after Mummy's death. There's nothing much to see now,' Deborah muttered.

She was so obviously on edge that Anderson decided this was the moment to deliver the big shock. 'I'm not sure I believe you,' he said slowly. Deborah looked at him with startled eyes. 'In fact, there's quite a lot you've told me that I don't believe, including the time you were out riding your horse. You said that you got home after your stepfather discovered your mother's body because you'd been riding. However, the owner of the stables says that on that particular morning you rode earlier than usual and had left the stables by 11 a.m. Where were you between 11 a.m. and 12.20 p.m. that day if you weren't riding your horse?'

Deborah couldn't have looked more stunned if Anderson had slapped her round the face. She looked at him like a trapped animal and then glanced round at the two women.

Chloe and Lin kept their faces impassive, and as the silence lengthened Deborah's nerve broke.

'I'm sorry,' she sobbed. 'I should have told you before but I was too frightened. You're right, I did ride earlier and I came straight home. I was here when Jeff brought Mummy back from the health club.'

Anderson could see no point in recriminations at this stage. At last Deborah was prepared to talk, all he had to do was keep her going. 'Tell me about it, Deborah,' he said encouragingly. 'Tell me exactly what happened.'

'I was in my room,' she said, swallowing hard. 'It was a mess and I knew I ought to tidy it up. Mummy was always saying that since I wasn't working the least I could do was learn to look after myself. Then I heard a car in the drive and I looked out to see who it was.

'I didn't recognise the car, but then Mummy and Jeff Phillips got out. When I realised they were coming in I decided I'd better not make a noise tidying up so I sat on the bed and read one of my horse magazines instead.

'They went through the hall into the kitchen. They'd only been in the house a few minutes when the shouting began. It was horrible, worse than when Mummy and Ralph used to argue. Mummy sounded so shrill, and she was calling him all sorts of names. I crept to the top of the stairs to listen to what it was about. The kitchen door was open and it was easy to overhear; neither of them knew anyone else was here so they weren't bothering to being careful.'

'Could you tell what the argument was about?' Anderson prompted.

Deborah looked even more distressed. 'I'd always thought Mummy was faithful to Ralph. She used to go on and on at him because she suspected he had a roving eye and then it turned out she'd been having an affair with this Jeff man for ages. It was obvious he'd decided to end it, and from the way she was shouting at him I think he could only have told her that morning. She said dreadful things to him.'

'Like what?' Lin asked.

'She was threatening him. She said she'd tell his boss and that he'd lose his job. He begged her not to, because of his family, and she said that she'd make sure his wife knew as well, if she didn't already. He said something about his wife not being well, and Mummy said that neither was she but that didn't seem to bother him. I'd never heard her speak like that before. It was horrible.'

'How long did this quarrel last?' asked Anderson.

'It seemed like ages, but it wasn't, not really. I suppose it only lasted about four or five minutes, and then it all went quiet. I thought that Mummy was probably crying. She never made a sound when she cried, tears just used to run down her face. After a few more minutes I heard footsteps on the drive and when I looked out of the window again I saw Jeff leaving. He wasn't running, but he was walking very quickly.'

'Did you go down to see how your mother was?' Anderson asked gently.

Deborah buried her head in her hands. 'No. I've gone over and over that, wondering if I could have saved her if I had, but I was afraid. The truth is she didn't like me very much. I think I reminded her of a time she wanted to forget, and I thought it was better to let her get over it on her own. If she'd realised that I'd heard everything, that I knew about her affair with Jeff, she'd never have forgiven me and I didn't want her to hate me more. But now I keep thinking that if she'd blacked out and was unconscious I could have saved her if I'd only had the courage to go down.'

'So you stayed in your room until your stepfather came home?'

'Yes. I waited there until both he and Tom were back, then I crept down the stairs and out through the front door before coming back in again.'

'And no one noticed that your car was here when they got back?'

'I keep mine in the second garage and the door was shut. They wouldn't have known whether it was there or not. Later on I moved it into the driveway. Your policeman didn't realise it hadn't been there all the time either.'

'Did your mother cry out at any stage? Did she tell Jeff to keep away from her or go away?' Anderson asked.

'Not as far as I can remember. There was this big quarrel and then total silence.'

'Did you leave your phone in the kitchen when you got back from the stables?' Anderson enquired.

'I suppose I must have done,' she said miserably, 'but I don't remember doing it.'

'Which means you came in through the back door?'

'Yes.' Deborah was crying again now, but Anderson knew that he had to keep going. If he let her have a break she might not be so eager to tell them all she knew when they resumed.

'Let's forget the quarrel for a minute,' he said, surprising Deborah, Chloe and Lin. 'You obviously know a lot more about what goes on in this family than I thought, so perhaps you can help me with something that's been puzzling me. Have you any idea why your stepbrother needed to borrow money from his father last year? After all, Ralph was very generous with you and I assume he was equally generous with his own son.'

'Well,' Deborah said awkwardly, 'it wasn't quite like that. I mean, Tom was at work and had a good salary. Ralph thought he should be able to manage on it, but Tom always said it wasn't enough. I think he did earn a lot for his age, but he was fond of betting on the horses and I think he had some trouble with one of the betting shops in Banstead. I heard him having a couple of rows with Mummy over that.'

Anderson was surprised. 'Why would he quarrel with your mother? Surely it was Ralph he would have talked to?'

'Yes, but Mummy was always looking for weaknesses in Tom. His mother drank, and she used to check up on how much he had when he went out with his friends, that kind of thing. When she heard he had problems with money she seemed to think it was related and I heard her telling him he'd better be careful or he'd end up like his mother.'

'Not very pleasant of her,' Lin Ford murmured.

Anderson turned his head sharply but, surprisingly, Deborah wasn't put out. 'Mummy wasn't really very nice,' she admitted in a low voice. 'People thought she was nice, because she was pretty, but they were wrong. I wanted her to be like she looked, but she couldn't be.'

'Did you ever help your stepbrother out, Deborah?' Chloe asked suddenly.

Deborah looked at Chloe, then back to Anderson. She seemed to be looking to him for guidance.

'You don't have to answer, Deborah,' he said gently. 'As I told you all at the beginning of this enquiry, Chloe is doing a thesis. She's only here because you allow her to sit in on the interviews. You're definitely not obliged to answer her questions. In fact, she isn't supposed to ask any.' He smiled at her as he said this, and Deborah relaxed, lapsing into silence.

Anderson allowed the silence to lengthen before tipping back his chair and, still smiling, he spoke to the waiting girl. 'As a matter of interest, did you ever help your brother out financially?' Out of the corner of his eye he saw that Chloe was watching him keenly, listening intently to every word. He couldn't help hoping that she appreciated his strategy.

Deborah moistened her lips with the tip of her tongue. 'Yes, sometimes,' she admitted.

'I assume his girlfriend is too young to be able to assist,' he continued thoughtfully.

'Girlfriend?' There was no doubting Deborah's surprise

'He does have one, doesn't he? I understood she was at the sixth-form college. If she isn't, then I want a good explanation from Tom as to why he's been seen hanging around there watching them play tennis.'

'There's no one special,' Deborah said firmly. 'He usually hangs out with a group. He doesn't want to get tied down young. That's what happened to his parents and he's afraid of making the same mistake as them.'

'Did he tell you this?' asked Lin.

'He's always telling me it,' Deborah exclaimed, and it was then Anderson realised she was keen on her own stepbrother and that Tom must have been making excuses for not becoming romantically involved with her while at the same time needing to keep borrowing her money. It would be interesting to find out precisely how much he'd had off the girl.

There was no doubt now that despite their physical dissimilarities Tom was a chip off the old block, and Anderson realised he'd probably underestimated him. As a detective he was happiest with hard, indisputable facts, but in this particular enquiry where they were at a premium, it might have been useful to have had a better knowledge of the way people were affected by circumstances and how this could affect their behaviour pattern.

'That's all for now,' he said, rising to his feet. 'We'll need a full statement from you and I have to talk to your stepbrother as soon as possible. When he gets back please ask him to ring me on any of these numbers and then to stay here until I arrive. Can I rely on you to do that?'

Deborah looked into his dark blue eyes and nodded before showing them out of the front door. 'How was Ralph killed?' she asked at the last moment. 'I mean, I know what happened, but why didn't he put up any kind of fight? He seems to have just sat in his car and let someone shoot him. It doesn't make sense.'

'No,' Anderson agreed. 'It doesn't make any sense at all.'

As they reached the car he started to call DS Kirby on the mobile. As he waited for him to reply he turned to Lin Ford. 'We'll have to bring Jeff Phillips in to assist us with enquiries after that statement of Deborah's. It contradicts everything he told us.'

'Do you think he killed both of them?' Lin asked.

'I'm not sure what to think,' said Anderson. 'Deborah lied about two things, so she may have lied about Jeff Phillips as well. The problem is I can't think why.'

'What did she lie about?' Chloe asked curiously.

'Deborah said she came in the back door and left her mobile in the kitchen by mistake. There's no way she would have used the back door. Jeff Phillips was adamant that Lisa regarded the back door as being for tradesmen only, and I've never seen it used by any family member. Also, I don't for one moment believe that she sells off all her wonderful designer clothes in Banstead. You can check that out Chloe. I'm sure you're more used to these charity shops than I am,' he added with a smile.

Chloe looked at his dark-green immaculately cut suit worn with a heavy cotton shirt and silk tie and smiled briefly back at him. 'It looks that way,' she admitted.

'Find out exactly how often they see Deborah, and how many outfits she takes in to them. If it isn't many, and I suspect it isn't, then go to the stables with Lin here, and check out the annual cost of keeping that horse of hers. Then, allowing an adequate amount for running her car and sundry expenses deduct the total the pair of you come up with from her thousand pounds a month. Finally, go and see her bank manager and find out how healthy her account is. If it isn't very healthy we can assume she's been helping Tom out in a big way.'

'But why would she do that?' asked Chloe.

'Because she's in love with him of course, but I suspect she's a little too mature even at eighteen for his particular taste. Ah, Kirby, what did you find out about Mitchell?' He listened intently for several minutes before terminating the call, and he didn't look happy.

'It seems that Don Mitchell has the summer flu, and was ill in bed yesterday morning. The hotel had to call a doctor who's verified that he had a high temperature and wasn't, in his opinion, capable of getting out of bed. Doctors have been wrong before, but it doesn't sound as though he could have gone and shot Ralph Allan, given the timescale. I'm going back to the station,' he added. 'It's time to take another look at our picture board.'

TEN

As Anderson and his team worked out their next moves, Tom Allan finally returned to The Chilterns in Mile Road. Watching him come up the path Deborah felt a mixture of emotions: the incredible sexual longing that his presence always evoked in her and, for the first time, a bitter resentment that like her mother before her, she might have been used for her money. Her mother had always warned her that would happen. Deborah, however, hadn't wanted to be like Lisa, and was sure her mother was wrong. It would be ironic if, after all that had happened, Lisa should be proved right in her assessment of men in general and Deborah was the one who was wrong.

'The police have been here,' she said the moment Tom came in the front door.

'I know. Did you tell them I had to go in to work?'

'Yes, but they weren't too impressed. Inspector Anderson asked me to tell you to ring him as soon as you got in and then to stay here until he came back to talk to you.'

'What the hell about?' Tom asked wearily. 'I don't know anything useful. I can make a few guesses, but so can they. What do they want to discuss, do you know?'

'Money, I think,' said Deborah.

Tom's expression darkened. 'What do you mean?'

'They knew you'd borrowed off Ralph last year, and then they guessed that you'd borrowed money off me. Inspector Anderson wants to know more about it.'

Tom shrugged. 'What's to tell? I gamble too much; it's the bad blood coming out in me. I hope you didn't go and say anything stupid, Debs.'

'I told them the truth for the first time,' Deborah said quietly.

Tom, who had gone into the kitchen and was making himself coffee, turned to look over his shoulder at her. 'Meaning what?'

'That I finally admitted being home before Mummy on the day she died.'

Tom nearly dropped the coffee jug. 'You said what?'

'That I was here when Mummy died.'

'What did you say that for?'

'Because it's the truth.'

He frowned. 'Then why didn't you tell them before? What's the point in keeping it secret for so long? Did you see anything important? If so they're going to think it a bit odd you didn't co-operate from the start aren't they? And why didn't you even tell Dad? Or me come to that?'

'I didn't want them to know the truth about Mummy,' Deborah said defensively. 'It was horrible admitting to them what she was really like and how mean she could be to people, especially you, Tom. And the fact that she was having an affair with Jeff Phillips. I was up in my bedroom when he brought her home, so I heard everything that went on.'

Tom looked stunned. He wandered back through the hall into the conservatory, finally sitting down in one of the large cane chairs and gazing out into the garden. 'So what exactly did you tell them?'

'I admitted that Jeff had come into the house with Mummy and that I heard them quarrelling. I said it was a noisy quarrel and she was saying some awful things. Then it went quiet. I explained that I didn't go down because I thought Mummy would be angry I'd been eavesdropping, but that I saw Jeff hurrying back to his car and driving off. It's the truth, Tom. That's what happened.'

'Then why lie to them, and to Dad and me? Why did you pretend you'd only just got back from horseriding later on? It's stupid to lie to the police. It always backfires and causes nothing but trouble.'

'Not as much trouble as the truth can cause people you care about and want to protect,' Deborah shouted.

Tom stared at her in silence for a moment and she moved closer to him, until she was able to reach out and touch his arm. Tom kept very still; even his breathing seemed to slow and it was like touching someone made of stone.

'You don't care for me at all, do you?' cried Deborah, the pain raw in her voice. 'All you've ever wanted off me is money.'

'That's not true. I like you, Debs. You've been good to me, and I think of you as my sister, but that's not what you want is it? You want me to love you differently, but I can't do that. I'm sorry things aren't the way you want them, but I've never lied to you and I've never used you. You offered me money at a time when I needed it, and I'm grateful, but that was your choice. You can't start using emotional blackmail on me because it won't work. You're just not my type,' he added desperately.

'Inspector Anderson knows what your type is,' Deborah retorted.

Tom went pale. 'He can't do.'

'I think you'll find when he comes to talk to you that he does. And if he's right then I'm probably not your sort. Mummy was right, men are horrible. I'm never going to marry. You can't trust anyone, not even the people closest to you.'

'No,' said Tom sadly. 'In the end, Debs, we're all on our own.'

Jeff Phillips sat in one of the interview rooms at Guildford station and glanced nervously about him. When Anderson and a woman DS had arrived at the health club and asked him to come down to the station to 'clarify a few points concerning his earlier statement,' he'd felt slightly nervous, but not as nervous as he felt now.

The door opened and Anderson and Joanna Blackheath came to join him. The constable sitting in the corner got to his feet for a moment and then took out his notebook and pencil. Anderson sat opposite Jeff, with Joanna on his left. The expression on Anderson's face was relaxed, almost friendly, but Joanna Blackheath was stern-faced.

'DS Blackheath is going to read out your original statement,' said Anderson. 'After she's done that I'd like you to tell me if there's anything in it you wish to change. Do you understand?'

'Yes,' Jeff muttered, and he listened as the DS recited his own words back to him.

'Now that you've had time to think about it,' Anderson said casually, 'do you still feel that's a fair and accurate account of what happened when you took Lisa Allan home?'

'Yes,' Jeff said more firmly.

Anderson straightened in his chair as he spoke. 'Before you answer any further questions I must caution you that you do not have to say anything. But it may harm your defence if you do not mention when questioned something which you later may rely on in court. Anything you do say may be given in evidence.'

Jeff stared at him. 'Am I under arrest?'

'No, Mr Phillips. You are also not obliged to remain at the station, but if you do choose to remain you are entitled to free legal advice,' Anderson said calmly.

'I don't need a lawyer. I haven't done anything wrong.'

'And you're willing to answer my questions?' Anderson asked.

Jeff waited a moment before nodding. 'Yes,' he agreed. 'What do you want to know?'

'Is it true that you didn't go into The Chilterns with Mrs Allan on the morning of her death?' Anderson asked.

'No,' Jeff muttered.

'Then your original statement was untrue?'

'Yes. I knew how bad it would look if I told the truth, but now I want to because as I didn't kill her if I tell the truth it can only help me, isn't that right?'

'It might have saved us a great deal of time if you'd taken that line in the beginning,' Joanna snapped.

'Perhaps you'd like to tell us what really did happen that morning,' Anderson suggested smoothly.

Jeff sighed heavily. He hoped he didn't look as dreadful as he felt. 'I drove Lisa home. We were quarrelling. When I told you before that she was quite happy for the affair to end that wasn't true. She was furious. Knowing about her heart condition I didn't want her going into the house all worked up and then perhaps being taken ill on her own, so I followed her inside to try and smooth things over.'

'And?' Joanna asked as Anderson remained silent, watching Jeff's face closely.

'It was pointless. I only made things worse. She started screaming about telling my boss and me losing my job. She even said she'd come round and tell Liz, my wife. No matter what I said she kept on shouting and swearing at me. I hadn't expected her to behave like that. She'd seemed so gentle and feminine at first, that was what attracted me to her, but she showed her real colours that Monday morning.'

'What did you do?' Anderson asked.

'There wasn't anything I could do,' Jeff said helplessly. 'In the end I realised I was only making things worse by staying. Lisa started banging around making coffee and I said I needed to use the bathroom. I walked straight out of the kitchen, along the hall and out the front door. I was grateful she didn't come running after me, I can tell you. The way she'd been behaving I thought she might throw a scene in her own front drive, but she probably didn't realise I'd gone until it was too late.'

'Did you see anyone else in the house or approaching the house at this time?' Anderson asked.

'No, no one. Lisa said both the men were at work and her daughter was out horseriding.'

'I see. I suppose you didn't happen to notice if there was a mobile phone on the kitchen worktop, did you?'

'Not on the worktop, no, but I saw one in the hall. I wouldn't normally have taken any notice only we'd had to ask people not to bring them into the gym studios when Lisa was there because of her pacemaker, so I was surprised to see one anywhere in her house.'

'Where exactly in the hall was it?' Anderson asked.

'On the top of the small bureau just inside the front door.'

'And was Mrs Allan alive when you left the house?'

'I've just told you she was! I couldn't believe it when I heard about her death and the time she was discovered. It didn't add up. How could anyone have killed her in the short time between me leaving and her husband arriving back?'

'Do you know Deborah Allan?' Anderson demanded abruptly.

Jeff looked baffled. 'No, not at all. Lisa said she was only interested in horseriding. She certainly never came to the health club.'

'Mr Phillips,' Anderson said softly. 'Are you quite sure that Lisa Allan was alive when you left?'

'Yes. I swear to God she was fine. She was worked up, well in a flaming temper to tell the truth, but she was very much alive. I wanted to end our affair, but I didn't want her dead. What would be the point?'

'Alive she could tell your boss and your wife. Dead she couldn't tell anyone.'

'She'd already told my wife, but I'm not a murderer!' Jeff Phillips insisted. 'I didn't kill her, and there's no way you can prove I did.'

Anderson got to his feet and signalled for Joanna to follow him out of the room. 'What do you think?' he asked her.

She was surprised to be asked, as Anderson didn't usually consult her, but she had her answer ready. 'I believe him. The story he's telling now tallies with the one Deborah gave us.'

'Yes, with the exception of the mobile phone which Deborah claims to have left in the kitchen but Jeff Phillips says he saw in the hall.'

'So do we charge him?' asked Joanna.

'No,' Anderson said swiftly. 'For one thing we've no real evidence against him apart from the fact that he lied about going into the house. He doesn't seem to realise how important the mobile phone is, and he certainly didn't have access to Lisa's beta-blockers at any stage.'

'Unless she lost them at the gym,' suggested Joanna.

'Possible, but unlikely I'd have thought. There's also the fact that according to DS Kirby he has a cast-iron alibi for the time of Ralph Allan's killing.'

'He doesn't have to have done both,' Joanna pointed out.

'No, but I'm beginning to think that Pippa Wright may have been in a position to do just that. We'll let Mr Phillips go once he's signed his statement. He won't run anywhere, not with two children and a crippled wife. Has Chloe come back yet?'

'She's waiting in your office.'

'Right. I'll see what she's found out, then collect you, and the three of us will pay a call on Tom Allan. According to his stepsister he's now back home and waiting for us. I have a feeling that, like Deborah, he may well know a lot more than he let on the first time we talked to him.'

Chloe was looking pleased with herself. 'We checked "Nearly New" in Banstead,' she said excitedly. 'According to them Deborah Allan has only used the shop twice, and even then she didn't sell many items. A couple of evening dresses, nice but not designer labels, and last summer she sold them quite a few casual dresses that she presumably felt she'd outgrown, age-wise I mean.'

'What about her financial position?'

'Lin did most of that side of things. She talked to the woman who runs the stables as you suggested, added on a generous amount for living expenses, and then saw Deborah's bank manager. He was reluctant to co-operate, but in the end he did. Deborah Allan has three hundred pounds in her current account and two thousand in her premium reserve.'

'And should there be more?' Anderson asked.

'Yes, absolutely,' Chloe declared. 'Lin worked out that Deborah should have had about eight thousand saved even if she'd only been getting her allowance at that rate for the past year. Let's be honest, a thousand pounds a month is an incredible sum and there's only a certain amount of hay a horse can eat.'

'Vet's bills?' asked Anderson.

'None of significance.'

'You and Lin have done a good job. Joanna and I are off to The Chilterns now to talk to Tom Allan. Do you want to come?'

'Try and stop me,' Chloe said. 'I suppose you know where this is all leading, but I haven't a clue.'

Before they left, Anderson put in a call to DS Kirby at the Reigate station and asked if anyone had checked out Pippa's alibi for the time of Lisa's murder.

'A couple of our officers did,' he confirmed. 'When questioned again none of the witnesses was quite so certain of the precise time they saw Miss Wright. It also transpires that she frequently left the office for an early lunch, but no one remembers seeing her drive away that day. One secretary is "almost certain" she saw her at 11.45, but admits it might have been 11.15. She's dyslexic,' he added in explanation.

'Thanks,' said Anderson. 'It's pretty much what I expected, nothing definite either way.'

As Anderson, Joanna and Chloe were about to set out on the now familiar route to The Chilterns, Anderson was caught in the car park by DS Walker. He was breathing rapidly. 'Glad I caught you, sir. There's been a bit of a breakthrough. That rep that Tom Allan was visiting on the day his stepmother was murdered is back from the Caribbean at last, and guess what? Tom never turned up to see him that day. Mr Taylor, the rep, wasn't surprised because Tom's done that before. It seems he isn't quite as conscientious about work as his father was, but Taylor would have reported it if he'd known about the killing. As he was abroad he didn't, of course, and it was only when we sent someone round to him that he realised it might be significant.'

'Yes,' said Anderson slowly, 'it might. What about the bottle of beta-blockers. Any fingerprints on that?'

'Only Deborah Allan's, sir.'

Anderson frowned. 'Not her mother's?'

'No, just hers.'

'Then the bottle was wiped clean before Deborah found it, which means someone else took the tablets and hid them, but whether they really hid them in the bottom of the wardrobe or not remains to be seen. Right, thanks Phil. We're off to Kingswood again. I've left all my notes on my desk, you'd better read through them and catch up on the things you've missed.'

Anderson noticed a look of puzzlement on Walker's face as he left. He guessed that the DS was wondering why it was Joanna and not him who was sitting in the car. The answer was simple, he was happier working with a woman, and despite his best efforts he hadn't found DS Walker someone he could relate to. Joanna Blackheath might keep herself to herself, but as far as Anderson was concerned that was something to be grateful for, and although she was somewhat abrasive he liked her attitude to her work. She was clearly bright, and he felt comfortable when she was with him.

Tom opened the front door to them himself. 'Sorry I missed you last time, but I was needed at work. It makes quite a change,' he added.

'Yes, your father's death must have had a big impact on your life,' remarked Anderson as Tom took them through into the front room.

'It has,' Tom agreed, signalling for his three visitors to sit down but choosing to stand himself. 'I'm afraid I've never liked the family business, and now I find myself running it, but not for long. My father was intending to sell the company anyway. I shall do the same, but without staying on to run it as Dad had planned.'

'What about the other employees?' asked Anderson.

'I imagine that whoever buys will do quite a bit of streamlining. There's some dead wood to be cut away, even I can see that.'

'Have you any idea how your father has left his money?' Joanna enquired.

'Of course. He was quite open about it. Originally everything was to go to Lisa. After she died he changed that immediately. He left the business and half his estate to me; the rest goes to Debs.'

'Which means that if your stepmother hadn't died, you wouldn't have benefitted from your father's death,' Anderson said mildly.

Tom flushed but kept his voice low. 'Yes, that's true. Luckily, though, I'm not so destitute that I had to commit a double murder in order to survive, if that's what you're suggesting.'

'I'm not suggesting anything at all, but since you've

brought the subject up is it really true that your finances were healthy before your father died?'

'Yes. I've always had a good job and there are a lot of company perks.'

'So you've never had to borrow money at any time?' Anderson queried.

'I wondered how long it would take you to get round to that. As a matter of fact, I have borrowed off Dad in the past. I've got a weakness for the horses and ended up way over my head. He bailed me out a couple of times, along with warnings about people paying more for weakness in their lives than for anything else. He thought I was weak, in case you hadn't guessed, and that I'd inherited my mother's weakness for addictions too.'

'Would you say you and your father had a good relationship?' asked Joanna.

'That would have been impossible with him, because he always knew best. Cloning would have provided the perfect answer for Dad. That way he could have had an entire family made up of replicas of himself. He pushed me at work, which was fair up to a point, and of course he was a compulsive womaniser but that didn't affect me. We got along all right with the occasional inevitable argument. That's the way most people existed alongside my father.'

'Including Deborah?' Anderson asked.

Tom shook his head. 'No, Debs got on with him without much trouble. He had a soft spot for her.'

'Meaning what?' Joanna demanded.

Tom looked surprised. 'What I say, that he was fond of her.' He stared at the policewoman for a moment and then laughed. 'Oh, I see, is that the way your mind's working? Well, he definitely wasn't having an affair with her. She was too young even for him.'

'And too old for you?' Anderson asked.

'I'm sorry?'

'I gather you like your girlfriends young, which explains

your predilection for hanging around outside the sixth-form college watching the young girls play tennis in their short skirts.'

'There's no law against looking, and they're over sixteen.'

'By a few months,' Anderson conceded. 'Tell me, do you have a special girlfriend?'

'No, I don't.'

'You prefer to go out in a crowd, is that right?'

For the first time Tom looked confused. 'Who told you that?'

'Is it true?' Anderson persisted.

'Sometimes.'

'Then perhaps you'd give me the names of your friends. I'd like to have a word with them.'

Tom looked flustered. 'I don't see why I should. What's that got to do with my father's murder? Or Lisa's?'

'Just the same, if you would give a list to DS Blackheath I'd be grateful,' said Anderson smoothly. Sensing that Tom was becoming rattled, Anderson pushed on. 'Did your stepsister ever give you any money to help out with gambling debts?'

With a sigh Tom finally sank into an armchair. 'OK, I admit it, yes she did. She offered me the money earlier this year when I was in trouble and I accepted it. I knew Dad wouldn't help again, he'd made that clear enough and I didn't know which way to turn. It was a mistake though. Deborah needs a lot of affection, that's what Dad realised I suppose, but the kind she wanted from me wasn't the brotherly sort and that's how I felt about her. Once she'd lent me money she felt entitled to press for a different relationship. It's made things quite awkward.'

'How much money did she give you?'

'Lend. It was a loan,' protested Tom. 'Not much, about three hundred or so.'

'And you didn't ask her for any more again?'

'Hardly, not once I realised what she wanted in return.'

Anderson leant forward in his chair and his tone altered, becoming paternal and concerned. 'This will probably come as rather a shock to you, Tom, but we have reason to believe that your stepsister may be implicated in the death of her mother.'

It clearly did come as a shock to the young man sitting opposite Anderson. For a moment he looked as though he was going to faint. 'That's rubbish!' he exclaimed. 'Deborah couldn't kill anything, not even a spider.'

'Most people are capable of murder if pushed too far,' Anderson said. 'On her own admission your stepsister was alone here with her mother after Jeff Phillips left. According to Mr Phillips, Lisa was alive and well but angry when he last saw her, yet by the time your father arrived here, less than fifteen minutes later, she was dead. In that short space of time someone had murdered her.'

'But surely Jeff Phillips is the most likely suspect,' Tom protested. 'You say he admits to having been here, and he and Lisa had been having an affair. He's got a motive. Debs hasn't.'

'There are two problems with that,' Anderson explained confidentially. 'One concerns the mobile phone, and the second far more difficult one to explain away is how Jeff Phillips could have had anything to do with the lack of beta-blockers in your stepmother's body. She told Sara Cooper that she'd lost them at home, but I doubt if Jeff had set foot in the house before that fatal morning. We have every reason to believe that your stepmother's murder was premeditated and therefore unlikely to be the sudden result of a quarrel. All of which means that Jeff Phillips doesn't fit the profile of the killer as we see him.'

'You thought my father had killed her,' said Tom, still very white. 'If that's an example of your profiling then it doesn't speak very highly of its efficiency.'

Anderson was aware that Chloe was watching to see how he took the rebuke, but although Tom's words had hit home he made sure that his expression didn't change. He still looked relaxed and friendly, as though he was trying to help Tom. 'Your father was only one of the suspects,' he said carefully.

'What about Pippa?' Tom continued. 'She could have killed both Lisa and my father. Deborah couldn't possibly have killed Dad. For a start she has an alibi, she really was at the stables that time, and secondly where would she get a gun from, let alone the knowledge to use it?'

'She's found her mother's missing pills, did you know that?' asked Joanna as Anderson sat silently watching Tom.

'No, she never told me. When did that happen?'

'Two days ago.'

Tom frowned. 'Where did she find them?'

'In the bottom of her mother's wardrobe. She thinks they rolled out of Lisa's pocket and under her shoes.'

'That doesn't prove anything, except that my stepmother was even dizzier than we thought if she managed to miss them there.'

'I doubt if she did,' said Anderson. 'Her prints had been wiped off the bottle. Someone took those pills and hid them.'

'In her wardrobe?' Tom asked incredulously.

'Probably not, which is another reason why we suspect your stepsister. She's lied to us right from the start, and for no good reason. Now she's claiming to be telling us the truth, but it isn't the whole truth and I believe that's because she can't face the whole truth. Killing your own mother must be very traumatic.'

'You're talking nonsense,' Tom protested. 'I know Debs. She simply isn't capable of murder, no matter what you say. There are lots of people with far more reason to kill Lisa than Deborah.'

'And your father?' Anderson asked softly.

'I can't imagine why my father was killed,' said Tom in a markedly different tone.

Anderson leant back in his chair again. 'You may be right, but it's interesting that while you can offer up several people who might have wanted to kill your stepmother you seem totally at a loss where your father's concerned. Bearing in mind the fact that your father was a womaniser, a cheating businessman and a bully I find this difficult to understand.'

'Well, Lisa's death was different,' said Tom. 'I honestly don't think you really understand what she was like.'

'I don't think I do,' Anderson agreed. 'Perhaps you could enlighten me?'

Pale and tense, Tom stood up and as he started to talk he paced around the room. 'She was always moody, and she distrusted everyone, even those closest to her. For some reason she seemed to think people were only interested in her money. I think her parents had brainwashed her about that and no matter how much Dad tried to reassure her she couldn't change her attitude.'

'Perhaps asking her for money to bail his firm out of trouble wasn't the kind of reassurance she needed,' Anderson said dryly.

'But she was difficult about everything,' Tom said despairingly. 'It was bad enough when she first married Dad, but after she became ill it was a thousand times worse. After she'd had two convulsions and lost her driving licence I suppose she felt dependent on others and that didn't suit her either. She wouldn't ever calm down and accept that everyone's life has ups and downs. She was very intolerant and used to get in a state about everything, which made her health even worse. It would have been easy to kill her you know,' he added suddenly.

Anderson felt the hairs on the back of his neck prickle. 'In what way, Tom?' he asked quietly.

'Well, as she hadn't been taking her pills she'd have been even more emotional than was normal. Before the pills almost anything could trigger off one of her turns, despite the pacemaker. I've been thinking about it a lot and I reckon it was an accident.'

'An accident?' Anderson queried softly.

'Yes,' said Tom, looking at the policeman with a sudden expression of despair on his face. 'Suppose she wasn't meant to die? Suppose someone only ever intended to frighten her?'

Anderson got to his feet. 'Tom, I think it might be a good idea if you came down to the station with us,' he said gently. 'We can talk about this more there.'

Tom looked almost haunted. 'I'm not sure . . . That is, I . . .'

'I think you need to talk this through, Tom,' said Anderson keeping his voice gentle. 'Here isn't the right place, you know that.'

During the entire course of the conversation Anderson had worked hard to gain Tom's trust. It paid off. Without any further argument he picked up a lightweight jacket and walked towards the door. 'You're right,' he conceded. 'It's difficult talking about your family when two of them are dead and you're sitting in a room where they used to sit. It's really difficult.'

The drive to the station was a silent one, which was what Anderson wanted. On arrival he told Chloe to wait in his office and proceeded to the interview room with Joanna and Tom.

Before they reached the interview room Tom began to look so ill that Anderson asked if he'd like to see a doctor, but Tom declined. 'I'm fine, it's probably the shock of Dad's death catching up with me. I've been so busy since he was killed I haven't had time to think about it much, but talking to you has brought it home to me.'

'Then you're happy to give us a statement?'

'Yes.'

At the start of the interview Joanna cautioned Tom and

asked him if he wanted a solicitor present but, like Jeff Phillips before him, Tom declined.

'Before we talk to you about what Lisa was like to live with,' Anderson said quietly, 'I'd like you to give us the list of your friends that we discussed earlier.'

Tom didn't respond.

'Is there any special reason why you don't want to name them?' Anderson continued. 'If you're worried that they'll get into trouble with us for some minor offences they may have committed in the past that's not what this is about. We simply want corroboration that you spend your spare time in a group rather than with one girl.'

'I can't give you their names,' said Tom, sounding on the verge of tears.

'Tell me why,' Anderson coaxed. 'Don't they exist? That's nothing to be ashamed of either. Plenty of young people pretend that they're more popular than they are. If you spend a lot of time on your own, or with one particular girl who happens to be rather young, we're not going to be shocked. All we want is the truth from you.'

'There is no group of friends, and no girlfriend either!' Tom exclaimed.

'No girlfriend? Then why were you hanging around watching the girls play tennis? Are you happier as a voyeur, is that it?' Anderson's voice was totally non-judgemental and Tom reacted to this with almost painful gratitude.

'It's not like you think at all,' he blurted out. 'I'm not interested in the girls there. I've never been interested in girls. My boyfriend is studying at the college. I go and watch when he's playing mixed tennis because one of the girls there is keen on him and sometimes I'm not sure that he's going to stay with me. He thinks he might not be gay. He is, he just doesn't want to accept it.'

'Did your father know this?' Anderson asked.

'Are you joking? My father despised me enough as it was. I was too quiet, too well-mannered for his liking. If he'd discovered I was a homosexual he'd have thrown me out of the firm and the home. He'd have seen it as a reflection on his own masculinity. Besides, I'd heard the way he talked about people like me. He wanted to see us all shot, like mad dogs. My father was not a man who'd moved with the times, and he was full of prejudices. That's how my trouble began. If I'd been able to tell him the truth it might have been different.

'There was this boy I had a relationship with. He lied to me about his age, and when it ended he told me that he was really underage and unless I paid him he was going to go to the police. I didn't have the kind of money he wanted, but I couldn't tell Dad the truth so I pretended I had gambling debts. He still made a fuss, but only in a half-hearted way. I think he was almost pleased I'd done something he could relate to.

'During the affair we'd taken photos of each other, and I'd used the automatic timer on my camera to take some of the pair of us. They were for me to keep but somehow this boy got hold of one of them. Even after my first payment he didn't return it, instead he demanded more money and said he'd not only tell the police but also send a copy to Dad. I had to go back to Dad a second time saying I'd run up gambling debts again. He did pay but he made it clear that it was the last time, a final payoff. In future he said that I had to settle my debts myself or take the consequences.

'I know I was stupid, blackmailers never stop, but I thought Pete – that's the boy – really loved me. He didn't, I realise that now, and as soon as he got a new boyfriend he told him all about me. He was older and egged Pete on to try and keep milking me. I got desperate, and that was when I turned to Deborah, but she didn't have the kind of money I needed. By that time I'd negotiated a price for the return of the photo. I told Pete and his friend if they didn't accept that then they could do what they liked. I was almost broke as it was.

'They agreed to that, but somehow I had to raise five thousand pounds by the end of June. I've never felt so trapped. I knew Dad wouldn't pay again and it wasn't fair to try and get more out of Deborah because she thought she was in love with me. Finally I made the terrible mistake of turning to Lisa. She had more money than anyone, and she'd never done anything for me. I told her that I was in debt again and that if I didn't pay up I'd get worked over. All she did was laugh. She said it might be a good idea if I took up martial arts and learnt to defend myself because she wasn't going to give me a penny. She also said she'd never liked me and that I gave her the creeps.'

'Not very pleasant,' Joanna said sympathetically.

'It was absolutely foul,' Tom confessed. 'I realised I'd made a bad mistake and it was then that I worked out my plan. I decided I had to force Lisa to pay, and in order to do that I had to make her vulnerable to pressure. I decided to hide her beta-blockers a week before I asked her for money a second time.'

'Where did you hide them?' asked Anderson.

'In the glove compartment of my car. I wasn't able to replace them for ages because of your men. In the end I shoved them in her wardrobe. Anyway, even after I'd done that I didn't think I'd go through with it. I was sure she'd make a fuss about her pills, or ring the doctor for more, but then I realised she wasn't taking anything because she started to get more worked up about things again. In a way that made me feel she was meant to give me money, that because everything was working out for me it was what I deserved. Dad had given Debs a lot, why shouldn't Lisa help me? Well, that was the way I was thinking by then.

'On the Monday morning I was due to see our rep. I'd missed calls to him before and I knew he wouldn't ring Dad straight away. The idea was that I'd call on him after lunch on my way back to work and say I'd got the time wrong, because Lisa was never meant to die.

'It all worked out so well at first. I was just pulling in to Mile Road when I saw Jeff's car driving out on to the main road. Of course I didn't know they'd quarrelled, I even thought Lisa might be in a good mood after seeing him. Then, as I walked through the front door, I saw Deborah's phone on the top of the bureau and I picked it up. It was like a gift, exactly what I needed. She must have left it there when she got in from horseriding, but I assumed it was from the night before. She was never normally home at that time on a Monday.

'I found Lisa in the kitchen. She was in a dreadful mood, swearing and sobbing about men in general and Jeff in particular. That put me off at first but then I realised it might work in my favour. Since she was already in a state she'd be easier to frighten, which was all I ever intended to do.

'I asked her straight out for the money, but she looked at me as though I was mad. "I've already said no once," she said. "You're a born loser, like your mother was and I'm not going to prop you up. All men are the same, you just want women for what you can get out of them, either sex or money. Maybe if your creditors catch up with you it will teach you a lesson. I certainly shan't lift a finger to help. You're nothing to me, we're not even related. In fact, Tom, I think I ought to tell your father. It's my duty as a loyal wife." She laughed then, because she knew what would happen to me if she carried out her threat. Dad would have chucked me out, and I realised that was what Lisa wanted.

'At that moment I hated her more than I'd ever hated anyone, so I moved right up to her and manoeuvred her towards the corner of the kitchen. That was when she first started to get nervous. I could see it in her eyes. She told me to get away or she'd tell Dad, but I ignored her. I kept asking for the money, and she went on shaking her head, but at least she'd stopped laughing at me. For the first time she was actually afraid of me, and in a strange way that made me feel good.

'Then suddenly her breathing changed. She started to struggle for air and I could see she was panicking. I told her that if she let me have the money I'd tell her where her pills were. You've never seen anyone look as stunned as she did then. I suppose she'd never thought me capable of doing anything so awful. She distrusted everyone, but she underestimated me badly.

'I'd expected her to give in immediately, but she didn't and that's why it all went wrong. It wasn't my fault. She started hitting out at me, and I had to pin her against the wall while I took Deborah's phone from my pocket. That terrified her, especially when I told her I was going to use it. She begged me not to, but she hadn't left me any choice. I wanted her to realise she couldn't get away with treating me the way she had. Dad had treated Debs like a daughter, she should have treated me like a son. I wasn't only after the money then, I wanted respect as well, do you see what I mean?'

'Yes, I do,' Anderson said quietly. 'Go on.'

'I dialled the speaking clock because it was the first number that came into my head. Then I held the phone up close to her so that she could hear the woman's voice, and all the time I kept asking her for the money. "Just give me the money and you'll be all right," I said. I must have repeated it three or four times, but she wasn't listening. Her eyes had glazed over and she seemed to be in a world of her own.

'Finally I lost my nerve. I could see how ill she was. She'd gone deathly white and her lips were turning blue so I yelled at her to agree to help me, that I was desperate, and for a split second she looked at me differently. I could see she respected me then, and I thought it was going to be okay. I switched off the phone but before I knew what was happening her knees had buckled and she'd gone into a convulsion. Then –' He stopped, a green sheen covering his ashen face as perspiration broke out on his forehead. 'Then,' he continued resolutely, 'she slid down the wall with her eyes wide open, staring at me in horror. Finally she let out one tiny breath and I realised it was all over. She was dead, but she kept on looking at me. It was grotesque, disgusting.

'I couldn't believe what had happened. It had started off so well and then everything got out of control. She was never meant to die. I swear to you I didn't want to kill her. I only wanted to frighten her. I deserved something, if not money then respect, but she never gave me anything. I didn't ask for love but at least she could have cared, couldn't she?'

He was weeping now but he didn't seem to realise and Anderson pushed a box of tissues across the desk to him. 'What about your father, Tom?'

Tom stared at him through tear-filled eyes. 'Dad? Do you honestly think I could ever kill another person after what happened in the kitchen that morning? I've no idea who killed my father, but I swear it wasn't me. Why would I kill him? He cared for me more than anyone else. It might not have been much, but it was better than nothing.'

'Charge him,' Anderson said to Joanna as he got to his feet. 'He's already been cautioned.'

Outside in the corridor Anderson took some deep breaths. It had been a harrowing interview, and he couldn't help feeling a tinge of pity for the young man who had never had a chance in life despite all his father's money. He was also shaken by the picture of Lisa that had emerged during the statement. It was so at odds with Anderson's assessment of her at their one and only meeting.

To make matters worse he believed that Tom was telling the truth about his father's death, which meant that now he had to bring in Pippa Wright, and he didn't relish that prospect. It was the next logical step, but it did make him wonder once more about his judgement where women were concerned.

ELEVEN

When Anderson returned to his office, he found Chloe waiting for him.

'Why's Tom been brought in?' she asked curiously.

Anderson sat down behind his desk. 'He's just confessed to killing his stepmother,' he replied calmly.

'Tom? But why? And didn't he have an alibi?' asked a stunned Chloe.

'No, he didn't have an alibi. As for the why, it's a complicated tale of homosexual love, blackmail and a stepmother who doesn't appear to have had an ounce of kindness in her for anyone, not even her own daughter let alone a stepson whose mother had committed suicide.'

'But he doesn't look like a murderer,' Chloe said stupidly.

'According to him he never intended to be one. I imagine he might get off on a plea of manslaughter, given Lisa's medical condition. The main factor against that is that he deliberately concealed her medication for a week before her death, which suggests premeditation. It was premeditated, he doesn't deny that, but only as a means of making his task easier. Listening to him talking about the moment she died I can't picture him as a cold-blooded killer either, but that's up to the court to decide. We've done our work.'

'Did he kill Ralph too?' Chloe asked fearfully.

Anderson sighed. 'He says not, and for what it's worth I believe him.'

'Then who did?'

Anderson understood only too well how much this mattered to Chloe. 'That's what we're about to try and find out,' he assured her.

'Are you charging anyone?'

Anderson struggled to keep his irritation under control. 'Chloe, surely you've learnt by now that charging people isn't that easy. You need a lot of proof, or a useful confession – like the one from poor Tom who couldn't wait to get it all off his chest – before you can do that. No, we're not charging anyone, but I'm bringing someone in to assist with our enquiries.'

'Who?'

'Pippa Wright.'

'Poor you,' Chloe said sympathetically.

Anderson looked at her sharply. 'What do you mean by that?'

'Well, you and she were friendly weren't you? At least, that's what Phil Walker said.'

'Did he really? I think he should learn more discretion if he intends to get on in the force,' Anderson remarked, mentally deciding that after this case he'd never work with DS Walker again. He had to be able to trust his colleagues, and having a DS alongside him who was a gossip was a nightmare, particularly for a man as private as Anderson.

Anderson sent Joanna and Walker to fetch Pippa in while he checked on what had been discovered about her phone calls during the time Ralph had been killed. The pathologist's report had been quite helpful, indicating that Ralph had died between 11 a.m. and 12.30 p.m. from a single shot through the head fired at close range, but not close enough to leave powder burns on his skin. It was difficult to conjure up a scenario where this would have happened to a streetwise man like Ralph Allan.

'She's in the interview room, sir,' said Joanna, putting her head round Anderson's door.

'Right, I'll be with you in a couple of minutes,' Anderson promised, checking his notes one last time. He knew the interview would be difficult, but with his personal knowledge of Pippa's personality it should be possible for him to get the truth out of her in the end.

She looked at him apprehensively when he walked into the room, then tried a tentative smile, to which he didn't respond. Her bottom lip trembled and Anderson knew that this was as much due to sexual desire as fear. Clearly Pippa Wright was still very attracted to him.

'I should remind you that you are still under caution following your last statement to us,' Anderson said briskly. Pippa nodded. 'Following recent events there are now additional questions that I need to ask you. Do you wish to have your solicitor present?'

'No,' said Pippa in a small voice.

'Very well. Perhaps you would tell me where you were between the hours of 11 a.m. and 12.30 p.m. on Monday last.'

'I was at home,' Pippa said patiently. 'I didn't go in to work because Ralph and I had agreed that it was time for me to look for another job. I spent the morning ringing round friends and contacts, doing some general networking.'

'Why had you decided to change your job?'

'Because my affair with Ralph had come to an end and it was going to be difficult for the pair of us to work together.'

'Who ended the affair?' Anderson asked.

'Ralph did.'

'Do you know why?'

She nodded. 'He said it would look bad after Lisa died. Ralph thought he was your prime suspect for her murder and that if you learned of our affair it would give him an additional motive. I felt it was a little late to do anything about it, but he was adamant.'

'Were you upset by this?'

'Of course I was,' replied Pippa, her voice suddenly stronger. 'I loved him, and I thought he felt the same about me. I was sorry his wife had died, but at the same time I couldn't help thinking that this meant we'd be able to be together permanently. Not straight away, of course, but later on. I'd have been a better wife to him than Lisa was. She wasn't a partner, she was one of those blonde fluffy women who are as hard as nails underneath and all she ever did was take from him.'

'While he was unfaithful to her,' Anderson remarked.

'That's not surprising. He wanted . . .' She stopped.

'He wanted what?' asked Anderson.

'The same as most men,' she muttered, but Anderson knew that she'd been about to reveal what kind of sex Ralph Allan enjoyed the most. It wasn't a subject he cared to linger over.

'In other words, you were angry with him?'

'Yes, I was.'

'Angry enough to kill him?'

'No! That isn't the kind of person I am. I was terribly hurt at first, then for a short time I thought perhaps it was a blessing. I was free to see other men and I even thought I'd found one who could make me really happy. He couldn't though. In the end they all let you down.' She looked directly at Anderson as she spoke.

'We've checked your phone calls during Monday morning,' Anderson told her. 'They make interesting reading. Most of them are early in the morning, leaving you plenty of time to drive to Headley Common and kill Ralph Allan before returning to make more calls. Fortunately for you there's one call made precisely in the middle of the period during which Ralph is believed to have died. However, that call was to a secretarial agency, and of course they wouldn't know if it really was you they spoke to or not.'

'There's no one else in my house,' said Pippa. 'I made that call, I can tell you every word that was said.'

'I'm sure you can. Strangely, one of your neighbours claims to have seen you drive away from your house in your white Carina twenty minutes before that call was made. She says you didn't return until gone twelve o'clock. Can you explain that?'

'She's mistaken,' Pippa replied, looking defiantly at Anderson. 'I never left the house that day.'

'When you and Ralph Allan were lovers, where did you meet?' Anderson asked her as she continued to stare at him.

'At my home.'

'Anywhere else?'

Pippa swallowed hard and on the top of the table her fingers were tightly interlaced. 'Sometimes,' she admitted.

'And where was that?'

'On Headley Common.'

'Where exactly on Headley Common?'

'If you go past the car park and along the road another twenty yards or so there's a place where you can pull off and you're almost immediately screened from passers-by by bushes. That's where we met up in our lunchtimes.'

'For sex?'

Pippa went red. 'Yes, if you must know, for sex. We didn't use it that often, but sometimes if we had a whole week when we couldn't meet of an evening we'd get desperate.'

'Did you know that the place where you and he used to meet is the exact spot where he was killed?' Anderson asked casually.

'No, how could I?' Pippa protested, but to Anderson's way of thinking she didn't look nearly shocked enough.

'I can't believe he would have driven there to meet anyone else,' he continued. 'I believe you rang him at the office, asked him to meet you there under some pretext and then drove there yourself and shot him.'

'Then how did I manage to make a telephone call from my house? Where did I get a gun from? And why didn't Ralph try and get away from me?'

'How do you know he didn't?' Anderson asked with interest. 'I don't remember any mention of the position in which he was found in the papers.'

Pippa looked terrified. 'There must have been! I didn't kill him, I swear that's the truth. I know nothing about guns, how could I have got hold of one let alone fired it accurately?'

'You received an incoming call at 10 a.m. that morning. The caller dialled 141 before ringing, making it impossible to trace. Who was that?' asked Anderson suddenly.

'I don't know what you're talking about.'

'Think, Miss Wright. Who rang you at ten that morning?'

'I can't remember. It might have been a friend.'

'Does this friend have a name?'

'Look, you're muddling me. I was concentrating on the calls I made. I haven't been thinking about people who rang me. You'll have to give me more time.'

'I don't believe you,' Anderson said sharply, and at the sound of authority in his voice Pippa's eyes became large and docile as she automatically fell into the role of dominated female. 'I think Don Mitchell rang you that morning,' he continued. 'I believe he'd arranged to have his son-in-law killed as he was certain Ralph had murdered his daughter, and you helped him set Ralph up. Isn't that right? You certainly rang Ralph's office a little after that call came through. Was that to set the trap that Don had arranged?'

'Don Mitchell? I've never spoken to Don Mitchell in my life,' said Pippa. 'I don't think you've got any idea who killed Ralph, it's all guesswork on your part.'

'If it wasn't Don,' said Anderson, 'then it was you. Your neighbour was quite definite about seeing you drive away from your house. Where were you going?'

'I never left the house that morning,' Pippa repeated doggedly.

'Where do you park your car?' asked Joanna.

'In a lock-up at the side of the house. There are three garages there, perhaps this neighbour saw one of the other cars. I think one of them is white.'

'It is,' Anderson confirmed. 'However, it wasn't in the garage that morning. The owner was involved in an accident a few weeks ago and the car has gone in for repair.'

Pippa's eyes met Anderson's for a moment, and she was the first to look away. 'Am I under arrest?' she asked suddenly.

'No.'

'Then I'd like to leave.'

'Before you do, I think I should tell you that your neighbour is also willing to testify that on the morning in question you got into your car wearing a cream linen jacket with a highly distinctive red and white polka-dot silk scarf at the neck. Do you own clothes that fit that description, Miss Wright?'

Pippa, who'd half-risen from her chair, sat down abruptly. 'Yes, I do,' she said in a small voice.

'Are they still in your possession?'

'Yes, but I wasn't wearing them that day. Your officers who interviewed me after Ralph's murder can testify to that.'

'How do you explain your neighbour's statement then?'

'I want to leave,' Pippa repeated.

Anderson glanced at Joanna and saw from the expression in her eyes that she expected him to make the move he was planning. 'Phillipa Wright, you are charged with the murder of Ralph Allan on Monday –'

'No!' screamed Pippa. 'It wasn't me. I swear it wasn't me. I had no idea he was going to be killed. I was only trying to help out. It seemed the right thing to do but I'm not going to take the blame. I loved Ralph, I'd never have murdered him, not even after what he did to me.'

Anderson continued charging her, but Pippa hardly seemed to listen. She kept shaking her head and shouting denials until finally, when Anderson had finished, she looked at him with such an expression of pain and betrayal that he realised she'd still imagined he was secretly on her side, and that his feelings for her were the same as they had been before Ralph's death.

'Listen, Pippa,' he said gently. 'Why don't you tell us the truth? If you didn't do it, you obviously know who did.'

'I was helping her, that's all,' Pippa said, struggling for composure. 'She rang me up you see, and told me that she needed to meet Ralph somewhere private because it wasn't possible to talk to him properly at The Chilterns. She said she needed time alone with him, but that he kept avoiding her, so we decided on a plan.

'I felt sorry for her. I knew how ruthless Ralph could be when he didn't want to do something, and if I'd been her I'd have wanted a chance to talk to him properly, but he was good at avoiding things he didn't want to do. She turned to me because she knew about our affair. That was the key to getting him to Headley Common.

'I rang him up at work and said that I wanted to meet him one last time at our usual place. I made it clear I knew our affair was over, but I suggested we had one last session as a farewell. I knew he wouldn't be able to resist. He'd started seeing that Chloe girl who's doing her thesis, did you know? Anyway, she wasn't his type; I guessed that he wasn't able to do all the things he liked with her yet. He always takes time to show what he enjoys, and he also liked making love on the common. Probably the risk of being seen added extra spice to the experience.'

'In other words, you lured him to his death?' said Joanna.

Anderson gave her a swift look and then turned back to Pippa. 'He went to Headley Common expecting to meet you, is that what you're saying?' His voice was incredibly warm and understanding.

'Yes,' said Pippa, at last beginning to relax.

'But it wasn't you?'

'No, that's what I've been saying all along. It had to look as though it was me when he first got there, otherwise he'd have driven straight off, so I lent her my jacket and scarf, and also my car. I thought she was just going to talk to him. There were things she needed to discuss, to get off her chest, and I wanted her to have that chance. But she betrayed me too, like everyone else. She killed him, and she never told me, not even when she came back with my car and my clothes. I knew nothing about it until your men turned up and told me. I haven't slept since. I keep wondering if Ralph thought it was me right up to the end, if he died believing I'd murdered him.'

'Who was it?' Anderson asked quietly. 'Who borrowed your car and your clothes?'

Pippa told him.

When Anderson found her Chloe was sitting with the desk sergeant, who was busily jotting down the various complaints he'd received from members of the public that day.

'Chloe, a quick word please,' he said tersely.

She went through into his office. 'What is it?'

'We're on our way with a warrant for the arrest of the person who killed Ralph Allan. Do you want to be there when it's served?'

Chloe's eyes lit up with gratitude. 'More than anything,' she said vehemently.

'Fine, but you mustn't interfere, interrupt or express your feelings visibly, understand?'

'I won't, but I realise why you love your work so much,' said Chloe as they left the building. 'You must be feeling really triumphant right now.' Anderson didn't reply, because the truth was that he wasn't feeling triumphant at all.

True to her word, Chloe kept silent on the journey, not

even showing any emotion when she realised where they were going. The girl on reception at the Mill House phoned up to the Mitchells and said that Mrs Mitchell would be down to see them immediately. This time Anderson had DS Walker with him, and the two men stood slightly apart from Chloe as Mary Mitchell came down the stairs and smiled her gentle smile at them both.

'Do come up,' she said warmly. 'My husband's much better now, and we're hoping to go back to London tomorrow so you caught us just in time. I hope you've got some good news for Don, he's feeling very low.'

Anderson didn't answer; instead he followed the well-dressed, middle-aged woman up the stairs and into the living room of the small suite she and Don were occupying. Don, looking pale and thinner in the face but just as antagonistic, glared at Anderson. 'What do you want?' he demanded.

'We're here in connection with the murder of your son-in-law, Ralph Allan,' Anderson replied.

'Not caught anyone for that either? When you catch his killer, give him a medal from me. You were going to let him get away with killing Lisa, despite what I kept telling you.'

'They were two separate murders,' said Anderson, keeping an eye on Mary. She was standing talking to Chloe who, still unaware of the bombshell that was about to be dropped on her, was making small talk. 'Neither killer was Ralph Allan.'

'I don't believe you. Made any arrests to prove it?'

'Earlier today we arrested Tom Allan for the murder of your daughter Lisa,' Anderson said, turning towards Mary Mitchell as he spoke.

Her face registered little. 'Tom? How sad, he seemed such a nice boy,' she said at last, clearly feeling some response was called for. 'I'd never have suspected him, not in a million years.'

'I know,' said Anderson. 'You believed it was Ralph, didn't you?'

'We both did,' added Don.

'You had no doubt?' DS Walker asked Mary Mitchell.

'None at all,' she confessed. 'It was the logical answer.'

'Like father like son,' said Don, struggling to his feet. 'If Lisa had never met that family she'd still be alive today, and I take my hat off to whoever killed Ralph. I should have done it years ago.'

'I think there's someone in this room who agrees with you,' said Anderson, aware that he'd never relished charging someone with murder less than he was relishing this. Finally he turned to Mary, who had moved to stand by her husband's side. 'Mary Mitchell, I have here a warrant for your arrest for the murder of Ralph Allan. You do not have to say anything. But it may harm your defence if you do not mention now something which you later rely on in court. Anything you do say may be given in evidence.'

While Mary Mitchell remained quite calm both Chloe and Don Mitchell looked as though they were about to faint. Don pulled his wife close to him. 'You must be out of your bloody mind, Anderson. I'm calling our solicitor right now. Mary, don't say a word. I told you he was a fool, but even I didn't realise quite how big a one. Don't worry, leave it all to me. We'll get you free in no time, and then we'll sue them for every penny they've got.'

Mary pulled away from her husband and when she spoke it was in the same well-modulated, calm tone she'd always used. 'There's no point in making a fuss, Don. The chief inspector's quite right. I did kill Ralph, and I don't regret it one bit. He deserved to die.'

Don stared at his wife as though he didn't know her, and it occurred to Anderson that probably none of them knew her. They'd all seen the surface, the woman formed by her birth and background, but underneath was a very different person.

'Mary, what are you saying?' Chloe asked, quite forgetting Anderson's instructions through sheer shock. Anderson didn't mind. He knew Mary had liked Chloe the first time she'd met her, and guessed she was more likely to talk to her than to him or his officers. That was partly why he'd brought her.

'I'm sorry my dear, but it's the truth. I shot Ralph through the head and when I drove away I'd never felt better in my life.'

'Stop it!' shouted Don. 'Don't talk, wait until we've got you a solicitor.'

'It won't make any difference,' his wife replied. 'A solicitor can't change what happened.'

'But Mary, Ralph didn't murder your daughter,' said a distraught Chloe. 'You might have thought he did, but it was Tom. That means you killed an innocent man.'

Mary Mitchell gave a strange smile. 'I don't think there's any such thing. Even if Ralph didn't kill my darling daughter he ruined the last few years of her life with his philandering and his lack of concern about her health. He married her for her money, then when she wouldn't give it to him he abused her. No one should think this was a tragic case of mistaken identity. Why should Lisa be dead and Ralph alive? I believe justice has been done. Sometimes it isn't possible for the legal system to do the right thing, and that's when we all have to do what we believe is right.'

'Mary, you don't know what you're saying,' Don protested angrily. He turned to Anderson. 'She doesn't even realise she's been cautioned. You can't use this drivel against her. She's certifiable; Lisa's death unbalanced her. She never killed Ralph, she hasn't got the guts for a start.'

'Be quiet, Don,' said Mary, her voice cool. 'Do you want to know why you disliked Ralph so much? It wasn't because of the way he treated Lisa, it was because the two of you were so alike. I've suffered for the past thirty-seven years, just as Lisa was suffering. I've watched you use my money to climb to the top of the ladder, and use my connections to get accepted into a society that's always despised you really but didn't dare say so because you were married to me.

'You've had affairs and thought I was too stupid to realise and you've treated me like a silly, fluffy woman who was at her happiest looking after you, Lisa and later Deborah. I wasn't though. I resented everything you did, and that's why I warned Lisa not to make the same mistakes as me. I'd ruined my life, but I didn't intend to let Ralph or any man ruin hers.'

For a moment Don was too taken aback to speak, but when he did there was vehemence in his voice. 'Then it's your fault Lisa died,' he shouted. 'If she'd been less obsessed with keeping her money to herself, if she'd given Deborah and even Tom some help now and again, she wouldn't be dead. You taught her to distrust everyone, and that's why she died.'

For the first time Mary Mitchell looked confused. She turned to Chloe beseechingly. 'That's not true, is it? It wasn't my fault. I helped her to be independent, that's all.'

'If course it wasn't your fault,' said Chloe, almost in tears. 'Lisa's death had nothing to do with you.'

Mary sighed with relief. 'No, I thought not. Don's only being unpleasant, as usual. I'll get my jacket, Chief Inspector, and then we'd better leave for the station.'

Anderson watched her with secret admiration as she got her things together and then flanked on one side by Walker and on the other by Anderson himself, she walked calmly out of the hotel and into the waiting police car, leaving behind a husband who had finally lost the one thing that he valued and relied on most in the world, but who hadn't realised it until it was too late.

TWELVE

Late that night, John Anderson and Chloe Wells sat on opposite sides of a table at his favourite Italian restaurant. The meal had been excellent, although Chloe had found she had little appetite, and now they were drinking coffee she finally felt relaxed enough to talk about the case.

Anderson had been a different man away from work. He'd displayed an unexpectedly dry sense of humour and a sensitivity towards Chloe that was totally unexpected. She could now accept his reputation at the station for being something of a ladies' man, because when he allowed himself to loosen up a little he was definitely good company, and even when she'd disliked him Chloe had accepted he was handsome in a conventional way. He still wasn't her type, but at least she appreciated his good points.

'Now that it's over, and I won't be coming to plague you any more, can we talk about the case?' she asked, getting out her cigarettes and then, at the look on his face, putting them hastily away again.

'Smoke if you like,' Anderson said with a smile. 'I was wondering how you'd got this far without one. We can talk about anything you like. What do you want to know?'

'Exactly how Mary Mitchell killed Ralph.'

Anderson's eyes looked piercingly into hers. 'Are you sure you want to know?' She nodded. 'She'd thought it through very well. There was no chance of Ralph agreeing to meet her so she put on a jacket and scarf that belonged to Pippa and then met him at a rendezvous Pippa had arranged with Ralph for them. He thought he was going to have one final exciting session of kinky sex and was already parked in his usual place, sitting in his driving seat with his window down feeling relaxed and one assumes quite excited.

'Mary drove off the road and found Ralph's car parked pointing towards her. She brought Pippa's car to a halt on Ralph's side of his Jaguar, positioning herself parallel to him. At this stage he must still have assumed she was Pippa. After all he was expecting Pippa, this was her car and the woman driver was wearing Pippa's clothes. It was a clever set-up. We won't ever know if he realised the truth at the last moment or not. My guess is that he did, but by then it was too late.

'Mary reached for her father's old service revolver, a family heirloom which she'd kept in working order and which was on the passenger seat next to her. Then she wound her window down and calmly shot Ralph through the forehead. She was close, but not close enough to cause powder burns, and that way there was no danger of her getting blood on herself. She knew his brains would cover the back of his own car. She was safe. All she had to do was get back to the Mill House before Don awoke from the sedative the doctor had given him.'

Chloe felt sick. 'How did she know all this?'

'She was brought up on a country estate, remember. She knew how to ride and shoot almost before she was out of her pram. It was easy for her and she says she had no more compunction about shooting Ralph than she would have had about shooting vermin on the family estate.'

'What about Pippa?' Chloe asked. 'Did she know what Mary was going to do?'

Anderson hesitated. 'To be honest with you, I'm not sure. In my opinion, for what that's worth, she didn't know at first, and Mary was unlikely to tell her when she got back with the car and the clothes. Once she heard the news though, Pippa must have guessed, but she kept quiet. You might think she kept quiet out of fear that we would have thought she was in on the plot from the start, but by remaining silent she made herself an accessory anyway.

'This entire business is riddled with mistakes; some were mine and some were made by the family. As a result Ralph died in retaliation for a murder that never really was, and both Pippa Wright and Deborah Allan have been charged as being accessories to murder.'

'Why Deborah?' Chloe queried.

'Deborah told us she heard every word Jeff Phillips said, and she did, which means that unless she had selective deafness she heard every word exchanged between Tom and Lisa as well. Then out of love for Tom, she tried to lead us in the wrong direction. She might have succeeded but for the two mistakes about using the back door and leaving her phone in the kitchen.'

'You got there in the end,' said Chloe. 'That must make you feel good.'

Anderson hesitated again. 'I made mistakes,' he confessed. 'I met Lisa two days before she died and I was attracted to her. I thought she was lovely to look at, very sweet, and that her husband was a chauvinist pig. When she died I carried those preconceived ideas over into the investigation. Perhaps if I hadn't done that Ralph wouldn't have died and Mary Mitchell and Pippa Wright wouldn't now find themselves charged with murder.

'It's rather ironic if you think about it. Lisa wasn't ever meant to die, but as a result of her death there are four people facing murder charges and an entire family's life is in ruins.'

'Did you like Pippa?' asked Chloe.

'In what way?' Anderson asked blandly.

'Forget it, it was something I heard that's all. I don't blame you if you did. I liked Ralph,' she said.

'I know,' said Anderson, 'and I'm sorry.' For a moment his hand touched hers lightly on the tabletop, then he called for the bill and within a few minutes he was driving her back to her parents' house.

Outside he cut the engine and turned towards her. 'I hope the thesis goes well.'

'So do I. It had better; it's not an experience I'd want to go through again. How you can do it day after day is beyond me. Don't you despair of human nature?'

'No,' Anderson said slowly. 'We see a lot of the bad side, but we see the good side too. I shall miss you,' he added unexpectedly.

'Not for long,' she replied breezily. 'You'll soon be busy on another case and I'll just be a memory. I hope you get what you want from life,' she added, kissing him on the cheek before getting out of the car and going inside to ring Phil Walker, who'd been pestering her for a date ever since they first met.

Anderson watched her go and thought about what she'd said. There were only two things he really wanted from life: the right woman and promotion. At this moment the right woman seemed nothing but a dream, but promotion was almost a certainty.

The next morning he had an appointment to see Chief Superintendent Eyer, and he was positive that the meeting was to offer him Parrish's job. Despite his mistakes early on in the Allan case everything had worked out well in the end and he'd managed to avoid offending anyone who mattered during the course of the investigation. His time had finally come, and it felt good.

As he drove away he reflected wryly on the fact that it was quite literally time which had helped to cause Lisa Allan's death, and he wondered if it was the first occasion when the expression 'time to kill' could have been used so accurately.

CRIME & PASSION

DEADLY AFFAIRS
by
Juliet Hastings
ISBN: 0 7535 0029 9
Publication date: 17 April 1997

Eddie Drax is a playboy businessman with a short fuse and a taste for blondes. A lot of people don't like him: ex-girlfriends, business rivals, even his colleagues. He's not an easy man to like. When Eddie is found asphyxiated at the wheel of his car, DCI John Anderson delves beneath the golf-clubbing, tree-lined respectability of suburban Surrey and uncovers the secret — and often complex — sex-lives of Drax's colleagues and associates.

He soon finds that Drax was murdered — and there are more killings to come. In the course of his investigations, Anderson becomes personally involved in Drax's circle of passionate women, jealous husbands and people who can't be trusted. He also has plenty of opportunities to find out more about his own sexual nature.

This is the first in the series of John Anderson mysteries.

CRIME & PASSION

A MOMENT OF MADNESS
by
Pan Pantziarka
ISBN: 0 7535 0024 8
Publication date: 17 April 1997

Tom Ryder is the charismatic head of the Ryder Forum – an organisation teaching slick management techniques to business people. Sarah Fairfax is investigating current management theories for a television programme called *Insight* and is attending a course at Ryder Hall. All the women on the course think Ryder is dynamic, powerful and extremely attractive. Sarah agrees, but this doesn't mean that she's won over by his evangelical spiel; in fact, she's rather cynical about the whole thing.

When one of the course attendees – a high-ranking civil servant – is found dead in his room from a drugs overdose, Detective Chief Inspector Anthony Vallance is called in to investigate. Everyone has something to hide, except for Sarah Fairfax who is also keen to find out the truth about this suspicious death. As the mystery deepens and another death occurs, Fairfax and Vallance compete to unearth the truth. They discover dark, erotic secrets, lethal dangers and, to their mutual irritation, each other.

This is the first in a series of Fairfax and Vallance mysteries.

CRIME & PASSION

INTIMATE ENEMIES
by
Juliet Hastings
ISBN: 0 7535 0034 5
Publication date: 15 May 1997

Francesca Lyons is found dead in her art gallery. The cause of death isn't obvious but her bound hands suggest foul play. The previous evening she had an argument with her husband, she had sex with someone, and two men left messages on the gallery's answering machine. Detective Chief Inspector Anderson has plenty of suspects but can't find anyone with a motive.

When Stephanie Pinkney, an art researcher, is found dead in similar circumstances, Anderson's colleagues are sure the culprit is a serial killer. But Anderson is convinced that the murders are connected with something else entirely. Unravelling the threads leads him to Andrea Maguire, a vulnerable, sensuous art dealer with a quick-tempered husband and unsatisfied desires. Anderson can prove Andrea isn't the killer and finds himself strongly attracted to her. Is he making an untypical and dangerous mistake?

***Intimate Enemies* is the second in the series of John Anderson mysteries.**

CRIME & PASSION

A TANGLED WEB
by
Pan Pantziarka
ISBN: 0 7535 0155 4
Publication date: 19 June 1997

Michael Cunliffe was ordinary. He was an accountant for a small charity. He had a pretty wife and an executive home in a leafy estate. Now he's been found dead: shot in the back of the head at close range. The murder bears the hallmark of a gangland execution.

DCI Vallance soon discovers Cunliffe wasn't ordinary at all. The police investigation lifts the veneer of suburban respectability to reveal blackmail, extortion, embezzlement, and a network of sexual intrigue. One of Cunliffe's businesses has been the subject of an investigation by the television programme, *Insight*, which means that Vallance has an excuse to get in touch again with Sarah Fairfax. Soon they're getting on each other's nerves and in each other's way, but they cannot help working well together.

***A Tangled Web* is the second in the series of Fairfax and Vallance mysteries.**

CRIME & PASSION

A WAITING GAME
by
Juliet Hastings
ISBN: 0 7535 0109 0
Publication date: 21 August 1997

A child is abducted and held to ransom. As the boy's mother is a prospective MP and his father is a friend of the Chief Constable, Detective Chief Inspector Anderson is required to wrap up the case cleanly and efficiently.

But the kidnappers, although cunning and well-organised, make up a triangle of lust and jealousy. Somehow Anderson's tactics are being betrayed to the kidnappers and, after a series of mishaps and errors and a violent death, Anderson's latest sexual conquest and his ex-wife become involved in the conspiracy. Anderson's legendary patience and willpower are stretched to the limit as he risks his own life trying to save others.

This is the third in the series of John Anderson mysteries.

CRIME & PASSION

TO DIE FOR
by
Peter Birch
ISBN: 0 7535 0034 5
Publication date: 18 September 1997

The cool and efficient Detective Chief Inspector is keen to re-establish his reputation as a skilled investigator. The body of Charles Draper has been found in the mud flats of a Devon estuary. The murdered man was a law-abiding citizen and there appears to be no motive for the killing. There are also very few clues.

When Anderson is sent to assist the Devon and Cornwall constabulary, he's led towards dubious evidence and suspects whose alibis are watertight. The investigation also brings him in contact with forensics assistant Anna Ferreira whose intellect and physical attractiveness makes her irresistible.

The only suspect is then found murdered. Local antiques dealer Nathan Cutts fits the murderer's profile but Anderson feels he's not the man they're looking for. Against the backdrop of windswept Dartmoor, the chase to catch a killer is on.

This is the fourth in the series of John Anderson novels.

CRIME & PASSION

TIME TO KILL
by
Margaret Bingley
ISBN: 0 7535 0164 3
Publication date: 16 October 1997

Lisa Allan's body is found in the corner of her kitchen by her husband, Ralph. Everyone knows Lisa was ill, suffering from a complicated heart condition, but no one expected her to die – least of all her doctor. DCI Anderson met Lisa socially only two days before her death. He found her desirable but disliked her husband on sight.

Two autopsy reports pose more questions than answers and as Anderson struggles to untangle the relationships of the dysfunctional Allan family, he becomes involved with Pippa Wright, Ralph's attractive PA and ex-mistress. When a second murder occurs, Anderson realises that getting to know Pippa was not one of his better ideas. Against a background of sexual intrigue and hidden secrets, he needs to harness all his skills and intuition if he is to ensure that justice is done.

This is the fifth in the series of John Anderson mysteries.

CRIME & PASSION

DAMAGED GOODS
by
Georgina Franks
ISBN: 0 7535 0124 4
Publication date: 20 November 1997

A high-performance car has spun out of control on a test drive. The driver has suffered multiple injuries and is suing Landor Motors for negligence. He says the airbag inflated for no reason, causing him to lose control of the car.

This is the third and most serious claim Landor Motors have had to make this year. The insurance company aren't happy, and they bring in Victoria Donovan to assist in their investigations.

Landor Motors is a high-profile car showroom situated in the stockbroker belt. But the Landor family have a history of untimely deaths and brooding resentments. Soon, Vic is up to her neck in a complex web of drug-dealing, sexual jealousy and deception involving Derek Landor's wayward and very attractive son. When Derek Landor is kidnapped, only Vic knows what's going on. Will anyone take her seriously before time runs out for Derek Landor?

This is the first Victoria Donovan mystery.

CRIME & PASSION

GAMES OF DECEIT
by
Pan Pantziarka
ISBN: 0 7535 0119 8
Publication date: 4 December 1997

Detective Chief Inspector Anthony Vallance and television journalist Sarah Fairfax team up once more when an old friend of Sarah's is caught up in the strange goings-on at the science park where she's working. Carol Davis says someone there is trying to kill her but the squeaky clean credentials of her colleagues don't tally with the dangerous and violent nature of the attacks.

When Vallance becomes sexually involved with Carol Davis, he begins to realise that she has a dark side to her nature: she's manipulative, kinky and possibly unstable. As Fairfax and Vallance peel away the layers of respectability to reveal a background of corporate coercion, deceit and neo-Nazism, they discover that Carol has not been telling the truth about the people she's working for. But who is going to reveal what's really going on when Carol winds up dead?

This is the third in the series of Fairfax and Vallance novels.